“I Like Your Form”

"I Like Your Form"
Confessions of a Personal Trainer

Based on a true story

JD Holmes

www.jdconfessions.com

Yin-Yang Publishing

ISBN-13: 978-0-9890716-0-4

Cover photograph by Marissa Stratton
Cover design by Jeff Kepler
Model credits: Victoria Sanders and Anthony Vazquez

To those both in and out of the fitness world
who made this possible

CONTENTS

1
WHO, ME?

Who would have thought that a job title would lead me to become one of the premier cocksmiths of my day? I do believe that I once held one of the greatest jobs a guy with little or no qualifications could ever have. Like most people, I wanted a job where I could make great money doing something that would not have me limping into my golden years. My ideal job would enable me to have a great time at work each day in a laid-back atmosphere where the preferred uniform was something I could lounge around in after work or on the weekends. It also wouldn't hurt to work with beautiful people every day. I was certain a job like this existed, but who the hell knew where to find it?

To say that I was lost when it came to finding employment after high school would be an understatement. I knew I didn't want to spend years in college racking up a ton of debt. I also wanted to be successful in something other than a typical nine-to-five job. I wanted to see the light sooner rather than later when it came to making good money and working the hours I wanted to work. From my late teens, I always wanted enough money in the bank to do whatever I wanted, whenever I wanted, and I didn't want to have to work twelve-hour days seven days a week to get to that financial state. I always thought that working hard didn't have to equate to working myself into the grave as I had seen so many of my relatives do over the years.

I didn't find this ideal job right away. After high school graduation, I kind of just floated along. How many people know exactly what they want to do for the rest of their lives before the age of twenty-five unless they already had it mapped out by their family? Fortunately, I made it out of Mom and Dad's basement just one year after high school, and I can proudly say I have yet to move back in. I got my fingers crossed that once this comes out I don't find myself living back at my parents' place.

Don't get me wrong. I wasn't thinking about being able to vacation in the Bahamas once a month or eat at The Capital Grille several nights a week, but I didn't want to have to save money for half a year just to be able to eat at a nice restaurant. I didn't want to have to max out a credit card just to take a vacation once a year either. I wasn't even an out-of-control spender. I drove a car that was well over ten years old, and I hated shopping for clothes. Unless my boxers had large enough holes in them, I refused to replace them, and I didn't gamble or piss away my money. I had one credit card with a limit so low you would barely consider it a credit card. So was it so wrong of me to just want to have money available to do shit when the occasion called for it? Let's face it, work sucks most of the time. So like any true-blooded male in his youth, I partied here and there, smoked a few bowls when the opportunity presented itself, and generally did what I needed to do to get by and weave my way through this journey called life.

The bar was never set high for me from an early age. I had zero direction from my parents. They assumed all I needed to learn about life would be taught to me while I languished in that institution otherwise known as public school. My memories of public school are filled with many bitter older adults who were mad at themselves for not living their dreams, and they took that anger out on poor chumps like me. Fuckers, I hope you are all happy with your pensions, and I can only pray you are not spending your golden years yelling at neighborhood kids for riding their bikes too close to your precious monkey trees.

What's a guy with no direction to do? Luckily, I didn't get into the kind of trouble that would have really put me behind the eight ball as an adult. God forbid I got a DUI or in some other type of legal trouble back in the day, who knows where I would have ended up? I didn't join the band in high school, so my musical talent wasn't going to land me a spot in a band anytime soon. Unless you consider that goddamned wooden stick with holes carved in it an instrument, I was screwed. Thanks a lot, Mom and Dad. With a little motivation and encouragement, I might have been the next Eddie Van Halen.

Sports? Sure, I played a little bit of everything, but to be good enough to make a living at it or at least get a free ride to college was about as unlikely as winning the lotto, considering I was just over five and a half feet tall and weighed just a hair over 150 pounds. I was, however, armed with decent enough looks, with bright blue eyes and a well-chiseled face, but that doesn't mean too much in a world full of Brad Pitts and Scarlett Johanssons. Growing up in a small suburb of Philadelphia kept the miraculous possibility of being "discovered" from happening. To this day, I'm positive I could have been cast as the next Derek Zoolander, as my extraordinary wavy black hair was a force to be reckoned with, in my own opinion. Sadly, even though I was a cross between Tom Cruise and Matthew McConaughey, I lacked the confidence necessary to try to make any money off it.

Unlike many of my friends who went away to college, I stayed home and went to the almighty community college, which was the logical extension for many high school grads like myself who didn't have a clue what the hell they were going to do. Occasionally, I took trips to see some friends who were upstate at college, and I was always in awe that they were allowed to sleep in the same building as these unbelievably hot members of the opposite sex. Not only that, but the parties on college campuses put any parties I'd been to back home to shame. I would go for a weekend and get a small glimpse of the debauchery that was freshman year away from home. On the long drive home, I would have a tough time not feeling jealous, as the following day I would find myself just a few miles away from my house at my community college class, sitting next to a girl my age who also happened to be a mother of three already. Fuck my life, I thought. There had to be a better way, only I had no idea what that way would be.

I tried my hand at a number of jobs after high school. First, I worked in a restaurant, which is the commonly traveled road people take when they need to make money but really can't do anything else. I figured where else would I be able to work with better-than-average-looking girls and have access to alcohol before turning twenty-one? I think it was Trip McNeely who said working at a restaurant was all fun and games with the added plus of money. I quickly discovered that I was capable of bussing a table with the best of them. I was busting my ass every night of the weekend and made enough money to get my own place, but I didn't have much money left over for anything else. Working in a restaurant also taught me some of the finer things in life, such as how to shotgun a beer with a straw. Throw in the usually coked-out manager, and there are bound to be some good times. But something was missing. I'm not sure if it was the shitty hours or the inability to even think about asking for a Friday night off, but I was desperate to find something that paid well without having to smell like I spent a night in a tobacco factory. Not to mention, dealing with the people who find their way into these establishments on weekends was enough to drive a guy insane. I'm not talking about your average asshole you meet in the street. I'm talking about those uptight schmucks who forget they are in a chain restaurant and give you an attitude about shit you have no control over, like how the steak tastes like shit. Did you really think you were getting the crème de la crème of filets for twelve dollars? You will truly never understand the depth of your intolerance of people until you have the pleasure of working in the service industry. Mind you, I was nothing but a peon busboy. I had less pull than the goddamned dishwasher. Little did I know my interactions with coworkers and customers alike would bode well for me in the near future.

Once I managed to find my own place, I wanted something more from my job. The good times at the restaurant soon came to an end. Management changed, and all of a sudden it was as if I was working at a five-star dining establishment. Gone were the after-hours shots and games of quarters after cleaning up. A friend of the family owned a sheet metal shop, so I figured what the hell? How bad could it be? I soon found out that this kind of work sucks unlike any other. There is probably no worse way to spend eight or ten hours doing essentially the same thing over and over again just to be able to put food on the table. One of my many boring tasks was putting pieces of metal through a huge electric sander—for eight fucking hours straight! Who the hell does this shit for twenty, maybe thirty years? I even started smoking cigarettes for the short time I was employed there just so that I could participate in the fifteen-minute smoke breaks every couple of hours to mix up the monotonous task at hand. Much to my astonishment, this is how a large percentage of our population earns a living. The guys I met at the shop had been working there for almost ten years! There they were, performing mind-numbing tasks thousands of times a day just to wake up the next day and do the same shit again. I realize that somebody's got to do these manual labor jobs, but other than laying down new sod in my yard twice a year, I couldn't see myself doing this shit day in and day out until my body just quit. This job wasn't all bad, as some of my coworkers would lighten the mood with their fucked-up sense of humor. But aside from laughing at the occasional wisecrack from the Russian guy who was right off the boat and sounded a little like Borat, there was nothing exciting going on that convinced me that was the way to go. It was a short-lived experiment in employment for me, as I was quickly onto the next job after a couple of months.

My next step up the career ladder had me on the front lines of a car wash, working side by side with several guys who were in a prison work-release program. As bad as that may sound, at least this job gave me the opportunity to break up the workday by switching from cleaning windows, interiors, and wheels to drying cars and even scrubbing the toilets. I wondered if my friends interning at big investment firms over the summers were forced to scrub the shitter on a Friday after a long week. Cleaning toilets wasn't the only thing that sucked about this job. Having to clean a brand-new car that belonged to a very well-off person who made it very clear where you stood on the food chain was not fun either. Thank you, Mr. Jerk-off, for pointing out that this job is bullshit and that you are obviously more important than I'll ever be. I also had numerous run-ins with people who seemed to enjoy breaking my balls about the most mundane details, like a piece of lint that got stuck on the bumper while I was drying the car with a towel. I'm sure this uptight asshole would think twice about saying something about this "mess" if my buddy Carlos, who had tattoos around his neck and spent a couple of years in jail, was the guilty party. Being the youngest guy working there and the only white guy on staff who wasn't a manager, I was known as "Hollywood" among my coworkers. I'm not sure if they called me that because they thought I looked like someone famous or because they thought all white people looked alike. Nevertheless, I knew my days there would be numbered. As much as I was fed up with my job situation, I had the responsibility of paying rent now, so quitting before getting another source of income was out of the question.

As I drove back to my apartment after a day's work at the 'wash, I couldn't help but notice the construction of what would be a brand-new gym, Precision Fitness. I belonged to a gym since my freshman year in high school and was religious about going three to four days a week. My fascination with fitness began thanks to my dad. He was a religious reader of *Muscle & Fitness*, so in between glancing at his issues of *Playboy*, I read all those bodybuilding magazines when I was growing up. Nothing like looking at pictures of huge, 'roided-up males to provide inspiration to America's youth. I was always intrigued by the classifieds at the back that claimed, "Add 20 pounds of muscle in two weeks with legal steroids!" or "Get ripped *without* picking up a weight!" Wow! There is such a thing as a legal steroid? Nice.

The advertisement that came flashing back to me as I passed the soon-to-open gym was the one that said, "Make up to $150 an hour personal training!" I remember even as a young kid thinking, You've got to be fucking kidding me. I could make that much money as a personal trainer? I even recall the advertisement also happened to show a guy with two beautiful women under each arm, which I thought could be a sign of things to come. What young kid wasn't mesmerized by sleek advertisements in the back of magazines? Don't tell me I'm the only asshole who was suckered in by the ad that read, "Make up to $1,000 a week stuffing envelopes." I figured what the hell? If it's anything like the countless pyramid schemes I had been sucked into through the years, what's the worst that could happen? In fact, I had boxes of water filters in my closet that were supposed to be the guaranteed "next big thing" to make you a millionaire, according to the very professional-looking brochure. Unfortunately, I'd been had one too many times by these advertisements to part with another few hundred dollars, which would have been difficult to cough up. I was getting desperate and needed to find another source of income because this car wash job just wasn't going to work for me much longer.

As it turns out, I didn't even have to get ripped off by one of those "Become a personal trainer for $500!" ads before landing my first job as a trainer. Having worked out for several years at a gym, I considered most of the people who worked there douchebags and I didn't want to become one of them. But I couldn't help but notice how simple the personal trainer's job appeared to be. I thought my chances of getting hired at Precision Fitness were slim, since my prior experience included a restaurant job and some manual labor jobs. But I had just turned twenty-one and had not done a whole hell of a lot with my life. So on an overcast day in the spring while driving home from that godforsaken car wash, one thing led to another and I found myself in a trailer on the construction site of the new building. With the gray afternoon clouds blocking out most of the light, I sat in the makeshift office and waited to be called in for an interview.

I was pretty fucking clueless at this point, since I had no idea what to do or how this job was actually accomplished. I would be lying to say I wasn't intimidated. Of course, I was just thinking about the most mundane details, like whether my biceps were on par with the other guys who had been interviewed. I can assure you, my interviews for the car wash and sheet metal shop were much less nerve-racking.

Both the general manager and the director of sales asked me a ton of questions that I had no idea how to answer, such as, "What makes you think you are cut out to be a personal trainer?"

"Um, I work out and I like it?" I wasn't very proficient in the art of the interview at this point in my life.

"How do you plan on retaining your clients over time?"

"Um, I'll show them neat workouts that will convince them to stay with me," I said.

"Are you certified as a personal trainer?"

"No, um, but I want to be."

After a battery of questions, which I seemed to answer with little to no confidence, and a few minutes of chatter, I got the good news: "JD, you seem like a stand-up guy. When can you start?"

Holy shit! I had just landed my first real job—one that didn't entail picking up dishes for four bucks an hour, coming home smelling like a tobacco factory, or running pieces of sheet metal through mechanical sanders. And just like that I became one of those douchebags in the gym. I would later find out that if you even remotely look like you've lifted a weight in the past six months and have the least bit of a personality—even a shitty one—it was pretty difficult to not get a job as a personal trainer back then. Things may have changed over the years, but when I got into personal training, it was as if gyms couldn't hire enough trainers, as times were good and people seemed to have money to burn. Little did I know that day would officially change me as a person and life as I once knew it would never be the same.

The beauty of starting a personal training job at a business in its infancy is that you have the luxury of an even playing field. Even though I didn't know the first thing about personal training, my coworkers had no idea I was clueless. I had no need to play catch-up or compete with some asshole who had been at the gym forever and always felt the need to remind you of that fact. This was all a relief in a business that comes down to sales. It can be quite the cutthroat business, as I would soon find out.

A good mix of guys and girls were hired as personal trainers to start this new venture, and we bonded quickly. The rest of the staff consisted of smooth-talking money handlers who must have had a ton of sales experience because they were able to get people who had barely any money to their name to continually shell out hundreds of dollars a month for personal training—on top of membership fees. Despite two full weeks of training before the gym's grand opening, I wasn't prepared for the shitstorm that would ensue when people started showing up. I felt like I was working in a foreign country where no one understood English.

Needless to say, I had no fucking clue how to close the deal, let alone train people for an hour and keep the shit interesting enough that they would want to come back. I was a disaster, and my managers assured me of this in our weekly meetings. Ah, yes. My first experience with weekly sales meetings was an eye-opener for sure. There is nothing worse than sitting in front of all your coworkers and having to explain why your numbers are less than everyone else's. While everyone else was doing great, I was missing something but didn't know what it was.

A month into the job, things were not looking good for me. My boss suggested I contact Rob, a trainer who worked at another location, and shadow him for a few days—unpaid, of course. As embarrassing as it was, I learned a lot by watching Rob. He had been training people for just two short years and was working at full capacity and then some. He wasn't much older than me, but he had all the confidence in the world. He was turning away clients left and right. The first thing I noticed about Rob was how he gave each client 100 percent of his attention from the beginning of the session right up until the end. Maybe because this was before the cell phone era, but Rob tuned out everything and everyone else around him while training his clients. He told me that for over twenty dollars an hour, the least he could do for his clients was give them his undivided attention. He also shared with me the infamous "act as if" principle: act as if you know what the hell you are doing even if you don't. He told me that people could give two shits about how much you know and how good your training methods are; if you don't pay attention to what they want, consider them gone after their first set of sessions. I took this advice and ran with it.

When I returned to work, I listened to everything that each of my clients wanted and I gave it to them and then some. They had my complete attention for that hour of their training. I wouldn't even glance up at the girl with the great ass on the treadmill. By the way, I am still amazed at the number of women who show more skin while working out at the gym than any other place they go. I don't even see women out at clubs revealing as much as some do when they are working out. I was blind to what some of these women really wanted when I first started training.

Instead of taking random classes at college, as I'd seen so many others do, I decided to take classes that would enhance my knowledge of what I was going to be doing for work. I enrolled in science classes, including anatomy and physiology, and nutrition classes. I had been stuck at this community college for two years now, and it was beginning to remind me more and more of a high school except that it allowed smoking on campus. In addition to classes that didn't seem like a waste of time, I tried to read as many books on training and bodybuilding as I could. This was back in the glory days when businesses gave somewhat of a shit about employees and spent money to send us to courses and seminars about fitness. Is it just me, or were things a lot better in the nineties than they are today?

Thanks to my brief couple of days shadowing Rob, not only did my fortunes turn for the better, but I also got busier than I ever thought I would be. Within just a few months, I had the best retention rate in our gym and had to increase my work hours to accommodate new clients. Everything was rolling and going smoothly. I finally found a way to make great money and had a job doing something I enjoyed. I actually looked forward to going to work, and that was a feeling I had always longed for. This was so far from the reality of my life just a few months earlier when I was applying Armor All to a set of whitewalls or clearing tables at a restaurant. I was in my early twenties and was able to support myself financially and then some. I was able to work part time but get paid like I was working full time. The perks of personal training were outstanding: a flexible schedule, more-than-tolerable coworkers, and the ability to meet people every day who could do any kind of favor you could imagine. Need legal advice? There were plenty of lawyers working out at the gym. Need a parking ticket adjusted? No big deal. There were more than a few police officers who would happily assist. For the first time in my life, I felt like I was moving forward

To say that I had one of the best blue-collar jobs would be an understatement. I even convinced myself for a New York minute that I had reached the top, that there would be no reason to ever need to look for another career, as I thought it couldn't get any better. Who makes over twenty dollars an hour these days with little or no education? I see people with degrees who barely pull this kind of money down. I fell into a job back when you could still get hired without having connections, multiple degrees, or years of experience. I didn't have aspirations of being the next Jack LaLanne or, God forbid, Richard Simmons. I have never hosted *The Biggest Loser*, appeared on Oprah uncovering the secrets of fitness, or been seen on a late-night infomercial touting a Gazelle. I could care less about training celebrities and peddling the latest workout fad on DVD. My primary goal was getting paid well without having to come home feeling like I worked at a construction site all day, and I was able to accomplish that goal just a few months after beginning my job as a personal trainer.

Like many of my fellow Generation-X counterparts, I was brought up in the early years of the technology boom. The *Revenge of the Nerds* stereotype—that all people involved with computers were geeks—was in full force, so I stuck with what I figured were the manlier endeavors, playing every sport and lifting weights in my formative years. I was fortunate enough to make the art of instructing other people to lift weights into a moneymaker years later. It wasn't long before I realized that most of the people who were paying for my services were making their money in the computer field. I immediately felt horrible about the way I used to talk shit about anyone who wore glasses or was book smart. Who would have thought those supposed "geeks" would have the last laugh? What the hell, at least I have done well enough in my career as a trainer that I look back with no regrets—well, maybe just a few. I have always considered myself lucky to be able to sustain a career in this industry for a long time, make great money, and get away with shit that would one day be fit for a book.

A diverse clientele crossed my path in my years as a personal trainer: from big to small, young to old, and completely fucking crazy. It was tough for me to grasp at first why some high-powered attorney with a seemingly endless collection of exotic cars was willing to pay nearly seventy-five dollars an hour for me to train him or why some CEO of a huge company would be happy with an uneducated guy like me as his personal trainer. These were the kinds of people who probably wouldn't give me the time of day in any other situation but were willing to pay me well for getting them into shape, and I wasn't about to complain. After getting over the initial shock of working with all types of clients all across the pay scale, I eventually found my niche with one particular demographic: women—and not just any women, but a particular group of women, which you will soon find out about.

I also trained countless clients who had no education but managed to make a ton of money. How many times have you looked at someone and wondered how the hell he got to be so successful after hearing him talk for thirty seconds? As a personal trainer, you get them all—fast talkers, slow talkers, business people, you name it. Anyone and everyone could use a personal trainer. Working regularly with all types of people from all walks of life was one of the highlights of the job and a great experience. I loved hearing how they made it in whatever avenue they pursued. Over time, I would learn more and more about the people I trained—what they liked, disliked, wanted from life, and so on. It was refreshing to hear the occasional story of someone who grew up poor and then somehow made it big and was able to live a life of luxury.

There happens to be a dark side to having these in-depth conversations with clients over the course of several months or sometimes years. Many times, these very innocent conversations can lead to something I only dreamed about before working as a personal trainer. I had no idea that some of the wealthy, attractive older women I trained were looking for a little more than just someone to talk to.

After being in the industry for several years and having trained hundreds of clients, I have come away with dozens of stories—some good, some bad, and some just unbelievable—that I have shared only with my close circle of friends; that is, until now. I'm finally ready to put the story out about the more memorable events that happened in my years as a personal trainer. I know there are plenty of client-trainer relationships that are G-rated, but there are more than a few who go down the path less traveled. I'm just waiting for the day I can feel better about myself knowing others in my profession cleared their own consciences and came clean about what happened on the job.

Unfortunately, I won't be talking about training any A-list celebrities, since my clients were average, everyday kind of people. At the height of my career, I trained someone who was considered D-list at best. Who hasn't seen the commercials with those "trainers to the stars" and ever wondered what really happens behind the scenes in those situations? I would love to hear the tale of Sandra Bullock's trainer and what's really going on in a day of the life of America's sweetheart. Do you think she didn't break down into the arms of her trusty personal trainer when she found out that biker husband of hers went on a mad tear? Perhaps she looked for some comfort in the rock who had been there over the years and managed to keep her looking unbelievable into her late forties. How about the trainer for Charlie Sheen who supposedly went to his house? How fucked up must that scene have been, and who wouldn't want to hear all about a day in the life of the Warlock? That shit would be fascinating.

This book is more about the people you come across every day, including some lawyers, students, the occasional opera singer, and quite a few housewives. It takes me from my days as a young buck tooling around in rookie ball all the way up to my short but illustrious career in the big leagues. Did I change along the way? Who couldn't change after going through what I went through? Who knows, maybe you have been in a similar situation and have a story of your own. I hope I can reach both clients and trainers alike. Maybe you can learn from some of my mistakes because, trust me, that's pretty much what they can be chalked up to. This book is also for all of you who are on the verge of signing up with a personal trainer and wonder what the hell goes on behind closed doors or, in some cases, one-way windows.

Just like many professions where there are those who hang on for way too long, personal training falls into that category. Let's face it—the industry is a young guy or girl's game. Those who are in great shape, are personable, and have a good head on their shoulders will go far in the profession. How many times have you gone into a gym and wondered, Why the hell is that person paying to work out with that guy? It's a sad fact, but I can relate to that guy or girl who holds on just a little too long because the truth is you will find that you put in a whole lot more for a whole lot less with most other jobs. Having worked several jobs now, I know it's difficult to give up something that you not only love to do but also make great money doing. Personal training takes a lot less talent than is needed to play a guitar but allows you to feel like a rock star. For me, personal training was one of the few jobs I held that made me feel like I was doing more than just working for a paycheck.

I grew up a huge Howard Stern fan and always envied how everyone on that show seemed to be having fun at work. Who wouldn't like to laugh and rub elbows with Hollywood types each and every day? I'm sure there was behind-the-scenes bullshit, but that's everywhere. By working as a personal trainer, I had the chance to work in a setting that felt somewhat similar to what is still the greatest show on earth.

So you may be thinking, What is so interesting about the life of a personal trainer that you can't read about in the life of, say, a doctor or lawyer? All I know is that I've trained quite a few doctors and lawyers, and many of them told me on more than one occasion that I had a great gig and not to give it up. They shared with me the downsides to their professions. While they had money, they didn't seem to have the least bit of fun on the job, and screwing around with clients usually meant the end of their job. The amount of shit that goes on in the average day for a personal trainer can be mind-numbing. Say you are training half a dozen clients. This translates into six very different personalities, meaning that from one hour to the next, you're hearing a distinct outlook on many topics. For example, let's say you have a gay male bartender, a coed from a private college, and a soon-to-be-divorced human resource manager. What do you think happens over the course of the next several hours? I'm probably overqualified at this point to throw a couch in my living room and charge a few hundred dollars an hour to listen to other people's problems.

I had a lot of shit thrown my way during my years as a personal trainer, and having little experience in the game of life equates to some bad decisions. To this day, I don't know what possessed me to do some of the things I did. I like to blame it on my age and overall inexperience in life. I can't say I wasn't warned when I first started. Within the first few weeks of the job, I remember sitting down for a one-on-one with my personal training manager, Larry. Larry was LL Cool J kind of cool. I believe he was one of the first people to start wearing sunglasses indoors. He explained to me how talking with female clients outside the gym could negatively affect the client-trainer relationship. Although there was nothing written stating my job would be in jeopardy if I found myself mixed up in shenanigans, he made it clear it would be in my best interest to maintain a "professional relationship" with my clients. Looking back, Larry wasn't bullshitting me, and something tells me that he was speaking from experience.

Since I had a slow start at first, there really weren't any opportunities for anything out of the ordinary to happen. It wasn't until I got busier, when I was focused on my job and everything was going right for me, that fate decided to intervene for the worst. We are faced with choices every day. Everything we decide to do in life comes down to a choice. You can go left or go right, you can sit still or get out there and go, but inevitably, you will one day look back and wonder about the choices you made in life. A better person would have been able to say no. A better person would have been looking down the road rather than at the next few hours. Maybe I wasn't the better man, but I did what I did. No matter what choices you make, they will always catch up to you in the end. You can think you are above the law, as they say, but life finds a way of forcing you to step in that pile of shit at some point. A Tim Tebow I was not.

I have worked as a personal trainer in two states, and while the scenery changes, the job and the innermost workings stay the same. People will always be people no matter what part of the country you are in. I have discovered that life is and always will be that perfect mix of sweet and sour. No matter how good you think things are going, you are just moments away from it all crashing down. Not everyone who works as a trainer is cut out for the job. As easy as it may appear, the job has stresses and expectations, which is why many trainers have traded in their gym shorts for a suit and tie and a life behind a desk.

Being one of the lucky ones in what can be a cutthroat business, I never realized how good I had it until I took my last client through his last set of lunges. Some people are just good at what they do. Even though personal training was something that didn't just come naturally to me, with a little help and a little experience, I was able to become a better-than-average trainer.

So sit back and see what it's like to work in the personal training industry. Filled with hijinks, high pay, and more fun than I have had at a job to date, personal training is easily one of the best—if not *the* best—jobs I have ever had. Just like most things in life, however, all things come to an end. That doesn't mean you can't take the advice I will give you throughout this book and take it to heart so that you can have a successful career of your own or at least be prepared for what you may encounter as either a trainer or a client. Remember, no matter how careful you are, you're always going to step in that pile of shit at some point in your life, and no one makes it through with clean shoes.

2
WHAT IT TAKES

As a personal trainer, you can have a flexible schedule, make good money, and work in a laid-back atmosphere with beautiful people. Sounds like a great deal, right? Not to mention, you are pretty much always guaranteed to have work. As long as beautiful celebrities grace the covers of magazines, people will always be willing to pay for personal trainers to help them "get in shape." The beauty of this generalized goal is that most people have nothing to shoot for other than the person with the great body who happened to be on the cover of *Us Weekly*. Much to their dismay, they will spend the rest of their lives trying to attain the physique of the hottest A-list celebrity and never become satisfied with the goals they do attain. With all the airbrushing and camera tricks these days, the asses of some of these celebrities will always be unattainable to the average person.

So what does it take to put together a workout plan for people and be good at it? This is a question that I asked myself when I first got the idea to apply for a personal training job. I happened to get extremely lucky by landing my first personal training job in a nurturing environment that taught me how to become a good trainer and encouraged continuing education. I know it sounds crazy. Here is a job that requires little formal training, and I find a company that is willing to pay my dumb ass to learn how to do my job better.

One might think that becoming a personal trainer takes about as much skill as becoming a high school guidance counselor. What exactly do these "guidance" counselors do? I remember my high school guidance counselor. She looked a little like Yoda but was nowhere near as insightful. She told me that, at the rate I was going, I wasn't going to be successful in life. Thanks a fuckin' lot, lady. I'm glad to see taxpayers' money going toward your salary and pension just so that you can take a wild guess on how I might fare in life. What the fuck is it that these people do when they aren't making some kid feel like shit? Needless to say, I'm still shocked I even made it out of high school with that type of encouragement. If anything, I still blame her for my inability to say no when a joint passed my way for the first time. Way to guide me down the path of success, but I digress.

To be a personal trainer, I initially thought you just had to look the part and have some experience working out so that you could throw together a program for a client. If you have participated in some kind of sport as a kid and didn't take a liking to Twinkies at a young age, you probably meet the physical requirements of the job. If you know how to operate a treadmill for your own use, then you have the ability to pass that knowledge on to a client. If you have picked up a weight at some point in your life, then you have some knowledge to share with a client, no matter how horrible your technique may be. These are the exact skills I possessed when I first started as a trainer, but I quickly discovered that they weren't going to cut it. I would say close to 90 percent of training isn't about your technical knowledge or creativity with designing a workout program but rather how well you get along with your clients and how you manage to keep them interested for that hour or so. If you're not the most talkative person, you may have some trouble holding on to clients. Sure, it helps if you look like someone who can grace the cover of a magazine, but if you are a tool, then it's only a matter of time before your clients move on to someone who is not a tool. But over the years, I've seen firsthand that even if you're the biggest jerk-off in the world, there is someone out there who, for whatever reason, will pay good money to work out with you. And there are quite a few jerk-offs out there today, aren't there?

Personal trainers might not realize at first that the business side of keeping clients happy is more important than the fancy moves they know on the TRX Suspension Trainer. It's not about wowing people with a ridiculous number of exercises that push them to the brink of vomiting. I've witnessed hundreds of trainers over the years, and in all honestly, most personal trainers take their jobs for granted and do the bare minimum to get by. They take a lackadaisical approach to training and don't even attempt to prepare beforehand what type of routine they are going to put their clients through. I remember some of the lazier trainers playing "repeater" with me on some occasions. If you are not familiar with that one, it's when you do exactly what the other person does. In the training world, this means just replicating the exact exercise you see another trainer doing and continuing to do so for the entire session. If you are a client, here's a warning for you: if your trainer isn't at least writing shit down during your session or doesn't have something written up prior to training with you, that is a red flag. With the going rate for a personal trainer these days at well over fifty dollars an hour, clients should expect some type of work from their trainer other than blurting out exercise after exercise. Of course, cutting corners is common in many jobs these days. Look around your office. How many people are doing honest work throughout the day? In a job where there is literally no accountability other than client retention, it's difficult to keep tabs on trainers. Most sales managers are only concerned about the bottom line; they don't really care if that fifty-year-old obese guy loses a single pound. As long as that guy continues to throw down his money each month for more training, no one is going to question what it is you're doing with him during his training sessions.

It sometimes takes a very long time for people to get tired of your bullshit before they ultimately fire you as their trainer. Unfortunately, so many clients fall through the cracks. If every personal trainer did their job from the get-go, there wouldn't be so many "my personal trainer sucked, and I didn't lose any weight" stories. The simple truth is that it's all about compatibility and your ability to be like a chameleon with each and every client. If your clients feel you are meeting their needs, even if their physical goals are not even close to being met, you will be training them for as long as you intend on being a personal trainer. If you can at least make your clients feel like they are progressing, even if they can't see any kind of objective proof, they will be more inclined to stick it out with you. I have found that it's all in the delivery and how you go about explaining to them what you are trying to help them accomplish. That being said, if you get caught up spending more time bullshitting with them, you can be certain that eventually they will find someone else to bullshit with who doesn't cost as much as you. As long as they continue to exercise regularly for the long haul, they are at least doing something healthy and will eventually see some type of progress. That is the bottom line when it comes to retaining clients.

Next up is the mind-boggling question of what certification to get. What's even more confusing to trainers than it is to clients is the large number of personal training certifications available today, for example, AFAA, NASM, ACE, and ISSA, to name a few. Each certification program has its own spin on what is the best approach to training. For example, when I was starting out, the whole "super slow" thing was all the rage. A medical doctor, who I'm sure had to be a pretty bright guy, once told me the super slow method was the best way to train, period. This method required you to spend ten seconds lifting a weight and four seconds bringing it back down, and then repeat the process four to six times. I may not have been lucky enough to receive an Ivy League education, but something tells me there is usually more than one way to get results when it comes to working out.

Nowadays, it seems you can't turn a corner without seeing a place that specializes in CrossFit. It's quite fun to flip large tires and throw shit around and have it count as a workout. To become a certified CrossFit trainer, you are required to attend not just the level 1 trainer course but also the level 2 *and* level 3 courses. These courses combined can cost you several thousands of dollars. You can go ahead and get whatever certification makes you feel better about yourself, but if you have no experience with sales and don't know how to work with clients, the going is sure to be rough. The fact that you can get an online certification today and begin your personal training career tomorrow is somewhat suspect. Although it's not as shady as backroom plastic surgeons performing illegal surgeries, it's not too reassuring knowing the guy or girl training you was able to answer fifty questions with an open book after spending a couple of hours online. How safe are you going to feel with a couple hundred pounds on your back and a trainer who was peddling carpet cleaning door-to-door just last week? Come on, what good does a certification really do for anyone? I think it's important to get some formal education on what you are doing so that you at least have some clue how the body works. Once you get some college-level classes in anatomy and biomechanics under your belt, then go ahead and go certification crazy if you have the extra dough to throw around. Unfortunately, just because you are certified in something doesn't mean you know what the fuck you are doing.

There are some schools of thought that argue most of what you need to learn about personal training you will learn on the job, not in college. I agree with this, but personally I would hate to be the guinea pig first client in that experiment. Without cracking open a single book on human anatomy, trainers are rolling the dice every time they train someone. Not knowing what the fuck is connected to what is pretty risky, especially when you throw in potentially heavy amounts of weight. With today's overly litigious society, I'm glad I was working back in a day before people would sue you for just about anything. One former client who was very overweight comes to mind. During one of our sessions, she told me she was going to try rock climbing. This woman had trouble walking at a slow speed on the treadmill with a very slight incline for more than five minutes. At this point in my life, I had never even studied physics, but I knew bad things would happen if she tried hanging onto anything that would require both of her feet to be off the ground. She wasn't talking about one of those fancy rock-climbing walls you see in some gyms. This was a real fucking mountain. I politely, without a hint of sarcasm, suggested that she should perhaps build up her endurance before attempting something like this heavy-duty challenge. Somehow, this got twisted into me calling her fat, and that is never good for business, as that marked the last time I ever saw that client. If McDonald's can get sued for making someone fat, I'm afraid I would be liable for somehow implying this woman was larger than life.

When I started working as a trainer, there were only a few avenues for formal education in the field. I had the National Academy of Sports Medicine (NASM) certification, courtesy of my new employer. In addition to having this weekend certification, I also knew I needed to learn what this job was all about, but there wasn't a college-level program available. So I did the next best thing and started taking courses in anatomy and nutrition at the community college, which at least forced me to learn something about what I was doing every day at work. A fair share of my training came from other trainers I worked with and managers who spent a ton of time with me when I was starting out. There is also shadowing; some trainers are more than happy to show future trainers the ins and outs of the business. You'd be surprised by how much you can learn after watching an experienced trainer at work for a couple of days. Besides, it beats the standard internship that is attached to many careers these days. There's nothing worse than interning for months and months just to be given the great news that you finally can't show up for free anymore: "Sorry, we don't have any positions right now, but you'll be the first to know when one opens up."

Among some of the important pieces of advice I got when I was starting out was to relate to the client as much as possible. This is easier said than done, especially if you're a nonpracticing Catholic from the not-so-great part of town and one of your clients is a wealthy Asian who has a difficult time with the English language. This took some time for me to figure out. After all, I was a barely educated kid having to essentially tell these people who were much older and smarter than me how to do something. I remember the first time I trained a physical therapist. I almost shit my pants thinking that she was going to question me about what I was going to have her do and that she was not going to fall for my usual bullshit lines. Oddly enough, I was in the clear. Turns out, she had never touched a weight in her life yet somehow instructed patients how to exercise.

Something you will find yourself doing when you are a trainer is saying unbelievably cheesy lines, such as "Great set!" "Pull your shoulders back!" and "Engage your core!" The list goes on and on. These lines will unconsciously come out of your mouth during training sessions. Next time you are at the gym, try listening in on some of the finer motivational lines a trainer will bark at his or her clients. "Two more!" "No, make that THREE more!" "PUSH!" "PULL!" You'll notice that this is always spoken by some overambitious trainer whose enthusiasm seems to match that of a Publishers Clearing House sweepstakes winner. I always get a kick out of the fired-up trainer who is giving his all to motivate a disinterested client. I really get a kick out of the simple yet complex line "On three," which has always screwed me up since the *Lethal Weapon* movies. In every gym across America, there is at least one incident of a bad liftoff thanks to the confusion this line gives to the simple task of starting an exercise. There is a whole lot more that comes out of a trainer than counting the number of reps.

I was a big posture freak, always advising my clients in between sets to sit up straight: "Sit up with your ears, shoulders, and hips in a straight line!" At the time, I had no idea what the fuck any of this meant, but it sounded great, especially when I followed it up with a few words about how important posture was. Many of my clients who were older than me and dead tired from the workday—and equally exhausted from the last set of box step-ups I made them do—would give me that "fuck off" look as they pretended to listen to what I was saying. I also had some choice lines that I reserved for some of my special clients. My personal favorite, which I only gave to the females who ironically would end up in bed with me at some point, was "I like your form." It doesn't sound like much, but in the heat of an hour-long workout, when they were dripping with sweat, I would slip this one in. I never said anything along the lines of "I like you," since that would be wrong, but somehow this line got lost in translation, and more than a few clients thought this was my way of inviting them to the pants party.

Once I got over my fear of training people who were older and wiser than myself, I began to find my training mojo. All I had to do was keep them stimulated and interested during that hour, and my sales guys would close even the cheapest of cheapskates. A package of training for $400 is too expensive? Not a problem. The sales guys would somehow upsell these clients on the $700 package but split the payment up.

If one client liked sports, I could talk about sports for the entire session without hesitation. If another liked weird shit on the Internet, I would ask about it with what seemed like genuine interest. Whatever it was my clients felt like talking about, I would shut up, listen, and occasionally interject to let them know I gave somewhat of a shit. After all, they were paying good money and the least I could do for them was entertain them with some type of conversation, like those strippers tend to do while making their rounds. No, they don't really like you. They are just trying to make you feel better about yourself and get paid in the process. Over the years, I have found that people love to talk to anyone who is remotely interested in listening. It really doesn't matter if you don't give two shits about the PGA Tour or upcoming election. Actively listening to clients talk about anything is the key to keeping them coming back for more.

There is a downside to this, however. Just like everyone loves to talk, I've seen trainers talk their clients' fucking ears off about things that really could have been left unsaid. This usually occurs when overaggressive trainers take the reins and hijack a client's hour to talk about whatever it is that they want to talk about. These types of trainers are usually larger, more muscular guys or gals. They somehow feel the need to talk about whatever is going on in their lives in an effort to impress their clients. They tend to attract clients who are very insecure and just want to be around someone they admire. I quickly learned it's best to leave my personal life out of conversations with clients. Only with a select few did I somehow feel compelled to let them in on whatever was going on in my life, and even then maybe I shouldn't have. I was not the type of trainer who would boast about my prominent features, my latest conquest over the weekend, or how hard I worked out earlier that day, as I have witnessed other trainers do firsthand. I could never figure out why people would pay very good money to listen to their trainer's shit and not even have a minute to get anything off their own chest. I'm sorry, but a job that pays better than most jobs available today and requires absolutely no higher education should entitle the customer to complete fucking silence if warranted. Not to say trainers can't converse with their clients, but it gets to be overkill when a one-hour session becomes happy hour and the topic of discussion is all about the trainer.

I've met and worked with personal trainers of all traits: boring, annoying, bitchy, cocky, dumb, and pretty fucking weird. You need to have a niche when it comes to training, whether it's training athletes, the obese, or middle-aged housewives. A trainer's unique character traits help attract a large number of clients from the gym floor. I happened to have carved out my own niche, but it wasn't by my own doing. I had been semi-successful with getting most clients to sign up with just a single free session, but I had a particularly high percentage of closing the deal (in more than one way) with females in their thirties and early forties. Being young and naïve about the whole situation, I did not discover until much later that I was set up by the management. They would prescreen all potential clients, and I always ended up with this demographic. There was one other male trainer close to my age who seemed to have a bunch of MILFs as well, but he had a concentration in well-off women in their twenties.

I didn't think much of it at the time. How was I to know I was thought of as the Dirk Diggler of the gym even though I wasn't hung as well? Sure, I was given the occasional guy or college student, but that was only a small portion of my clientele. It seemed the managers had a perfect client fit for all the trainers. Just like you wouldn't go into the ninth inning without Mariano, you wouldn't send your rookie trainer to close a CEO who is looking for a permanent training schedule.

I've been around long enough to notice that women want a good-looking, preferably younger male trainer and guys want a nicely toned, hot female trainer. Now, why do you suppose this is? These days, I have to laugh at what I witness in gyms: women literally throwing themselves at young trainers and men just as guilty as their female counterparts. Does this get to be somewhat problematic when it comes to running a successful personal training business? Of course it does. You cannot fuck around with your clientele if you intend on keeping them for the long term. That's pretty much where I fucked up, and you're about to hear about the unexpected pitfalls that you will encounter when you have nearly half a dozen horny women who are willing to give you anything you want for what seems to be nothing in return. I had no idea how easy getting laid would be. It was almost as if I was a celebrity or famous athlete and all I had to do was wink at some chick and she would end up in bed with me.

For most of my time in the business, I lacked self-control. Most of the thinking I did back in those days was definitely done by the other head. I found it to be extremely difficult to say no to an attractive older woman who not only told me what she was going to do to me but also went into great detail about how she was going to do it. How many times does a guy get to hear "I want to suck your dick" from a woman he barely knows and who happens to be paying him? This was no oriental spa where you have to pay before you play; this was the complete opposite. Call me what you will, but I think I'm speaking for the majority. If you asked a bunch of guys between the ages of eighteen and twenty-five what they would have done in my place, I bet that close to 99 percent would probably make the same decisions I did. Those who didn't were maybe either still trying to discover themselves or a little confused.

Do female trainers have it any different? If anything, they have it even worse. I remember the great Chris Rock once said that every guy a girl meets after she turns thirteen is trying to fuck her. You have to consider that female trainers usually have a better-than-average body and are dealing with the testosterone-laden atmosphere of the gym where endorphins are flowing and hormones are being secreted, making just the thought of sex even better than what it already is. The biggest difference between male and female trainers is that most females are used to having guys throw themselves at them in every way possible just to get a little bit of sugar. Guys spend most of their youth trying to stick their member into anything that is willing, whereas girls are trying to deflect as many of these members away as possible. Women are usually more selective than males when it comes to picking a partner for sex. It's bad enough that women have to deal with the incessant catcalls of men every time they leave the house, and inside the gym it doesn't get much better. The whole scene is probably the equivalent of going into a club on a Friday night. So how do female trainers deal with this at work? I've seen several types of approaches.

My personal favorite is the thick-skinned bitch attitude. This type of girl lets guys know immediately where they stand. If she's not single, she usually runs the show at home. She is bossy and doesn't take shit. If her man wants steak for dinner, guess what? Too fuckin' bad because the chicken is already defrosted. I have worked with quite a few of these girls, and for some reason, they always seem to be dating a very skinny, usually soft-spoken guy. I have seen these girls with their hardened exterior, but this is sometimes a nonreliable deterrent, as males for some unknown reason seem to like the constant rejection and push their efforts into overdrive to achieve the outcome they desire. I have no idea how some guys deal with and even enjoy this type of chase. I was never one for persistence. When shit hits the fan, I choose to step out of the way rather than take it in the face. No means no in my opinion, and I don't think persistence ever pays off when trying to scoring with girls. It's funny to watch a man's determination to make something happen when clearly there is no chance. Just look at the guy who is trying to work his magic with the ladies he meets in bars. He truly deserves an A for effort for still trying after a girl tells him to fuck off. These thick-skinned chicks aren't always cool and understanding—they can be straight up bitches when it comes down to it, but for some reason, there is always an abundance of dudes who like the attitude and will put up with it for, well, sometimes forever.

Next we have the cool chick who attempts to be one of the guys by talking about guy stuff: sex, sports, and movies. I'm not talking about *Titanic*; I'm talking about guy flicks starring Stallone or Van Damme. These chicks can act like your best buddy, and I've seen them rope clients into believing they have an inside track to their snatch. But don't be fooled, as these types of female trainers are very business oriented. They know exactly what they are doing, similar to those girls who spin around poles on the weekends and sometimes end up on your lap and begin to tell you their life story. Just remember, no matter how cool they may present themselves to you, they still sit down to pee. These female trainers are very well versed in playing the game, and as long as the checks are clearing, they will put on this show for as long as it takes. They are flirtatious and seem to make any poor schmo feel that, if he hangs in there just long enough, he might get lucky. Unfortunately, this girl is never going to give the client more than a hug, which is just the right affectionate signal to keep him on the roster for years to come. The male clientele who are usually assigned to these female trainers are your insecure, haven't-been-laid-in-years types. They are probably still living at home with mom and dad, and it just so happens that these are the same guys who go to strip clubs and actually think the girls like them.

Last but not least, we have the female trainer who makes the same mistake I did. She ends up sleeping with one or maybe a few of her clients. This usually ends in disaster quicker than it does for male trainers. Why? Well, feelings are usually a little more complex in this situation. Either the guy or girl gets a little too into it, and that's the end of it. Not to say it always happens, but female trainers tend to wear their feelings on their sleeve. You can tell immediately when something is bothering them, and when it comes to sex, there is always something that can cause hurt feelings. Unlike my situation, it's the female trainer who ends up getting attached to her client quickly. I never had the kinds of feelings for my clients that would lead to scenes of jealous rage, which I have seen happen to a coworker of mine. I know it sounds like quite the double standard, but it really is a man's world. Sorry, girls. You can have a lot in life, but it's hard for you to get away with the type of shit your male counterparts do when you travel down the often-twisted road of personal training.

I'm not trying to sound sexist, so I will say that guys do run into all kinds of bullshit when this type of juvenile behavior occurs and clothes come off. It may not show its ugly head for some time, but it will almost certainly end badly. I can say that I personally dealt with whatever came my way in a manner that wasn't discernible to the outside world unless of course it all came to a head at the gym, which was the case for me once. Don't be mistaken, however. The possible scenario of sex with a client is like a mirage. It may look good from a distance, but as you get closer, you might be surprised. It will come back to bite you in the ass when you least expect it, no matter how sly you think you may be. However, today there seems to be more and more people who appear to have no conscience at all. For all I know, they may not lose a second thought on fucking multiple people and never looking back. You can watch *The Secret* a million times and think all the positive shit possible no matter what's going on in your life, but when you're dabbling in someone else's property, it will take more than the right attitude and positive attraction to bail you out. You can fuck up a million times and get away with it, but your luck will run out at some point. I've done it quite a few times and am lucky enough to have walked away with minimal scarring, but I can tell you, I know many others who have not been as lucky. I've seen it bring a man to his knees begging his wife for forgiveness after getting caught balls deep in a client.

At the end of the day, a successful personal trainer is someone who takes the job seriously, even if it is a very laid-back and personable profession. I'm sure that these types of trainers exist, although I personally do not know any of them. The best advice I can give to anyone is to run the other way when a scenario that resembles any one of the escapades you are about to read begins to unfold in front of your own eyes. And yes, even something as innocent as a hummer in the backseat of your client's car is more than enough to get you in trouble. Aside from having to meet the monthly quota or occasional demand from your manager, personal training is a job that doesn't have many boundaries but takes a motivated individual to be successful. I had a great run and got paid top dollar to have fun every day at work. It was the best job I ever had, but unfortunately, I fucked it up to where it would be impossible to make it a career. Maybe it's true that if you really enjoy what you do on a daily basis you will be successful no matter what. Be yourself, but if you're an asshole, you might find the going a little tough. Just be cool, and don't try too hard. If you find yourself trying too hard, maybe you should look into being a guidance counselor.

3
LIKE A VIRGIN

Growing up, I listened to more than my fair share of likely bullshit stories from my friends about how they got laid within minutes of meeting a girl. Who didn't have a friend who got a blow job while vacationing in Niagara Falls with his family when he was just thirteen? Whether it was true will always be a mystery. It wasn't common back then for kids to carry around cameras on vacation, so I never saw proof of such events. Being a late bloomer, I was in awe of these guys' tales of late-night encounters with someone who always seemed to be a few years older. Such stories have occupied the minds of millions of pubescent males who were just trying to stick that thing in something other than their right or left hand.

I was never one to get in on the action before the others. It's not that I didn't try. My attempts, however, were horrible. It didn't take long to figure out that maneuvering my package in such a way that a girl would have to make contact with it wasn't the way to score. I would eventually get laid near the tail end of high school, but making it happen was a whole other story. One early strikeout was the one that stung the most. It was the summer after I graduated high school, and I was hanging out with friends at a local parking lot off the beaten path. I managed to wipe the girl's name from my memory, but I haven't forgotten her face. She was this beautiful thin blonde girl who was considered to be one of the best-looking girls at school. We were drinking on the hood of my Camaro (classy, right?). I remember locking lips with her, the scent of wild berry Mad Dog 20/20 on her breath, and letting my hand run down below when she cut me off—and not just with one swift move of her hand. She stopped to tell me when I was mid-tongue that she didn't like me like that. Fuck!

As it turns out, I was always the girlfriend type and my own worst enemy when it came to getting laid. Even a one-night stand would somehow wind up being my girlfriend a few days later. I attribute this to my shyness around the opposite sex—or my idiotic thought that I was good looking enough that a woman would make the first move if she were interested in me. How is a kid to know that his mother was full of shit when she said he was the most handsome kid in the whole world?

A young man's gotta do what a young man's gotta do when it comes to taming his beast below. When I was about twelve years old, I discovered my father's old *Playboy*s buried in the basement, and I never forgot the very detailed picture of a neatly trimmed bush or the story about a guy who went into a hair salon and got laid by a perfect stranger. Yes, at a young age, I actually read what was printed in nudie magazines and didn't just stare at the large boobies. In my own fantasyland, I actually thought this was something that could happen to me.

Even though my parents' basement held an endless supply of boobie books to educate me on what was where, I had no idea how to get these beautiful creatures to disrobe in front of me. With little training in my high school years, I was officially inept in the art of scoring in my early twenties. Larry, my personal training manager at Precision Fitness, warned me about how much tail I would find myself swimming among. He told me that I would be getting up close and personal with some of my clients after a few weeks or months of training them. I doubted everything Larry told me, and I quickly assured him that nothing like that would happen to me, as I was determined to be on my best behavior at all times. I also let him know that I lacked the skills necessary to accomplish sealing the deal with women. Despite how much I expressed my lack of lady luck, Larry must have seen something in me that reminded him of his early training days and felt the need to give me a fair warning. I had no idea that what Larry was warning me about would actually happen to me. Larry told me that, in his years as a trainer, he found himself in some precarious situations without much effort on his part. Had I only listened to Larry, maybe all this would have only happened in a dream. Maybe I could have spared myself the soap opera–ish shit that would eventually transpire over the better part of my twenties.

Initially upon starting my job and after Larry's stay-away-from-the-tail speech, I was a little slow. *Slow* meaning I didn't even think about extracurricular activities with my clients. In fact, I only had two or three clients total in the opening month of the gym. I was more concerned with building up a clientele than I was with getting laid at work. After all, I wanted to make the boss happy for taking a chance on someone like me with absolutely no qualifications.

I even can recall a few instances in my early training career where I passed up getting laid. One of my first outings with a client consisted of going to a Mexican cantina and getting pretty much hammered. Her name was Joan, and she was a hot twenty-nine-year-old who I had been training for a few months. Joan was tall with long black hair. She had an innocent look about her, although she had a somewhat crazy sense of humor during our training sessions. Nothing like a girl who drops the occasional

F-bomb every now and then. She had recently finished law school and was working the hellish hours required of a new lawyer. Her body was just right, if you ask me, even before beginning to train. I'm guessing she was going through that phase single women go through in their late twenties when they realize every taco counts and their odds of finding a mate would improve if they took a little more care of their bodies. Joan and I became pretty close, so when she invited me to have some drinks after work one night, I was ecstatic. This was the first time in my young history that someone of the opposite sex had asked me out. At the time, I had no idea that she would be the first of many female clients to ask me out. I had no expectations that night, and we ended up having a great time. A pitcher of margaritas is always a good time, in my opinion, but it's all the more fun with a girl like Joan. Now I'm not going to say I most certainly could have went to bed with her that night, but I'm sure something could have happened with a little prying. If I had pulled the old stretching the arm out/putting the arm around her move, something tells me she would have been more than happy to perhaps give me a handy. This was one of the first times in all my naivety where I witnessed what alcohol can do to bring things to the next level. Although there was some mutual flirtation going on, we kept the conversation light and steered clear of the topic of sex, and nothing ever transpired. That was my first encounter with a client outside work, and all I did was say yes to an invitation by a hot older woman. My, how things managed to turn around quickly for me, and little did I know that this wasn't even the tip of the iceberg. Even though nothing happened that night, I saw that with a few drinks and laughs, and maybe with a little provocation, some after-hours workouts might be in the cards.

Joan and I never went out again, and I can honestly say I am happy that nothing transpired after our little rendezvous. Even though Joan was single, hot, and educated, she was a good person and I would've had a difficult time involving her in the fucked-up web I was about to weave. She seemed a little too good of a catch for an average Joe like myself. For all I know, I could be way off and maybe she thought I was the prude that night. I never did get to find out, as several months after our "date," Joan took a new job that required more travel, thus ending our training. If only I pursued Joan just a little more, things might have been perfect for me. Couple of kids by now, her attorney's fees affording a nice-sized home for us in the suburbs, and whatever else it is that you are expected to do in life. If only things were that easy for me.

Had I taken the experience I had with Joan and kept that same mind-set with my other clients, I would have avoided the drama that was about to happen. I would quickly learn that if a situation came up that seemed too good to be true, it probably was. Why did I even have to entertain these women when they started to ask questions about sex? I couldn't keep my mouth shut and ended up making what might have been nothing more than a drink between friends more like a scene from a porn movie. Things had just started going well at work. I was on a roll, getting busier and busier, and my bosses were saying good things about me rather than making me feel like shit. Like many before my time and many more after me, I had my cake but decided to eat it, too.

Enter Sabrina. When I first met her, I had no idea she would open the gate to a pasture full of more-than-willing and eager women. Sabrina was a successful thirty-three-year-old woman who I had been training for several months. I started training her as business finally began picking up for me, so I was in the zone at the time and oblivious to anything other than signing up new clients and keeping them happy. I had no idea to what lengths I would end up going to keep some of them happy. Sabrina was the perfect image of your average, upper-income housewife, except that she wasn't a housewife at all. In fact, she worked in management at a large insurance firm and was the breadwinner in her relationship. Sabrina had been married for a little over a year, and her husband decided to change careers, so she was footing the bills while he went back to school. Sabrina was an attractive brunette with deep-blue eyes. Like many of my clients, she wasn't in bad shape at all. In fact, one would question why she was even interested in a personal trainer in the first place, considering her hectic work schedule and all the other things she had to take care of because her husband was busy with school. Of course, these are all questions I would never ask her. In fact, I was more than happy to train someone three to four days a week, even if she was in better shape than I was, as long as she was a paying customer.

Spending all this time with Sabrina allowed a close relationship to develop between the two of us. Similar to training with Joan, Sabrina and I would share a few laughs and have a good time during each session. I never really pried about her personal life during our sessions. She would talk to me, and I spent the hour listening. At first, our conversations were innocent enough. Things changed one day when Sabrina opened up about her husband. Little did I know that this would be a huge red flag for all you husbands out there. When a woman begins to talk about her husband in a somewhat demeaning way to another man, if it doesn't mark the end of her marriage, it most definitely means that infidelity is just a heartbeat away. Even though Sabrina had not been married long, it was obvious to me that she was unhappy in her marriage. How this happens in just over a year of marriage I will never know. I had no idea if it was a sexual or emotional thing or something else that was lacking at home, but Sabrina constantly brought up her dissatisfaction toward her husband.

"I like giving blow jobs, but my husband doesn't like them," she told me.

Did I just hear what I think I fucking heard? First, I can't remember a woman telling me she enjoyed giving a blow job, ever. Second, what kind of guy in his right mind doesn't like getting a BJ? I might have told Sabrina one day that I liked her form while she was doing dead lifts, but this was more than my testosterone-filled mind could handle. So caught up in my disbelief, I had no idea I was playing right into her twisted little plot. I went on and on about not only how much I loved to be on the receiving end of a blow job but also how a guy who didn't like blow jobs really wasn't a guy, in my opinion. I didn't think much of it, but I unknowingly unlocked Pandora's box full of shit just from being a patient listener.

After a few weeks of Sabrina ranting on and on about her husband and me trying to sympathize with her, Sabrina then started to shift the conversations toward me. She began asking questions about my personal life, including my girlfriend. I had been dating Danielle for close to a year. We met at one of those shitty parties you end up going to if you don't leave town for college. Once again, one night in bed ended up being a long-term relationship for me. She was a couple of years younger than me, so going out to drink anywhere other than a local dive that was notorious for selling to minors didn't happen all that much. Danielle was in nursing school and still lived at home with her parents. As much as I enjoyed spending time with her, seeing how she was my girlfriend, Danielle had been wearing on my nerves for the past few months. I don't know, maybe it was the "I'm wanting to get married soon" line she threw out that turned me off. Needless to say, when Sabrina asked about my girlfriend, my only response was how my girlfriend *didn't* like giving me head.

Being the eternal pessimist that I was, it wasn't difficult for me to find problems with any situation in my life. I felt more and more comfortable with Sabrina as our training sessions went on, so I had no problem opening up to her about my feelings toward my girlfriend and other aspects of my life. This back and forth banter continued for several months. The innocent flirting that I assumed was harmless became more and more real as comments would get more descriptive each time.

It was almost a year to the day that I had started my first personal training job when Sabrina invited me out for drinks one Friday night with her and her coworkers. What was the worst that could happen? If I was able to have a platonic relationship and innocent outing with Joan, I certainly should be able to have one with Sabrina. How was I supposed to know that meeting someone out for drinks was code for "I want whatever you have in your pants"? I expected things to go just the same as they had with Joan. Maybe a little flirting with a hug or two at most and maybe, if I was lucky, a little kiss with or without tongue.

Our plans were to meet at this restaurant lounge that was most notable for being a haven for aging lounge lizards. It was a place with a reputation where both attached and unattached women were looking for dick, and there were plenty of willing participants. The place must have been off the chains in the mid-seventies, but now it was just a sad scene for all in attendance. I didn't give much thought to this, as I was zeroed in on Sabrina that evening. When I entered the dimly lit bar, Sabrina was alone, which I thought was strange, since she was supposed to be meeting up with some of her coworkers. She was also a little more dressed up than I expected her to be, since she was supposedly coming right from work. She also had god only knows what type of perfume on, but it was the kind that gets any guy slightly aroused. I was and will continue to be a sucker for the scent of a woman. Just the right scent will give me a soft-on and put me in the mood anytime. I asked her where her friends were, and she said they were on their way, so we made ourselves comfortable in the oversized lounge chairs covered in cheap dark cherry red fabric and ordered drinks.

Several hours and several drinks later, it was apparent Sabrina's friends were not coming. In my defense, I was set up for failure on this one. I'm not much of a drinker, so I was feeling more than buzzed by now. Something told me right then and there that Sabrina wasn't going to be happy with just a hug and a little peck on the cheek goodnight. She wanted something, and I was getting more nervous by the minute, as the whole idea of casual sex was new to me. I didn't know what to do for obvious reasons: Sabrina was married, and I had a girlfriend. Had I thought about cheating on Danielle? The thought had crossed my mind from time to time, but I was never as close to doing it as I was now. Sabrina was looking a little red in the eyes as well, and I could tell we were most likely either at or around our legal limit.

We decided to leave the bar after nearly four hours and a hefty tab to pay, which she paid, by the way. This was the moment of truth. Perhaps a better man would have been able to part ways with nothing more than a handshake or hug, but Sabrina was looking at me with those puppy eyes as we stood in front of her car. It was as if she was subconsciously asking me to take her back to my place and do whatever I wanted to her. At least that's what I was thinking. I'm sure the mushrooms I indulged in during my high school years had a hand in my fucked-up way of thinking that night.

This was the first time in my life where I could have my way with an attractive older woman and she would be more than happy to accommodate me. With just the thought of this, combined with that rich aroma of her perfume and more than enough drinks, I was incapable of making an educated decision. Uh-oh, this was really happening to me. I had never been with anyone who had a significant other, let alone someone who was married. Even back in my high school days, I never thought about screwing around with another guy's girl. It just never seemed like a good idea to me. I'll be the first to admit I was more than a little hesitant at first. Not only did I have a girlfriend, but I also couldn't imagine how Sabrina's husband would feel when he found out his wife performed acts on some guy that he probably hasn't had himself in god knows how long—or worse, has never even thought she was capable of. In all my years watching movies and hearing stories, I found that this scenario never works out well for the participants. Would it turn out like it does in the movies, with someone ending up dead? All kinds of crazy thoughts were racing through my inebriated state of mind.

I somehow rationalized that since we both had someone else in our lives, it really wasn't a big deal. Using the Baba Booey math method, I calculated that 1 plus 1 times 2 somehow canceled the whole equation. What the fuck was I thinking? That sounds like the thought process of a total asshole if you put me in that same situation today.

I decided to use one of the many trusted lines I'd heard in movies—one that would come in handy for me down the road: "How about we stop by my apartment for a nightcap?"

A nightcap, really? Who the fuck was I? Magnum, P.I.? I didn't even really know what the hell it meant, but I thought it sounded cool. Having my own place for the first time in my life was also a key component in this equation, as I feel things wouldn't have happened the way they did for me if I had to inform Sabrina that I still lived at home with my parents.

Sabrina said yes so quickly that I doubt she gave it a second thought. That was it, and the deal was done. It was that simple. I didn't have to beg, ask twice, or jump through hoops. All I had to do was ask and I got it. Compared to my current relationship, this was much simpler. I felt a strange sense of accomplishment in that I was able to convince a married woman to let me have my way with her. In my current relationship, it was rather difficult to get anything I wanted. Sure, I was getting laid, but Danielle also managed to give me more headaches than I cared to deal with, as she was your typical nineteen-year-old who could manage making a trip to the movies complicated. I was tired of dealing with bullshit, and Sabrina had me thinking that there would be no bullshit involved with her. I'm confident that I could have asked Sabrina for a blow job in the parking lot of the bar and not gotten any resistance.

Since we had driven separately to the bar, Sabrina followed me back to my apartment in her car, despite us both probably being over the legal drinking limit. This short ride wasn't long enough for either of us to come to our senses. I was playing through several possible outcomes to this situation, the best being a one-time stint in the sheets with this woman and the worst being her husband hiring a hit man to take me out. That may sound outlandish, but I watched a lot of movies and felt they had to be based on at least an ounce of realism. After all, if I were married, I would like to think that whoever managed to get his unit anywhere near my wife would suffer severe repercussions.

When we arrived at my apartment, we made our way to my living room. I was fortunate enough to not have roommates at the time. How the small things in life, like not having roommates, no matter how shitty the place, can make you happy. I had a habit of keeping dirty laundry in the closet, so at least the place wasn't as messy as one would think, but it was still filled with secondhand furniture and neon-lit beer signs. The small supply of liquor that I kept on hand came in handy for the first time in my life other than the occasional times I would have to monitor my underage girlfriend's alcohol consumption. At this moment, I would like to show my level of maturity by mixing vodka with Sprite as opposed to Gatorade or whatever open juice was in my refrigerator. I poured a couple of drinks, and we sat down on the couch and continued with our conversation, which turned from our significant others to what types of crazy shit we had done in the past. Seeing how Sabrina had a decade plus on me, her stories had me in awe. The best thing I could come up with was how I tried to score with the interpreter for the deaf girl I went to high school with. I didn't really know what to say when Sabrina told me about hooking up with a cruise ship captain, and it wasn't on one of those little hour or so harbor tours. It was one of those huge cruise liners in which no one working on the ship seems to be from the United States.

After about five minutes of sitting on the couch and talking, Sabrina grabbed the back of my head with such force that I was caught off guard. No music, no television, and barely a few minutes of small talk, and it was on. My eyes were wide open as she kissed me and rubbed her hands all over my body. Her hands went from my chest and then quickly down to my crotch. She was acting as if she had been deprived of sex for years. Was this how all older women were? I began to think that I should start dating upward, as it was a nice change to not feel like I was forcing my wiener into my girlfriend's personal space to get him some attention. I had never experienced a woman be that aggressive with me, so I went from soft to hard quicker than I ever imagined possible. I'll never know how dudes in porn manage to keep only a semi after several minutes of a girl sucking and tugging.

Within minutes, Sabrina's mouth made its way down my neck as she began to pull my shirt over my head. She then slowly began to slide down to the floor, kissing my stomach as she worked her way down and kneeled in front of me. I was so turned on at this point that I was facing due north. Slightly embarrassed by my quick wood, I tried to act as if everything was cool by getting her attention off my crotch for a moment so that I could tuck him in real quick. This couldn't be further from the truth. I was somewhat nervous about the ferocity of her attack, yet I was more aroused than I had been in some time. She quickly unbuckled my belt and sensually rubbed me with one hand as she slowly unzipped my fly with the other. I must have sprung out of my pants like a rod. Holy shit! I only saw things like this in porn movies. Who would have thought it could happen to me?

I'm not gonna lie to you. I possibly could have intervened at this moment, but my self-control was out the window at this juncture. After all, my dick was exposed and her hand was on it—what was I going to do? I closed my eyes, and before I knew it, she took me in her mouth. Her moaning sounded as if I was doing all the work. I was in this buzzed, amazed state of mind just wondering how I won the equivalent of the lotto to any twenty-one-year-old guy. She seemed to know her way around downstairs better than anyone I had been with up until then. I wondered if all older women were as well versed as Sabrina when it came to blow jobs.

As I opened my eyes and watched in awe, I couldn't think about anything except trying to hold myself in so that I could make this unbelievable feeling last just a bit longer. She used the right combination of fast and slow movements that had me on the cusp of eruption. If I had my stopwatch going, I could probably confirm that this whole event took less than two minutes from shirt off to blast off, but let me tell you, those two minutes made me feel as if life was complete for a short time afterward. I could have died a happy man at that moment. Sabrina proceeded to make this the ultimate night by finishing the job, which was more than unexpected. I couldn't remember the last time I got a blow job that didn't end with the girl running to bathroom to loudly spit out my load. Even my own girlfriend didn't swallow. After I finished, I couldn't help but wonder what was going through Sabrina's mind knowing she just swallowed some guy's batch while her husband was who knows where.

Knowing that Sabrina had to go home afterward actually made it all the better. We were able to avoid that momentary awkwardness after intimacy. Should I stay or should I go? There wasn't even a question, since she had to get home to her husband. After walking her to the door and giving her a hug, since I didn't want to go near that mouth of hers, I was left to myself in my post-climactic state of euphoria. Thoughts were rolling around in my head, mainly about her husband and my girlfriend. What the hell was this guy going to think when his wife got home late at night, all dressed up, and half in the bag with funky-smelling breath?

On the other hand, what was my girlfriend going to think of me being "out with some people from work" and not calling her when I got home? Oh, well. Problems that could be left for another day. It's funny how at twenty-one you could simply trivialize the concept of extramarital affairs. Besides, according to all the major media outlets, cheating was commonplace among couples. My thinking was if I didn't do it, chances were that my girlfriend would be cheating on me soon enough. This may sound asinine, but like most guys, I didn't even consider the long-term consequences of my actions. My priority was to rehydrate and then call it a night.

Prior to Sabrina's next appointment a few days later, I was so anxious and thought it was the end of her training and possibly the end of my job. Since this was the first time I had contact with a client outside the gym that resulted in something, I had no idea what to expect. Was she going to be pissed at me for not calling? Was she going to be livid because I didn't return the favor after she swallowed? Did she think I was a joke because I blew my load in two minutes? Was she unimpressed with the size of my package?

Turns out, not only was she perfectly okay with everything, but she was also somewhat dude-like in her attitude about the whole ordeal. She made it very clear that if something happened again, great. If not, oh well, no harm done. Are you fucking kidding me? There is no way I'm going to get away with getting oral from a married woman with no consequences. She even brought me dinner at work that night. This was too much for my young mind to comprehend. Had things gone terribly at that first training session after our little get-together, there is probably a huge possibility that I would have ceased all interaction with clients outside of work and the story would be over. Unfortunately, things went so well that I began thinking this type of behavior was okay, and I would come to expect nothing less.

Sabrina took great pride in making me happy for some reason or another, and apparently I was filling some type of void in her life. We continued our training for quite some time. I was still coping with the fact that Sabrina was a married woman and, by the looks of things, had no intentions of becoming unmarried, but I never would have expected the antics that were about to occur over the next several months. They were reminiscent of a sorority girl at her first frat party. What can I say? I was hooked. Each after-hours encounter with Sabrina would top the previous, and my interest would heighten after each night with her. After what felt like countless blow jobs, we finally ended up doing the deed. This was fucked up in so many ways because it happened at her place, when her husband was out of town.

My friend Joey and I met Sabrina and some of her friends at a bar near her place. Even Joey, who knew no bounds, thought how messed up this would be if it ended up at her place. Sure enough, after more than a few vodka tonics, we made our way to her place, which was this very posh condo on the water a few blocks away. Joey and I were dumbfounded as we scanned the inside of her third-floor condo with water views from each room. Unlike my cheap furniture and wall art appropriate for a frat house, Sabrina had pricy furniture and paintings that just looked expensive, even if they looked like a second grader threw paint at a canvas. Joey was the ideal wingman, as he was well versed in how to keep that potential cock-blocking girlfriend at bay while I tried to get laid. He was smart enough to put on MTV, which was known for playing music videos in that era. Sabrina wasted no time showing me to her bedroom. As she closed the door behind her, she kissed me and, without looking, unbuttoned my pants and pulled out my cock. She stroked me as we made our descent and laid down on the bed. Wait a second, isn't this where she sleeps with her husband? Before I could think twice about it, she went down on me and I stopped thinking those crazy thoughts.

As she came up for air, I peeled off her top and then pulled down her shorts and white lace panties in one swift movement. Instead of going back down on me, Sabrina straddled me and slid right down on my cock. She was so wet, there was no question I had the right hole. Wait a second, shouldn't I be wearing a prophylactic or whatever it is they call those things? Those thoughts were pushed out of my mind as Sabrina's nails dug into my chest while she slid up and down on top of me. I had no idea if Sabrina's friend and Joey could hear Sabrina's moans as she fucked me in her husband's bed. All I could hear was Poison's "Nothin' But a Good Time" playing in the other room.

The vodka must have been the good stuff because I held out for some time. The vertical blinds over the sliding glass door in Sabrina's room weren't drawn completely, so the moon's reflection off the water lit up the inside of her room. I could see Sabrina's better-than-average rack as she rode me, and for the first time, I began to appreciate the work I had done, as her body was looking quite toned in the moon's white light.

After maybe fifteen minutes, I should have given her the signal to jump off, but instead I let loose inside her. Wow. This was something else. Afterward, Sabrina seemed undeterred by the load inside her. She just laid there on top of me for a minute or two before climbing off and disappearing into the bathroom for a few minutes. What is her husband thinking? I thought. This woman is amazing! It wasn't until years later that I realized this concept. Everyone loves the situation they are currently *not* in. What guy wouldn't like to be sleeping with Mila Kunis instead of his girlfriend or wife, no matter how beautiful she is? The same principle goes for women. This ongoing cycle of wanting more sucks. It ruins relationships and fucks things up for people who are trying to do things the right way. I know, spoken like a true asshole, considering the circumstances I put myself in.

I then got up and, without wiping myself off (I know, that's nasty), put my clothes back on. When Sabrina returned from the bathroom still naked, I got the feeling she wanted a little more.

"You have to leave?" she asked as she laid back down on her bed, as if to say I was welcome to have seconds. For a second, I thought about giving her another go, as round two usually lasts a little longer than round one for me.

"I'm a little worn out and have a little bit of a drive to get Joey back," I said without much confidence.

"You can stay here for a little while and take a nap if you want," she said, patting the pillow next to her.

Fuck! I was walking right into a booby trap. I thought for a minute about what position I would like her in next, but with some regret, I said with a smile, "Maybe next time. I'll be seeing you soon." With that, I said good-bye, wrangled Joey, and tried to make sense of this great night as we made the journey back home.

Being with Sabrina was as simple as asking for an extra napkin at a restaurant. With great service, the napkin appears on the spot without waiting long at all. Every few weeks or so, I would get my fix with little or no effort. Sabrina and I would use the covert question, "Want to meet up for drinks later?" I knew when this question was asked, I would be getting off in one way or another that day. With the two of us already in relationships, you might wonder how we were able to get away from our partners so easily and meet up a few times each month. Even today, I can't believe I was able to get away so easily from my girlfriend and Sabrina from her husband. I am now acutely aware of when a girlfriend is on the fritz and beginning to stray. It's a shitty thing to admit, especially from the guy who found himself in the middle of an affair.

Little did I know this small rock in the road would turn into a huge fucking rock the size you see chasing Indiana Jones, with Sabrina being the catalyst to it all. What happens to a guy like me in a situation where he is training several attractive women at one time? Sabrina opened my eyes to a world I would soon be immersed in. Spending several hours a week, week after week, with these women often led to close relationships. Most of the women I trained admired that I would just listen to them, even if they were essentially paying me to. All of my attention was theirs for an entire hour. This was sometimes more attention than they would get in a week from anyone else in their lives. Now, it wasn't like this with every female client I had. If that were the case, I would have a stable larger than Hef's. The women who were happy in their relationships at home kept a comfortable distance. Sure, we had a great time and would joke around, but things were kept on a professional level with no underlying flirtation. On the other hand, the longer I trained some of these unhappy women, the more details they chose to share with me. They would open up and eventually want to take our relationship outside the gym. Sabrina was just the first to introduce me to this appealing yet risky lifestyle.

After watching *Risky Business*, what younger guy didn't want some older woman to come along and rattle his senses? Sure, it is all fun and games when neither of the two parties are involved in another relationship, but shit gets dicey when you factor in other people. Seeing how Sabrina and I both had someone else in our lives, deceit became a daily habit. In fact, I ended up finding myself lying even when I had no reason to lie. What the fuck was happening to me? Every encounter Sabrina and I had was prefaced by some elaborate tale, such as meeting friends my girlfriend had never met or even going to concerts with people whom I barely knew. I can tell you, I felt awkward asking dudes I barely knew to cover for me just in case my girlfriend actually met them and asked about whatever it was that we were supposedly doing.

Meanwhile, some of my coworkers were catching on to the vibes Sabrina was throwing my way. It was more than just a little innocent smile or laughter after a stupid joke. It was very apparent to everyone at work that this woman was into me, and I'm not gonna lie to you, I was into her too—married or not. I loved spending time with her. Not only was she giving me anything I wanted, whenever I wanted it, but she also did it with a smile. Unlike my relationship with Danielle, which had become more work than play, it was a sweet relief to see Sabrina three to four times a week for our regular workouts and talk about all kinds of shit, from work life to everyday life. Top it off with the occasional quickie in the backseat of her car, and I was in heaven. Yes, a better man would have ended his current relationship if he intended to pursue this type of lifestyle, but I somehow thought in my own twisted way that what I was doing was okay.

All the while, something started happening. I began using the same approach I had used on Sabrina with my other female clients. There are no secrets here; this is not something you can learn by reading some self-help book and realizing shortly afterward it really didn't help you. It's not written in an old, leather-bound book located in the basement of your high school library. The knowledge I'm about to drop is priceless, and it's not some confusing shit you are going to have to read an entire two hundred pages to understand. I simply became more interested in what my clients had to say even though deep down I could care less about what came out of their mouths. I didn't push or prod with annoying questions, nor did I begin with in-depth questions about their feelings or thoughts. I just asked about things such as how work was or how their weekend was and then simply listened. I didn't offer advice; I just let them talk about whatever the hell it was they wanted to talk about. I would not talk about myself unless I was asked. Seeing how they were paying me great money, it was the least I could do, in my mind. If I just shut the hell up about myself and gave them my undivided attention, it made a world of a difference to these people. As the weeks went on, these women would begin to divulge more and more information about their lives. This would be followed by the need for them to talk to me on the phone occasionally, which would lead to conversations outside the gym, which could eventually lead to the bedroom, or car, or office…

Sabrina was just the first to lead me astray from my girlfriend, but she would not be the last. One would think I would have learned that living a life of sin and lies is an express ticket to hell. I had played with fire and got away without getting burned, so I opted for more. I was looking forward to my next round of Russian roulette. As a matter of fact, I was quickly gathering a stable full of women who wanted more than a workout in the gym. Growing up in a Catholic household, I had those early impressions of what would happen to me if I fucked up and had to come front and center with each encounter I had with a client. I'm sure you've heard of all those rules, including those ten written ones. I was breaking a handful of them each time I got together with a client, and a part of me felt guilty immediately afterward. Somehow, though, the guilt didn't set in until after orgasm. It was the kind of situation where you do something once, and no matter how wrong it is, you figure how bad could it be if you do it again and again? I would like to say that any guy in his twenties would be guilty of the same crime. Besides, it's not like I was some kid who offered to off his teacher's husband in exchange for a blow job. I just thought of it as giving Sabrina something she wasn't getting at home.

Sabrina and I would have multiple rendezvous over the course of my time at Precision Fitness. Because she was the first client I slept with, I felt an attraction to her like that of a high school girl who gives up her virginity to a guy who she knows deep down is only going to be around for so long. I felt an obligation to Sabrina that lasted for quite a while. No matter who else I was sleeping with or what was going on in my life, if Sabrina called and needed some personal attention, I was more than happy to give it to her. She would be my number one in the rotation for some time.

Luckily, this all happened at a time before the TV show *Cheaters*, which catches poor bastards literally in the act! Talk about fucked up. Sabrina's husband and a TV crew could have caught me in the act with my pants around my ankles.

We even had tentative plans to meet up at some beachside resort, which would have been a bad move in retrospect. Luckily, that trip never happened. We had never spent more than several hours together, let alone an extended period of time. An event like that would have brought our relationship to a new level, one that neither of us truly wanted. It all came to an end via a letter I received about a year after I moved. It was a classic Dear John letter, one that to this day I wish I had kept. But I remember the content vividly. Sabrina said she was tired of running around behind her husband's back and wanted to have kids, of all things. I'll never know how someone goes from not only blowing but also banging another guy for nearly a year to wanting to have kids with her husband. Although the letter came to me somewhat as a surprise, I felt a sense of relief, like I escaped a potentially harmful situation had this progressed any further. I had made it out of this particular situation unscathed, but I would like to blame Sabrina for being my personal guide down the road to hell, as things would have turned out much differently in the long run if I wasn't so eagerly pursued that first night. Here's to you, Sabrina. May your kids never know the truth about their mom.

4
CARIBBEAN QUEEN

Billy Ocean couldn't have sung it any better. What does a young guy do with an exotic woman from the islands and whose sex drive is off the charts? I had never been to the Bahamas, but I always envisioned the women to be quite freaky. Sure, I had heard about friends who visited the islands and got a lot more than they could ever imagine from a local girl, but how was I to know an islander would find her way to me on the mainland?

I would find out firsthand while personal training at Precision fitness that lightning really can strike the same place twice. Shortly after starting to train Sabrina, I started to train yet another housewife. She was a mother of two in her thirties. Unlike the other housewives I was training, Raquel was flirtatious from the very start and made her expectations clear from the get-go. Hearing things like, "You must not have any trouble getting girls" and, "Your arms look great in that shirt" were very foreign to a guy like me. Still somewhat in denial about what was going on around me and what I was becoming, I didn't think for a second that training with Raquel would go the same way as it had with Sabrina. After all, Raquel may have been married, but unlike Sabrina, she had kids, so she probably had to draw the line somewhere, right? Within moments of our initial meeting, the tone was set for what was to come.

Our gym had small offices where we would take clients' measurements and calculate body fat, among other things. During our initial consultation, Raquel didn't hesitate to pull off her shirt when I barely had the request out of my mouth so that I could take her measurements. To my surprise, she had these humongous knockers that caused me to do a double take. Fortunately, she had a sports bra on, which made me feel somewhat less awkward about the situation. But I could not help but stare at the two huge items in front of me as I tried to take her measurements without accidentally grazing them. They were definitely aftermarket parts, and something told me Raquel was very willing to show them to anyone who desired a peek. To top it off, she didn't have the body of your average mother of two. I was a little intimidated at first, as Raquel had a body that seemed appropriate for a professional basketball player, not some average guy like myself. Raquel was tall compared to most girls I had been with—she was at least five foot nine and would be considered leggy, as her well-built legs had not an ounce of fat on them. If she wore heels, forget about it; my face would be parallel with those funbags. Her hair was long and braided, but I would soon discover that she would do her hair differently almost weekly, which made her all the more intriguing. Sometimes she wore her hair like your typical islander but with very clean braids that made her look both sexy and sophisticated. Other times, she would dye it light and wear it down, letting it flow like an eighties model. Raquel would always have her long nails freshly done each time I saw her—they were long in a good way, not the Jackie Joyner-Kersee way. She also had this athletic build that was similar to Venus Williams. If I somehow found myself naked with her, I could only hope to keep up, as it appeared she might require hours in bed to be satisfied.

She was not Halle Berry black but more like Grace Jones black. It was close to winter, so I was pasty white and envisioned us entwined in bed looking like the yin-yang sign.

I had always fantasized about being with an island girl. I always imagined the sex would be crazy and similar to that seen online at YouPorn or whatever your favorite site may be. Having an exotic woman on top of me screaming for me to fuck her harder was something I wanted to experience firsthand. I also spent some time working in a restaurant kitchen and remembered a story about one of the cook's visits to Jamaica, which was more than memorable thanks to him meeting one local lady. With all these crazy thoughts racing around in my one-track mind, I tried my best to play it safe seeing how Raquel was married. With Sabrina still in the mix, I had no desire to be with another married woman, so I did not show any type of interest. That wouldn't keep Raquel at bay for long, as she was very up front with her needs. Not only was she looking to tone up, but she was also looking for something on the side. At this early stage in my career, I was thinking the game could be played for some time before one party or the other made a move. I had every intention of keeping her clothes on by deflecting her numerous requests. Within the first week of training Raquel, she made her case as to why I should sleep with her. One week was all that it took for this woman to decide she wanted my dick as opposed to her husband's.

During one of the first couple workouts, when we barely knew anything about each other, Raquel requested I squire her about town. "There's this great little bar that just opened that I really want to go to," she said.

Really? Shouldn't she ask her husband to take her rather than some guy she just met who definitely does not want to be anyone's husband? I attempted to dodge the questions between sets of pull-ups and bent-over rows, but Raquel wasn't going to let me off the hook without an answer. This whole scene was something out of a movie for me, as I was still in disbelief at how things had transpired with Sabrina. Aside from the usual "I'm unhappy with my husband" spiel, Raquel made it a point to let me know that, even though she was closer to forty than thirty, she felt like she was still in college. I had something to do with Danielle, my actual girlfriend, that weekend, so I was able to get out of this invite, but something told me Raquel wouldn't always accept no for an answer.

A session never went by where she didn't talk about sex. Where to do it, how to do it, you name it. I tried to contain my excitement and thankfully never pitched a tent while training her, but I'd be lying to say I didn't have a soft-on more than once. She was a hot older woman, dressed in little clothing, telling me what she wanted to do in bed. Raquel was a big fan of spandex bicycle shorts, more than likely because they seemed to direct attention to her finely tuned quads and calves. A skimpy spaghetti strap tank top was all that held back her huge breasts from freedom. How could I not be somewhat intrigued? Not only that, but stories of her college years when she experimented with other girls were the icing on the cake. Could I reach unchartered territory by accomplishing a threesome with Raquel and someone else? For a minute, I really thought Raquel was a retired porn star, with her above-average body and her tales that seemed fit for print in dirty magazines.

I didn't dive right in, although I easily could have. I still had a conscience at this point, along with a girlfriend. The guilt of being with Sabrina was also on my mind. I thought about not only how pissed off Raquel's husband would be but also how her two young kids would handle it if anything happened between us. How do you not grow up fucked in the head knowing that your mom boned her personal trainer behind your dad's back? I didn't think much of consequences at this point in my life, but something told me that absolutely nothing good would come out of sleeping with a married woman with kids. Unfortunately, Raquel didn't seem to share my view on this matter. In fact, she was persistent in her quest for cock, and that's when things got complicated. Raquel put her efforts in full gear. All I could think of to deter me from another bad decision was that I was in no shape to be a father figure to anyone at this point; I probably couldn't even manage to take care of a dog. But Raquel was constantly on the offensive. She constantly asked me to join her for drinks (in other words, "Let's fuck"). I had never been with a woman of color, let alone someone as horny as Raquel. Her sexy overtones were becoming more and more difficult to resist. Although she didn't sound like a phone sex operator, I wouldn't be shocked to find out that Raquel is making some extra money these days on some 900-number giving guys wood over the phone.

For about a month or so, I managed to dodge Raquel's attempts before we saw each other naked. It was more than likely because my girlfriend pissed me off for some reason or another that I ended up accepting one of Raquel's requests to meet up at a bar for drinks. Dammit! If Danielle just had enough sense not to piss me off that day, all this could have been avoided. How dare she! I know—what kind of asshole does this again with a married woman, and what type of shitty excuse is that?

I would always find an excuse to fuck around on my girlfriend, and I was getting better and better at bullshitting her. It's one thing to go out with friends every now and then but two to three nights a week sometimes? And always without even giving her the chance to come? She had to have known something was up, but if she did, she never brought it up. Now that I had given into Raquel's demands and was going to meet up with her outside the gym, I couldn't forget about the time I needed to allocate to meet up with Sabrina if the occasion presented itself. I was learning the art of juggling without proper training but doing my best to keep all parties satisfied.

It was a cold Thursday evening in the middle of winter, which meant the crowd at the bar would more than likely be sparse. Raquel had picked a bar that happened to be pretty close to my apartment. I hadn't been there before but was confident I wouldn't run into anyone who may know me. Once again, I found myself tucked away back in the darkness of what resembled a Mexican saloon, and I was still amazed at how a well-made pitcher of margaritas could bring my guard down in less than thirty minutes. Maybe it was the tequila. Maybe it was the constant buildup of sex talk between us, but things were well on their way to the next level. Sitting in a corner of this tiny watering hole, Raquel and I quickly went from buzzed to fully intoxicated.

One of the many surprises that night was something I had not anticipated happening in a million years. When I went up to the bar and put in an order, none other than the girl I went to my prom with was serving drinks. I could only imagine what was going through her head when she saw me sitting with a woman nearly fifteen years my senior. Although Raquel didn't look old, I still looked like I was in high school, so it might have looked as if I was out with my mother's friend. This girl was a couple of years ahead of me, and I remember being scared as hell asking her to my prom. Oh, well. I didn't get laid the night of my prom, but I had a feeling it was bound to happen this night. Turns out, that girl ended up fucking my stepbrother, but that's another story.

Raquel and I spent several hours drinking and talking. We touched on our significant others, among other things, but most of the conversation was about sex—what was our favorite position, what we liked and didn't like in bed, and so on. Lucky for me, she wasn't into the backdoor entry, as my only experience with that felt like getting my dick caught in a mousetrap. After a couple of pitchers, it looked as though we would touch on quite a few of the different positions we had discussed, in due time. It seemed as though Raquel had heard enough about my relationship and what my likes were in the bedroom. Now she only wanted to get to know what was hiding beneath my pants.

For just a split second, I assumed we would part ways, but then Raquel asked if she could see where I lived.

Next thing I knew, Raquel was following me back to my apartment. I was smart enough to always meet my clients out separately. Once again, the ten-minute drive to my apartment was obviously not long enough to get Raquel to think about what she was about to do. I did have something up my sleeve to boost my performance that night. I had heard about this herb that supposedly increased the blood flow to your member. Mind you, these were the days before the little blue pills that give you hours of solid wood. Before our meeting at the bar, I popped a few yohimbe pills and hoped for the best.

When we arrived at my apartment, Raquel wasted no time getting right to the point. No after-hours drinks, no small talk. It was as if Raquel needed to get laid and be on her way before midnight or she would turn into a gremlin. Immediately upon sitting down next to me on the living room couch, Raquel pulled up her shirt to show me her breasts. Mind you, this was on the same couch just a few shorts weeks ago that Sabrina had me in exactly the same precarious position. Who would have thought this couch of mine would end up having a history like a Hollywood casting couch? She was wearing one of those shirts with a built-in bra, so when it came off, those two enormous chocolate mounds were staring me right in the face. She sure was proud of these items she must have just gotten within the last year. She then casually talked about how real they looked and felt and told me to touch them.

"I told the doctor to make them feel as real as possible," she said, as if I needed any coaxing. I was a virgin to fake breasts, so you can imagine the excitement that I felt rush through my body when I was given the green light to cop a feel. She didn't have to ask twice, as I was already making my way toward her beautiful knockers before the words were out of her mouth.

By now, my unit was poking through my jeans, and the second I put my hands on her tits, I almost exploded. I felt like I was back in high school with my first girlfriend when I came faster than Jim in *American Pie*. I hoped the pills I took would somehow help things stay in for a little longer than usual. Raquel just sat back on the couch and let me feel around a little bit as I complimented her perfectly rounded breasts. I was mesmerized by the softness yet firmness that kept these D-size breasts perfectly afloat.

"These feel so soft and smooth, and they don't feel fake at all!" I said, as if I was critiquing art. I was about to comment on how they felt better than my girlfriend's small-but-adequate, real breasts when I thought better of possibly ruining the mood. I was at the point of no return; I then started to lick her tits like a baby. I felt as if I just hit the lotto—twice. For a guy who didn't get much action, this was hard to comprehend. I then went for the pants, which Raquel willingly helped me remove.

"You've got me so fucking hot right now. I'm going to fuck you all night," she said as she looked straight into my eyes. I was too astonished to be hearing this to even think about responding. Guys, take note: there never is a good response, and it's best to let the woman do the talking. Her body seemed to know exactly what it was doing, as she was in the perfect position for me to have my way with her. Did I mention I'm a huge fan of blow jobs? With Raquel completely naked and reclined on my couch, I stood up and pulled my pants down. I must have looked like a young Ron Jeremy, only with a much more fit body but unfortunately half a hedgehog downstairs. She wasted no time and grabbed my ass with both hands to pull me inside her mouth. All I could hope for now was to hold on a little longer. Even though I was more than a few drinks in and probably legally drunk, I had become so aroused over the course of the past few hours that I was ready to lose it, but somehow nothing happened. Dammit, should I have excused myself to the bathroom to clear the round that had been in the chamber for some time to get the full effect of this yohimbe? The instructions weren't too clear from what I recall. Too late for all that now. Standing there, pants around my ankles, I started thinking of anything to keep my mind off of what was going on. Who had the most receiving yards in last week's Eagles game? When was Bruce Springsteen coming to town to play a concert?

After a few minutes, I pulled Raquel's head off my dick, which seemed to turn her on even more, if that was possible. I grabbed her legs to pull them up onto the couch. She was now spread-eagle on my couch. As dark as she was, I couldn't help but notice the pink between her thighs. Her legs were so long I could only put one of them to rest on my shoulder while the other hung over the edge of the couch on the floor. I leaned forward with her one leg on my shoulder and slipped inside her. She went absolutely crazy, so I mixed up my technique and went at it with the half in–half out move. A few seconds later, I entered completely. It was as if I struck gold. Could I have hit the G-spot my first time in? Did I manage to grow an extra couple of inches from the long buildup combined with tequila and yohimbe? This really was a little better than what I had been used to in that I had made it past the BJ and on to the next round without a nap in between.

I don't know if every girl from the islands is that crazy, but I recommend it to anyone. Raquel was not only completely confident in her sexuality, but she also gave it a little extra, including moaning and groaning that could put Anna Kournikova to shame. Her hand pulled me closer as if to get me deeper and deeper inside of her. I felt like I was starring in my first adult film. If only I had a camcorder.

After my time on top, which seemed to be more than five minutes or at least enough time to cause a cramp in my hamstring, Raquel pushed me off, threw me down on the couch, and straddled me. This was also still new for me—having a woman take command of the situation. I just went with it and enjoyed the ride. The sight of her huge, voluptuous breasts bouncing in front of my face had me in awe. She was fucking me in a way I had never imagined. Her hips slid up and down and back and forth with greater speed each cycle. Somehow I managed to hold on despite a load that was no longer in the chamber but making its way through the barrel. I had to keep my eyes closed, as this was what I had always thought sex with a stripper would be like ever since my father took me to Scores for the first time. This was beyond hot, and not the Paris Hilton type of hot. Raquel worked her hips in a way that I only thought possible with trained professionals. As she sped up, her moans became more and more intense. Before I knew it, she screamed as if she had been shot and her wild hip thrusts came to a sudden stop. As much as I tried, I couldn't hold out any longer. The yohimbe and tequila had done an effective job in giving me more than enough time of pure pleasure, but I lost it inside her. Within seconds of Raquel climaxing, I didn't think to get her off my lap and finish on those beautiful breasts. After I came, I thought of the possibility of having just impregnated a married woman. I quickly wiped that possible scenario out of my mind. After all, I felt like I just ran a mile in a full sprint and was exhausted.

Condom, what condom? Raquel didn't make any hint of using one, so like your typical jackass twenty-one-year-old guy, I thought it was okay. Of course, I immediately felt guilty afterward. Raquel must have sensed me returning to normal size while still inside her and slowly got up to get dressed. Nothing dripped out of her as she got off me. Was she going to get whatever I just left inside of her out? As I put on my clothes, I curiously waited for Raquel to ask me where the bathroom was. Thankfully, after just one awkward minute of silence, Raquel asked where she could find the bathroom. While she was in the bathroom, I wondered what a married woman was going to do with some other guy's load stored up inside her. I didn't want to think of the possibilities as I walked her out of my place after she returned from the bathroom.

Raquel came back to the gym the following Monday for her appointment. There was no resentment, ill feelings, or guilt that I sensed at any level. I was two for two, not bad in the grand scheme of things. In fact, I had opened up a world of possibilities, as Raquel was looking to expand on our first sexual encounter. She even offered to bring a friend to join in. Jackpot! This woman really was a freak. This was shit you only see in pornos. I had spent many years taking care of myself watching videos of two girls satisfying a man. I had dreamed of this moment for some time. Don't look at me like I'm disgusting. If a straight guy in his twenties never thought of this, something was really wrong. Raquel and I continued our affair, but I'm not gonna lie to you, the threesome never did pan out for some reason or another. It is the one thing on my sexual checklist that eludes me to this day.

As we continued to train, the advances became more and more obvious to others I worked with. Unlike Sabrina, who continued to be subtle in her hints to get together, Raquel acted as if she wanted everyone to know she wanted to bone. In fact, a coworker happened to walk by when Raquel and I were talking in one of the offices and couldn't help but notice Raquel's hand on my cock. When my coworker asked me later what the hell was going on, I simply responded by saying, "At least my pants were still on."

Not only was the physical attraction strong, but Raquel was also getting inside my head. She was unhappy in her marriage of close to a decade, and I was in a dead-end relationship. Danielle was looking for marriage, and it was more and more apparent that I wasn't even close to that point. After seeing these past couple of ladies I was training in action, I had all the proof I needed that marriage wasn't always all it's made out to be. Raquel and I would talk about how it was not only okay to fuck around behind our significant others' backs but it was also their fault! Being the naïve, young buck I was, I bought into this shit. Raquel was starting to show her craziness, but I was so wrapped up in what she could do in the bedroom that I dismissed every obvious sign.

Raquel dropped the line that is certain to be the dagger in every relationship: "If it wasn't for my kids, I would be divorced." In addition to this, she also talked about us moving far away somewhere together. This would probably scare the shit out of most people, especially coming from a married woman with a few kids, but I was undeterred in my sexual journey. Every time we had an encounter outside the gym, I justified my actions by thinking that it wasn't my fault, that somehow my girlfriend drove me to another woman's bed. I hoped she was happy that she made my penis enter another woman!

After about a half dozen meetings with Raquel outside the gym, this running around began to wear on me. I can't tell if it was because of the constant lying to my girlfriend or the way Raquel treated me like a boyfriend rather than some guy she was fucking aside from her husband. I was constantly coming up with these elaborate stories as to why I wouldn't be able to go out on a Friday or Saturday night. With the advent of the cell phone, I have no idea how I would have been able to pull that shit off today. I couldn't imagine having a fucking cell phone read "12 missed calls" over the course of a night. I was feeling more and more stressed out about everything and beginning to think about what was happening to me. I was becoming that guy. We have all heard about that guy who just spends his life fucking around, pressing his luck by spending time in another guy's girl. This could not end well for me, particularly when you add married women to the mix. Raquel had passed her tryouts with flying colors and was in the game day rotation. At this point, I can tell you it was getting a little out of hand, but I thought I could handle this and more. I was young and unwise to the ways of the world, but I had the adulation of my coworkers and friends, so I went all in.

From the time I got with Raquel, there were a couple more women who climbed onboard, such as two more attractive housewives and one overeager insurance agent. And, of course, there was Sabrina, who was my first and got attention regularly. It was beginning to look like a stable full of women. Aside from having a girlfriend, who I was still sleeping with albeit not too often, I was quickly garnering a list of regulars who I could depend on and could sleep with on cue. One may think that this is the greatest feeling in the world, and for a short while, it was. I had no idea how big this thing would get and how out of control it would become. I was still enamored that I could have the best of both worlds. With these other women, I could do all those things that my girlfriend was opposed to doing, and these women were more than happy to assist me.

For some reason, I never could get used to the fact that these women had husbands yet they were still doing what they were doing. My life was reminding me of that Diane Lane movie that made every guy feel like shit. I was the other guy. I felt like an asshole. No matter what the situation was for these women, I couldn't imagine what was so bad it drove them into my apartment on a Friday night. I was beginning to feel more guilt each time something like this happened, yet I would find myself doing it more and more, with more and more women. Maybe I'm naïve and my current girlfriend is sucking someone else's dick while I'm watching *Rocky IV* for the 867th time on TNT on a Saturday night. Maybe the same shit I was a willing participant of in the past is happening to me this day. Have you ever had a significant other tell you she's going out with friends, and then she stays out until after midnight, ends up getting hammered, and fucks another guy while you're at home watching SportsCenter? I'd rather not think about it.

What exactly was I doing to reap these unbelievable rewards? I was training these women a couple of times a week and listening to whatever it was that they wanted to talk about for that hour. That was about it. I wasn't exactly going out of my way to impress any of these women. I didn't have some awesome haircut. I didn't dress to impress. I didn't spit out cheesy lines or put forth much effort at all. I could think of nothing that I was doing other than giving them attention. Since they were paying for my time, it was the least I could do. Considering just a few short years ago in high school I was pulling out all the stops just for a hand job, I could not believe how far I'd come in the realm of boning. Could I have been a better man and said no once I picked up on their advances? I'm sure I could have. If I was happy in my own relationship, I could have maybe avoided this mess. I went from being an ordinary, average guy to a sex symbol, albeit on a much smaller scale than George Clooney. It was an X-rated version of the eighties classic with the pizza delivery guy who gave his customers a little something extra when they ordered extra anchovies.

Rather than try to get myself out of this situation the honorable way by manning up and apologizing to everyone involved, I searched for an easy out. I contemplated moving somewhere far from the Philadelphia suburb where I was currently living. I was twenty-two years old now and figured it would be a great time to get out. My girlfriend knew that I wasn't happy living near the same town I grew up in and that I wanted to move one day. There was something about spending my adult years so close to where I grew up that never did sit well with me, as I always hoped for bigger and better things. I worked myself up into a paranoid state on a regular basis with each client who was getting extra attention. But I was making some great money at the gym, and it was going to be a tough thing to give up. I assumed the worst—that some angry husband would pay me a visit at my apartment on some random Thursday night while my girlfriend was over and it would all come to an end like the finale of some Lifetime movie.

As I rolled these crazy scenarios around in my head, one of the most awkward situations happened one weekend. Never had I bumped into a client outside the gym by accident; it was always an arranged meeting. I was out with my girlfriend one Sunday afternoon walking around a spring fair in the center of town. It was as if one of these crazy scenarios I had been milling around in my head finally came to fruition. Danielle and I were walking along, minding our own business, when out of the blue I heard my name called out from a distance. My first reaction was to act as if I didn't hear a thing, but before I knew it, Raquel was right there with her husband and daughters. You have got to be shitting me. Did she really just call out to me in public with her entire family? Why would she even think about doing this? She could have easily avoided me with no trouble at all seeing how it was a crowded event. As shocked as I was, I maintained a smile, introduced my girlfriend, and shook the hand of the guy whose wife I had just boned a couple of weeks prior and a handful of times before that. Thankfully, it was a brief exchange, and we were on our way without any awkwardness, but I was clearly shaken. All I could think about was how fucking guilty I felt. I truly was a jerk-off. As Raquel and her family walked away, part of me just wanted to come clean to my girlfriend, but I was too much of a pussy. Besides, a couple of weeks ago, my girlfriend and I were at odds for some reason or another, so I felt justified at the time. Now I just felt like shit.

After I made plans to relocate to another state, I finally decided to break it off with Raquel. I chose to tell her at an Italian restaurant, which happened to serve some of the finest limoncello I've had in the states. I figured this would be the classy thing to do in this situation rather than tell her at the gym, where shit could have seriously hit the fan. Raquel showed up dressed to kill wearing a tight red dress that accentuated her well-defined curves. She was also wearing one of those exotic scents that get the most holy of men to break their vows.

There I was, ready to say that this could no longer go on, that this was wrong, so on and so forth, but her perfectly implanted breasts seemed to be winking at me under her almost see-through dress. Fuck. I was stuck between a rock and a hard place. Anyone who has ever slept with someone he or she shouldn't have slept with while in a relationship knows this feeling. Doing it once was already bad enough, but Raquel and I had done the deed several times, so what was one more time going to do? Besides, if I was going to get caught by an angry spouse or my girlfriend, I might as well have the satisfaction of an unbelievable lay one more time and store it in the back of my mind for some cold, lonely night in the future. We even met at a restaurant for the sake of staying somewhat sober, as a bar would have sent the wrong message. Unfortunately for me, I chose a restaurant with a bar. One drink later and quite a few of Raquel's not-so-subtle brushes against my pants had us in the backseat of her car.

We took a short drive to a spot near the river that was very well secluded. Raquel had the perfect car for any type of sexual activity you could imagine—an oversized SUV with the darkest window tint you could get. It didn't help that once I told Raquel I was moving, she said, "Here's your going-away present" as she pulled her dress over her shoulders. It was well after midnight and almost completely pitch black inside her car, but I could still notice her black lingerie. Anyone who has had the privilege of seeing black lingerie on a hot black woman knows exactly what I'm talking about.

Before I knew it, my head was between her legs and I was well on my way to another act of adultery. I shocked myself as I pulled her black, see-through panties down her long, shapely legs and went down on her. Raquel was the first client I went down on. It's not that I wasn't a fan of going down there, but there was something in my fucked-up train of thought that made me think that act was off-limits to everyone *except* my actual girlfriend. I know—I sound like a high school girl who will do everything with a guy except let him into her pants. I was so caught up in the moment that I didn't even think about the smell down there, if there was one. I was a man on a mission, and after a little while, I emerged from below and pulled my fully aroused unit out for some play. Raquel was so wound up that I slid in easily as I lay on top of her and gave her all I could. No condom, no worries. With plenty of room in the backseat of her car, I was able to comfortably get on top and move around freely.

Just like the first time we fucked in my apartment, Raquel was wild as ever as I thrust in and out. Her moans were so loud, it probably sounded like someone was getting killed inside that car. She also screamed out lines like the ones you hear in any porno clip. "Fuck me like a dirty slut" and "You like that wet pussy?" were among the choice lines I remembered hearing that night. Luckily, I didn't have it in me to respond, since I don't think I could have come up with anything that would have sounded even remotely cool in that situation. It didn't take long for me to cum inside her as she scratched my back to a point I'm certain there were visible marks for some time afterward. Oh, well. It was a hell of a going-away present.

Raquel was one of the clients who tried to keep in contact with me after I moved away, and I have to admit, she was the first person I ever had phone sex with. After settling into my new job and new place, I got a call from Raquel one late Saturday afternoon. Hearing that voice of hers, which was soft and sexy but still sounded innocent, and remembering her huge, pendulous breasts, I was slightly aroused as I talked to her. I have no idea how it happened, but we got to talking about sex. Raquel didn't hold back on giving me what felt like a replay of our last encounter. I felt the way I did back when I was in middle school and stayed at my grandparents' place for the summer and got in trouble for ringing up a $100 phone bill by calling one of those 900-numbers I saw in the back of *Hustler*. Now here I was in my early twenties with my hands on my dick giving him a massage while talking to Raquel. After a couple of minutes, I finished on a piece of dirty clothing I had lying around. Immediately afterward, I felt just as guilty as I did when I first finished off inside her on my couch. That phone call was the last time I had contact with Raquel. I reminded myself of why I moved away in the first place. I had made a promise to myself that I was going to try to live on the straight and narrow path from here on out, but little did I know that path would become a little more twisted than I ever could imagine.

5
MY FIRST COUGAR

It's funny how when guys are young, they dream of being with an older woman, but when they are older, the last thing they want is to sleep with an older woman. By no real authority, a cougar is a woman over the age of thirty-five who seeks out sexual relations with younger men. In my early training career, the women I bedded were all older than me but never by more than about ten years or so. I was about to get my first taste of a forty-something-year-old.

This all happened right around the time that Stifler's mom first turned heads, but no feature film could have prepared me for what would soon unfold. What younger guy wouldn't want an older woman to show him the ropes? The world of personal training consists of many older women looking to improve their physique in order to attract the eye of a younger man. As a young guy still relatively new to the industry, I was unaware of the mystique of the cougar. Cougars don't even have to be the most attractive women in the room, but they exude sexual confidence in such a way that when they talk to you, you become mesmerized. Let's face it, no matter how hot that young coed is, there is a huge chance she may just lie there as you do what you need to do. There's nothing like a hot older woman who not only will talk like a dirty pirate whore but will also do things to you that you didn't know were possible.

At the time I met Michelle, I still hadn't moved away, but I was about to walk the plank again at Precision Fitness. Michelle's subtle hints at wanting me naked were not quickly picked up by a rookie such as myself. She would give me a once over, but her stare would linger before making a remark such as, "I bet your legs are in amazing shape." With Michelle, I never even got a chance to use my horrible lines, since she always beat me to the chase. Still, I needed a little more of an invitation to know I had the green light. Before long, I learned that if you just roll with the conversation, you will soon end up rolling around in bed with these types of women. Even though most of the clients I had slept with were several years older than me, I didn't consider any of them bona fide cougars. I really wanted to see what a real cougar was like, so just to be on the safe side and to ensure a memorable encounter, I upped the ante of the customary ten-year age difference to twenty years.

Every gym is full of cougars. I can only hope that one day the woman I'm with does not get dressed up to go to the gym, as this will be a red flag that bad things are on the horizon. These women are also the biggest source of potential income for personal trainers. If they are married, they usually have an expendable income, and if they are single, they have even more money to burn on looking good. Having trained just a handful of people at this point, I didn't have a lot of these clients, but this would soon be another area I where considered myself an expert.

Michelle was a forty-four-year-old divorcee who was already in shape before she began training. I know what you're thinking—how is it that every woman I found myself training was already in good shape? Keep in mind that I wasn't fucking every female who came my way; I just chose to fuck the ones who already looked pretty good, as I have never been accused of being a chubby chaser. Seeing how Michelle was already in good shape, I should have taken this as an obvious sign that she was maybe looking for a little more than just personal training. Michelle was a petite woman around one hundred pounds with reddish-blonde hair and always seemed to wear matching gym outfits that showed her subtle curves. Some days she wore very short blue shorts with a white T-shirt with blue trim or tight black spandex shorts with the equally form-fitting black top. She had a nice, firm-looking backside but lacked in the chest department. Listen to me critiquing girls like Hef probably does as he pans through hundreds of naked snapshots daily. The only thing I needed now was the laser pointer for the official title of a sexual tyrannosaurus.

My training relationship with Michelle began innocently enough like most did. Michelle would talk about the guy she was seeing but was quick to point out that it was nothing serious and that she wasn't exactly too happy with him. She had a job in finance, and this guy she was seeing was some real estate mogul. This was one of the first times I realized that money doesn't always guarantee stability in a relationship. Here was a very successful woman who was dating a successful man, yet she was looking for something more. Are you fucking kidding me? You mean to tell me that you could have a boatload of money and still have to worry about your woman straying? This does not bode well for me if by some chance I fall into money one day. All this time I was under the impression that a fat wallet would guarantee a faithful partner. Little did I know.

At first, Michelle intimidated me. She reminded me of Lita Ford in her prime, hair all feathered out like one of those gals you used to see in the front row of a Poison concert back in the eighties. You could tell Michelle could still party like it was 1985. Not only did she look the part, but after a few training sessions, it was also apparent that Michelle knew how to party. On occasion, in the middle of a training session, she would share some of her tales of excess involving that white powdery substance and nights that lasted until the sun came up. She was not only wild and sexy, but she also had the smarts to go along with it.

For some time, Michelle and I shared a very professional relationship. Our conversations didn't even hint at sex, and even though she was making steady passes, I was oblivious, so it didn't seem possible to me that we might be in bed together soon. I was so uneducated in the ways of the world that I didn't think this woman wanted to hang out with me on more than a platonic level.

Then one day Michelle asked me out to dinner for my birthday. I was naïve enough to think that she didn't want anything else other than to take me out, since she was close to my mother's age. So we made plans to go out one weekend later on in the month.

Now here is where the pieces of the puzzle began to fall together. During one of our training sessions, Michelle told me how she broke up with the guy she had been seeing. Over the course of the next week or two, Michelle began to look a little different when she came in to work out. Aside from the eighties-style workout gear, she managed to kick it up a notch. She usually wore perfume to the gym, but now she was wearing a little more makeup and, for some reason, her breasts looked a little bigger. Was she stuffing those puppies or using tape to plaster them up? I did my best to maintain my professionalism despite her hints of wanting a little more.

During one of our sessions, Michelle jokingly said that she had a niece who would be perfect for me. She was closer to my age and in college. Michelle showed me a picture of her niece, and sure enough, this girl was smoking hot. But how could I let Michelle know I was interested? Sensing Michelle was into me, I held back my excitement because I didn't want to offend her and lose her as a client. I didn't really know what to say to this, so I kept a tight lip and didn't request a meeting with her niece. It was also becoming clearer that Michelle wanted more than my charming personality. I was starting to pick up more and more on her innuendos as she began to open up a little and talk about sex while working out.

Michelle was confusing the hell out of me, so I asked Larry for some advice on the developing situation. He became a Miyagi-like figure to me on this epic journey. I knew I could always count on him for a no-bullshit, to-the-point answer to any question I had, especially when it came to girls. I told him that Michelle had been sending me subtle messages over the past few weeks and that I was beginning to think she wanted something more than just training.

"Are you fuckin' serious? She's been wanting to fuck from day one. I knew the first time she started training with your ass you were going to get laid if you wanted. You see anyone else in this gym wearing shorts that short when they're working out? I think I almost saw some camel toe last week," Larry said.

Once I heard it from him, I realized my suspicions were right. I guess I was just a little nervous about the whole situation. Yes, I had slept with clients who were older than me but never one this close to my mom's age. This was about to take my game to a whole new level. I was a little apprehensive about what a forty-four-year-old vagina looked and felt like, as if it would be any different. I recently became old enough to drink legally, and I honestly didn't know if I was ready for something like this.

It was getting closer and closer to my scheduled dinner with Michelle. I didn't want to call it a date. I didn't really know what the fuck to call it. Not only did I have to worry about my girlfriend finding out, but I also didn't know what to expect from Michelle. Although I had been out with other clients before, those outings were usually spur of the moment and hadn't been planned so far in advance. Was this going to be a one and done? Would she get what she wanted and then never return to the gym, and then I'd be down a client? Should I have just told Michelle that I was interested in her niece when given the opportunity? Even more importantly, would Michelle end up being my girlfriend? Holy shit! It was like starting freshman year all over again. To prepare for the big night, I watched *Risky Business* again to pick up any last-minute tips. Other than Larry, I didn't have any other friends who could relate to me on this matter. Sure, they all thought it was cool, but none had ever traveled down the path I was about to go down.

The night of our dinner unfolded just like any other Friday night. My girlfriend was working the late shift, and even though she would not be done until well after midnight, I wanted to cover all my bases just in case I somehow got caught. There was this guy Darren who worked at the front desk. I would often tell my girlfriend that I was hanging out with him on nights I was doing things with clients. He became my fall guy. I wasn't really friends with him, but he was trustworthy in the rare situation that my girlfriend came into the gym and asked him about where we had gone. He always had the story we rehearsed down pat.

I didn't have to be into work until nine o'clock the following morning. The scene was set. For all I knew, this would be nothing more than a friendly dinner between two friends, ending with a hug or perhaps an innocent peck on the cheek goodnight. If only I had been that lucky. Even though I had slept with a few clients, I still thought that somehow, someway, this was going to be different.

I met Michelle at her place, where she was decked out, to say the least. She doubled up on her usual dose of perfume that was a step away from the pungent concoction known as sex panther and was wearing an outfit that looked like she had to iron it on piece by piece. We took her car and drove for quite a while off the beaten path, which I was extremely happy about, since this reduced the risk of being seen by anyone I knew. It's not that I was embarrassed, but I didn't want to risk one of my other clients seeing me out in public with someone else. I still wanted to keep that mystique about myself and didn't want to look like some gallivanting philanderer. As Michelle drove us to the restaurant, the feeling in my gut was beginning to change. I was beginning to sense that I was going to fuck this woman at some point this evening and that it was guaranteed to happen, just like the sunset and sunrise.

I wasn't too familiar with sushi at this point in my life. I had eaten a California roll here and there but didn't realize the aphrodisiac effect of certain types of fish. I couldn't tell you what the fuck was what. We had a boatload of the shit brought to the table. Some tasted great, others like tire, and one reminded me of an eraser I mistakenly ate as a kid. But whatever the case, something brought a little extra blood downstairs. This time I didn't have any herbal extracts or pills at my disposal. I'm not saying I never popped a chubby during class while looking at the blonde in the front row, but this was a little different. Honestly, I don't even remember much about the little details because we had been downing sake throughout dinner with the occasional sake bomb every now and then. The dinner conversation seemed innocent enough at the time. I recall the sex talk didn't begin until after the boat disappeared from the table. All I know is that I wanted to get laid after dinner, and it was going to have to happen soon, as I was beginning to feel another boner from just the images in my mind of Michelle butt naked with her big hair. It was as if the sushi also had some type of hallucinogenic effect on me.

It started in the car. This is where I hit the point of no return. On the ride back to Michelle's place, so that I could pick up my car, the conversation quickly shifted to personal favorites in the bedroom. Michelle actually initiated the conversation, asking about what I liked and disliked and all kinds of shit. She then proceeded to tell me about her favorite position, which happened to be reverse cowgirl, and how much she liked to fuck. This seemed odd to me, since she was close to my parents' age and was telling me how much she liked to fuck. I couldn't imagine my mom and stepdad doing the hunka chunka in the living room, but I tried to remain focused. As I mentioned earlier, I already had a semi in the restaurant. By this point, I was rock hard. I was hoping she would just give me head in the car to get it over with, but this didn't happen. Maybe I should have asked politely for a blow job, as it would have taken the edge off. The sexual tension was steadily rising, as was my package. I didn't know how much more of this I could take. A twenty-minute car ride felt like hours. I don't think I have ever had a wet dream to this point in my life. I felt like I was ready to explode in my pants.

By the time we got to Michelle's house, I was at the breaking point. It didn't take much convincing for me to follow her inside. I don't even think she formally invited me in; she just gave me that look—that look all guys love that silently says, "Let's fuck!" I quickly had to perform a tuck to hide my wood as I made my way through the door. As soon as we walked into her house, Michelle wrapped her arms around me, began kissing my neck, and then made her way to my lips. She was aggressive, showing a confidence similar to Raquel's. I didn't really know what to do, so I just went along with it. Having a nice buzz and being on the cusp of ejaculation, I overlooked the wet, sloppy kissing as her tongue seemed to snake around inside my mouth. I let her do all the work. Eventually, her hands made their way down to my pants and she worked them inside. Shit! This buildup felt like my first time when I was a junior in high school. Yes, I know what you may be thinking—that it should take more than a woman's hand on my cock to get me that excited. What can I say? I could barely contain myself.

Soon we were standing at the bottom of her staircase, and she methodically stroked me with one hand and used the other to pull my shirt off. She kissed her way from my neck and quickly made a beeline down to my cock. Yep, my eyes were as wide open as yours are reading this. She gave me head on the stairs like no other. I managed to hold onto the railing and pretend as if this was something that had happened to me before. Again, my mind was in shambles as I attempted to think of anything to keep this going. I was seconds from liftoff. I had to pull back quickly to get her lips off me, which, by the way, was no easy feat when semi-reclined on the staircase. She was smiling and could barely contain her excitement. To think I did absolutely nothing to get this woman worked up was amazing to me. As much as I wanted to get it over with, I was very curious as to what the main course would entail. Should I just blow my load and hope to do better after the intermission? Should have and could have, which would have made me feel a little better about myself.

Michelle led me upstairs to her bedroom, which had one of those huge, four-post beds, the kind that make any guy go crazy, since it can be used for various positions and gives you something to hold onto during sex. Michelle pushed me onto her bed and, in a quick move similar to Superman, went from fully clothed to stark naked. She hopped on top of me in the reverse cowgirl position. I slid into her with ease, as she was more worked up than any other girl I had ever been with. Judging by her wetness, I can honestly say this cougar was more than ready to go. I lay there in awe as she fucked me. I had a beautiful view of this woman bouncing up and down, sliding back and forth, and borderline screaming. Her tight little backside covered most of my cock as she rode me, and I stared at her narrow waist and her long hair, which she pulled back with both hands.

Unfortunately, it was over before I knew it. I couldn't contain myself. I tried thinking of the last Chuck Norris movie I saw, my fifth-grade teacher, anything I could to get my mind off what was happening to me. It wasn't until after that I realized I forgot to think about Roseanne Barr naked. Whatever I tried didn't work. I had about as much control as any twenty-one-year-old guy could while getting fucked by someone more than twenty years his senior. I lost it inside her, sans condom. The things you do when you're in your twenties.

Michelle realized the party was over when I went completely soft and slipped out. To my surprise, Michelle wasn't ready to give up. Just like I saw in many movies but hadn't experienced myself, she went right back down on me and gave it her all to get me going for round two. Whatever wetness and juices that were down there were still present when she took me in her mouth again. Astonished at the lack of hygiene, I felt as if I was in the midst of my own porn shoot and looked for the hidden camera. She could have tried for an hour straight, but there was nothing left in the tank. With the drinking, the sushi, and the shock of what just happened, I was spent. A short intermission would not have brought me up to speed. Nothing but a three- to four-hour nap was going to get me in the mood again. That book of tantric secrets I had scanned through a few days prior really let me down.

I was too embarrassed to say much, so I just said, "That was great." Sure, maybe for me, but I couldn't say the same for Michelle. I wasn't sure what exactly she was thinking. I couldn't have been the worst she ever had, right? I quickly got dressed and gave her a hug good-bye, since I wasn't going anywhere near that mouth until she brushed her teeth and gargled for a minute or two. Next thing I knew, I was driving back to my apartment, wanting to call all my friends to tell them what just happened.

Unlike my previous sexual feats, this one had special meaning, since I never imagined I would have a cougar. The following week in the gym, I was a little giddy and couldn't help but share the news with my coworkers, including Larry. He expressed his congratulations as if I was now part of a select fraternity. I'm not gonna lie, my manhood felt like it had crept up to the upper echelon where many want to be but few ever reach. Aside from a threesome, this was huge for every young, *Maxim*-reading, alpha male out there. My following training session with Michelle was no different from any other, except for the look she gave me when I said hello—it was a look that said, "Hi, I just fucked you, and if you're lucky, I might just do it again."

Training was beginning to pick up, and I was running out of time to train anyone else. I also had been dabbling in quite a few extracurricular activities with Sabrina and Raquel, among others, and now I was introducing another one to the group. I was still dating Danielle, too. For the first time in my life, much to my chagrin, I didn't know if I was able to keep up with this porn-star lifestyle. There weren't enough hours in the week. Not to mention, none of those fancy meds such as Cialis were around to get you going for days at a time. I was wearing myself out and finding it difficult to keep each one satisfied. The many who have traveled down the road I have know that a cougar is difficult to please. She is looking for a much younger partner to satisfy her newly found sex drive. If you can't accommodate her, there are many other fish in the sea.

I continued to train Michelle, and we maintained a good working relationship. We also had a few extra training sessions outside the gym, but she was not what I would consider a regular. Sometimes we would go several weeks if not a month or so before getting together. I can't really tell you what the reason was, but something tells me she was looking for a little more than what I could give her. But when her options were limited, she knew where to turn to get at least a little satisfaction.

Oddly enough, several years after I moved away, Michelle and I ended up rendezvousing again when I was back in town for my cousin's wedding. Not having a whole lot of time off, I was going to make it a quick trip: fly in on Friday and fly back on Sunday night. I used to keep what some refer to as a "black book." It was an actual little black book, as cell phones were still considered a luxury at that time. While packing up my things for the trip, I pulled out my black book and scanned through my list of former clients. I didn't even think about trying to get a hold of those whom I knew were married, even though the thought of Sabrina going down on me in some parking lot was something I wouldn't mind at all. I came across Michelle's name and figured what the hell. So I gave her a ring, and surprisingly, she was still single and ready to go. With little notice, I arranged for her to meet up with my friends and me at a bar the night before the wedding.

It had been close to two years since I had last seen her, so I can't tell you what I expected. I knew a few important things going into this: Number one, she wasn't going to be fat. That was the most important requirement going in. Her body type was that of a petite gymnast, so unless she fell off the deep end within the past two years, there was no way she would look much different. After all, she was in her mid-forties, so there was little chance I would be shocked when I saw her. Number two, she had to be completely unattached, since I didn't want to deal with any potential bullshit, even if I was living on the West Coast.

I was hanging out in a downtown bar with my cousins and friends when Michelle walked in. Not only did she look exactly the same as I remembered her, but her fuckin' hair still made her look like one of the chicks in an eighties music video! I came to find out later that the part of town where Michelle was from was stuck in somewhat of a time warp, as that hairdo apparently was still as popular as ever. You can imagine the looks and comments I got shortly after she arrived when I pronounced not only had we slept together in the past but we also would be sleeping together tonight. I recall my cousin looking dumbfounded, as he was a few years younger than me, so seeing me with someone his mother's age seemed odd, to say the least.

After just a couple of drinks and some reminiscing of the good old days, I bluntly asked Michelle for a ride home. She knew exactly what I was thinking and didn't hesitate for a moment when I asked her. Strangely enough, during the car ride back, we were too wrapped up in conversation for me to realize I ended up at her house. Ah, yes. As we pulled up to her house, the memories came back to me from our first time together. This time I was determined to show her what a couple more years of experience had done for me. I was sure that I would be able to make this a night she truly remembered. Without as much as a word, she took my hand and led me up to the front door. I was fairly buzzed at this point but by no means intoxicated. I was well aware of the situation and what I needed to do. As long as my trusted steed was up to the task, this would be a good time for both parties involved.

The place looked the same as I remembered it with maybe a few new pieces of décor here and there. Everything seemed to fall into place when I spotted the staircase on which Michelle helped mold me into the man I had become. I followed Michelle up the stairs to her bedroom. There was something different about her room. The oversized bed in the middle of the room had the familiar four long posts on each corner, but now it was covered in a white, satin-like canopy that reminded me of a bed that royalty slept in. This was going to be a first for me. I felt like this go-round was going to be much different. Not only did I think this bed was awesome and something I had only seen in magazines, but I was also ready to give Michelle something to really remember me by.

Michelle pulled one side of the canopy open, which I took as an invitation to sit down on the bed. She excused herself to the bathroom and, on her way, lit a candle on the table next to the bed. The candle was an unspoken answer to my question of whether I was going to get laid. As if I needed more reassurance. So I took off my shoes and got comfortable on the bed. And yes, I had a boner. Michelle returned from the bathroom a few moments later wearing nothing but one of those see-through Victoria's Secret–type outfits. It wasn't the kind that makes a girl look like a fairy in a Peter Pan movie but rather the kind with the "fuck me" straps around the legs and the tight top that squeezes those knockers so hard together they look twice their normal size. Wow, I had more than a boner now.

Michelle slowly made her way over to the bed. Like the first time we had sex, she took full advantage of me. I let her take the reins yet again. In her sexy outfit that put most women in their mid-forties to shame, she crawled on top of me and immediately went for the pants. No kissy face, no hand manipulation, just right down to business. I was so spoiled that if this type of thing didn't happen within a few minutes of getting together with a woman, I would stop and check if there was something wrong. Kneeling over my midsection, Michelle pulled down my pants, put her hand around the base of my cock, and put it right inside her mouth.

My eyes rolled into the back of my head as my head went back to the pillow. Michelle went to work with her hand and mouth in such a way that I was yet again astonished because it seems that no matter how many blow jobs I get, there always seems to be one that tops the last best one. How is it that I called this woman just a few days ago after not talking to her for a couple of years and now I had her lips wrapped around my cock? It was something I'll never understand, but who was I to question why?

After just a few minutes, Michelle sat up on her knees. I propped myself up on one elbow and reached forward with the other hand toward her crotchless underwear. The candlelight illuminated the room just enough so that I could see Michelle was more than willing to let a finger or two inside. Michelle was so wet down there that my finger slid in with such ease that I couldn't believe this soon-to-be senior cougar was capable of getting that wet that fast. Michelle let me play around inside her for a couple of minutes until she had enough.

Without taking off her outfit, in one swift maneuver she turned her back toward me and slid down my forty-five-degree-angled cock with ease. Within seconds, I knew this was trouble. I knew Michelle was a big fan of the reverse cowgirl position, but as much as I enjoyed the position, I didn't have much control over the situation. With any other position, I was able to slow the pace to allow for a prolonged session. No way was I going to let this end like our first time. I was fortunate enough to have had a few chances to make up for my first time with Michelle, but this was certainly going to be my last, since I wasn't planning on coming back to this neck of the woods anytime soon. Michelle let out moans that compounded the feeling of pleasure I was having. Watching her bounce up and down on top of me in her slutty outfit was more than I could handle. With a quick "Oh, yeah!" I was done.

I know there are guys out there, like Sting, for example, who can supposedly keep going and going and going using tantric techniques, but once I came, I was finished. Using the force to the best of my ability, I tried to will my quickly shrinking hog to keep pressing on. It was no use. Michelle realized the party was over, and without the use of assistive devices or illegal substances, I was done for the night. Michelle, the trooper she was, tried some mouth resuscitation on me, but it just wasn't happening. I know I've had some early takeoffs in my career, but this was the first time I managed to buttonhook the same person with another early exit. Asking her for a ride back to my cousin's house was difficult, as I had a tough time making eye contact with her. Michelle got changed and willingly drove me across town well after three o'clock in the morning. Embarrassed as I was, I tried not to sound like a total tool when we said good-bye. I didn't want to promise her another round down the road, and something tells me she probably had enough of me by now. After a quick hug good-bye, Michelle drove off. That was the last I saw or heard from her.

You can imagine the tales at my cousin's wedding the next day. I felt a small bit of celebrity status as I fielded questions from many guests at the wedding. I didn't hold back. I told them the truth about my quick trigger and the shameful request for a fifteen-mile ride at three o'clock in the morning after a big letdown. Did I get laid? Yes, I did. Did I feel pretty good? Of course. I got laid—who wouldn't feel good?

But did I feel a little bit of shame having let down a cougar? Absolutely. Throughout my life, I would see and conquer all types of women, leaving them the satisfaction they had been searching for. But for some reason, I couldn't tame the wild beast otherwise known as the cougar.

Michelle, here's to you. May you find a young man who manages to stay hard for the hours you require. You may not have been fulfilled, but I can assure you that you taught me things I didn't know were possible. I'm most certain you are the hottest resident in the fifty-five and up community you must be living in these days. Thanks for being my first but not my last cougar.

6
A GYM LIFE

"What would you say you do here?" Everyone has a job that would warrant this question be asked at some point. Honestly, who doesn't want a job where you get paid and still have enough time to get shit done for yourself while on the clock? I'm not saying all jobs are filled with enormous amounts of downtime, but some are more boring than others and have you watching the clock praying for the next four hours to go by quicker than the first four. I have a relative who works in security, and I get random calls from him while he's pulling up to Dairy Queen or parked along a beachfront scanning the grounds for the best pair of fake breasts he can find. When I check my e-mail, I notice an influx of chain e-mails (the ones with those goddamned unlucky curses if I don't forward the message to ten friends) at all hours of the workday from friends with office jobs.

During my career as a personal trainer, I got a lot of shit thrown my way from friends with what they liked to call "real" jobs. These friends took the traditional route of going away to college immediately after high school and then fell into whatever field they had studied. Most of them, however, absolutely hated their postcollege lives, as they found themselves waking up each morning to go to a job they despised. Whenever they talked to me, I sensed the occasional hint of jealousy. After all, I was getting paid to essentially "hang out" with people, as they put it.

I can understand how most people don't view personal training as a real job. As one friend put it, "Here's your job in a nutshell: 'One, two, three—keep your head up—four, five…" For some time, I actually agreed. It doesn't take more than a monkey to count to ten. If you're going for higher reps, you may have to count to fifteen or twenty, which sometimes gets tricky. Sometimes you even have to man a stopwatch and clock off thirty seconds. When you think about it, it's not too hard at all. With all the fancy equipment available today, you have more than enough exercises at your disposal to throw at your clients for a long time before they get bored.

Not to mention, you can get paid extremely well for this kind of work. Most jobs that don't require you to have a degree or special skills will rarely give you more than ten dollars an hour. Personal trainers can easily make triple that to start, and the pay escalates rapidly. In defense of my constantly criticized profession, I, along with many others I worked with, spent many hours off the clock not only learning what the hell it was I was doing but also designing programs for each client. I would spend countless hours going over my clients' workouts and changing them each month so that they were never doing the same routine twice. This isn't something you will find these days unless you are training at a high-end gym or taking some type of group exercise class.

I'm not alone when I say most jobs these days are the equivalent of McJobs (i.e., unstimulating, low-paying jobs with few prospects), even if you went to school for half a dozen years. In talking with friends and clients over the years, I have found that only about 20 percent of them actually enjoy their jobs. Many jobs that require you to work your ass off are pretty much thankless and not that lucrative. You won't get immediate rewards in terms of money or gratification, except maybe at your year-end review at which time you hope your company is on the upswing and throws you a bone. But let's be serious. It may have been quite some time since you received some type of incentive from your job other than being told, "You should be thankful you have a job." Have you ever been required to work on Christmas or Thanksgiving and not gotten rewarded for all your hard work? In this day and age, we all know someone who wakes up at the crack of dawn with the angst of yet another unhappy day ahead. Maybe you even feel that way yourself.

Maybe I just know a lot of people who are unhappy with their jobs, but being a personal trainer at least gave me some sense of freedom in that my schedule was flexible, so I didn't feel handcuffed like most nine-to-fivers do. You're either a worker or an owner, and there are a million reasons why being a worker can suck the life right out of you.

Personal training is a job whose definition is still unclear not only to the trainers but also to the clients themselves. Each trainer does his or her own thing with each client, whether or not it is safe. Clients have no idea what to expect when they meet their trainer for the first time. One person's session may be similar to boot camp in the Marine Corps, while another's may consist of doing a couple of stretches in the back corner of the gym and then talking about life for the rest of the time.

It wasn't until the last decade or so that you could truly make a career out of personal training and use it as a stepping stone to some other avenue, such as sales or health care. There is no single unifying body or association. In fact, you can have a GED and manage to have a great career as a trainer. Take a daylong seminar on a Saturday and voila, welcome to your new career the following Monday. Some colleges have programs that are geared toward being a personal trainer, but you would be hard-pressed to find an instructor who really put in time working as a trainer and can give students a real-life picture of what the job is really like.

Then there is the huge spectrum of what is the right thing to do with your clients. Ask ten different trainers their philosophies, and you will get ten different approaches to training. You have the large, muscle-bound types and then those hippy-like individuals who try to get you in touch with your inner Zen. Personal trainers come in all shapes and sizes. What tells you that one trainer is better than the other? The jury is still out. And I'm sure everyone who has had a trainer for years will vouch for their trainer and say he or she is "great," regardless of the shape they are in.

It's the little things that set trainers apart from one another. Does your trainer spend part of the time you are paying for talking on the phone? Does he strike up a conversation with someone other than you while you are paying him for his time? Or does he seem to be working out himself while he is training you, concentrating more on what he is doing instead of what you are doing? These things may seem as obvious as not wearing a half shirt to the gym if you're a guy and definitely not if you're a woman who has some muffin top going on. The bottom line is there are no rules and regulations in this profession. Since there is no blueprint on how to be a trainer, only a gym's manual or some so-called expert's take on what you should do, people do whatever the hell they want. Trainers can spend an hour on a treadmill next to their clients or spend the time bullshitting with them while seated on a Swiss ball. I've seen some trainers sit on a ball while their client sits on a ball across from them; the client does about two sets of crunches, and then they talk for a half hour until the trainer says, "Good job!" and walks the client to the door. I've also seen some trainers mash their clients to the ground, and within fifteen minutes their clients are dripping in sweat.

So many trainers take their positions for granted and act nonchalant while training their clients. Whether it is admiring an attractive treadmill jogger while their client struggles to lift a bar off his chest or conversing with another coworker in the middle of an appointment, they routinely spend much of their clients' paid time on their own activities. I'm not gonna lie to you; I've been guilty of this type of behavior from time to time, especially when I first started. Have you ever gotten so comfortable around certain people that you tend to forget you're actually at work? I learned right away to give 100 percent of my attention to all my clients, since I experienced the displeasure of getting called out by someone early on. During my first month on the job, I was training a middle-aged woman who must have been a librarian. Larry happened to be next to me training someone, but he was not really paying attention to his client perform a set of dead lifts. I remember asking Larry a question about scheduling. At most, it was a thirty-second interruption. This woman looked at me as if I called her fat. She rolled her eyes once my attention returned to her and was pretty quiet the rest of the session. She didn't come back to train after that, so from that day on, I gave every client my undivided attention once they walked through the door.

With the waistlines of Americans getting bigger each year, there is a large need for personal trainers all over the country. Unfortunately, if you're some poor soul living in rural Iowa reading this, you may have to relocate to the nearest big city or at least a large suburban area to become a successful trainer unless you don't mind getting paid in apple pies. In today's economy, I have noticed one thing: people either have a lot of money or they don't have much but rely on credit to do the things they want to do. The bottom line is people who are adamant about taking care of their bodies will do so no matter what the cost.

Like finding a hair stylist, personal training is different for everyone. What works for one person doesn't work for another, but there is a difference between an eight-dollar haircut and a thirty-dollar haircut. Turns out, there is no right and wrong. In each trainer's mind, his way is the best way. I even know of some trainers who had long careers in totally unrelated fields, like real estate, caught the workout bug, and became personal trainers overnight. Even if they got workout routines from the pages of *Muscle & Fitness* or on the Internet, it doesn't matter if it really works for their clients as long as they are getting paid. Many of these second or third career-change trainers aren't too likely to put in a ton of work to get the experience they need to really know how to become a solid trainer. I'm not saying they will never be great trainers, but like anything else in life, very few are great at what they do the first day they show up on the job, including myself. But if you think you are going to walk into a gym and be busy, think again. You are going to have to put some effort in if you actually want to be successful. We all can't be Jillian what's-her-face now can we?

Although the gym environment doesn't appear to be a very stressful workplace, it can be about as demanding as a car dealership. Imagine sitting in a room full of people with a dry erase board on an easel and your name written in either black or red. You better hope your name is in black or else be ready to expect an uncomfortable and oftentimes embarrassing speech from your manager in front of all your coworkers. This was my trial by fire on-the-job training when I began personal training. Every week we would have these sales meetings and talk about how each trainer was progressing toward his or her goals. Luckily, I was in school full time and only had a part-time position, so my quota was a little less than the other full-timers. I won't forget how I was publicly ridiculed that first month for not selling a single session of personal training. My managers let me know that this was not only unacceptable, but also that they had never seen anything like it. I felt like I was sitting in the middle of the room naked after getting out of a cold pool and my sad, shriveled member was on display for all to mock. Here's a quick breakdown of how this whole process went: Let's say my monthly goal was $4,000 in training sales, which was always a goal they set for me. Now, unless I sold at least $1,000 a week in personal training packages, I would be in the red and get lectured about having to "step it up" or whatever their bullshit motivational phrase of the week was in an attempt to get me to reach the monthly goal. It may not sound like much, but seeing yourself in the red time and time again was not only depressing but also made you wonder if your job was safe. Luckily, after that rough start, I picked up quickly and filled up so that I was booked up weeks in advanced. After just about six months on the job, I was rolling, and other than working more hours, there was nothing I could do to make my quota higher.

I've taken certification after certification and attended courses and seminars all to improve my training methods, but the best knowledge I attained was that from experience working with different people and reading books on my own. Personal training was my first job that taught me how to read people, how to give them what they wanted, and how to let them know that they couldn't get to where they wanted to go without me. This was drilled into my head early on, and it carried me throughout my years as a personal trainer. If you give people what they want and make their time spent with you enjoyable rather than work-like, they are more apt to stick with you until you decide to retire. Clients for life are much more valuable than clients who will be around for a short while. Early in my training career, if I were given the choice of training a middle-aged housewife who needed to lose a few extra pounds or a smoking-hot sorority girl who was home for the summer, I would have chosen the sorority girl in a heartbeat. I would have given her more attention and focus than the chubby housewife. I soon learned that was a big mistake. Those flaky younger girls are more likely to cancel regularly and end up never seeing you once they return to school. Those housewives are your bread and butter. Make them happy, and they will refer several friends to you, and those friends will in turn refer even more friends to you.

Will some clients drop off the face of the earth? Sure. I've wondered why some clients never returned, but odds are the older, wiser clients are usually more willing to stay and pay. I gave them my all, but some people, for some reason, never even returned a phone call afterward. As upsetting as it was to have several people work out with me once and never return, I continued to put in the work necessary to become successful. I think, at most, I was 0 for 20 before closing my first client, which in reality isn't that bad but feels horrible while you're going through it.

Believe it or not, there is a lot of work that should go into each and every client. Technically, research should go into each client's health history to determine which exercises are going to be the safest and most effective for each client. Does this happen regularly? Hell no! I knew trainers who would jokingly dub their workouts the "ball extravaganza," which entailed a full half hour of Swiss ball exercises in no particular order. This approach would then be used for each and every client on that trainer's schedule for the day. In the personal trainer's defense, I know plenty of people who have utterly mindless jobs that do not include any actual work all day, so the next time you think about giving those nicely toned, tightly clothed trainers shit for not really working, think long and hard about what you do for work all day.

Let's not forget the little things about the job that keep it from ever getting old. There is a plethora of characters who comprise the dysfunctional environment of every gym. Somewhere in the corner of many gyms you will notice facilities dedicated to a clan of fitness enthusiasts who wear spandex shorts with the activity they are about to participate in written along the side. I'm talking about spinners, of course. It is one of those sects that will make you feel inadequate when you first arrive with your cutoff shorts and nonmatching top. It has a cult-like following of people who seem to eat, live, and breathe cycling in place like a hamster on a wheel to nowhere. If you are one of those people who wear those shorts that actually say the activity you are doing, well, I don't know what to say to you.

Spinners are not the only ones who provide plenty of fodder for the staff to talk about. Let's not forget those involved in yoga. I enjoy stretching as much as the next guy or gal and consider it an important part of every fitness routine, but throwing out "Namaste" instead of a simple "Hello"? Last I checked, we are living in the United States, not Nepal. If the chanting were kept to a minimum, I would feel a little better about the whole situation. I also don't mind the smell of burning incense if it means I'll be getting some, but sucking that in for an hour while putting my body in some precarious positions isn't something I care for. Who doesn't want to be more grounded and more in touch with life on a different level than the unfortunate materialistic mentality of today? All I'm saying is that it gets old.

Since many clients come to the gym on their way to or from work, they rely on their trainer for much more than just exercise. Trainers need to address the emotional needs of their clients as well. There is no more surefire way to end a trainer-client relationship quicker than pushing clients to do three extra pull-ups after they told you they had an awful day at work, especially for those less stable individuals. It takes several sessions to figure out your clients. Initially, they may put on a show and pretend to "love" exercise. It won't be long until you see your clients' true colors. Many people don't enjoy working out, but they realize they have to. You can call it a "lifestyle," but let's face it, working out essentially turns into work the older you get. People are willing to do only as little as possible to trim down or tone up, and it's your responsibility to make that happen. Push them too far, and they will drop you like a bad habit. Don't push them enough, and the next day you will see them training with that guy who has the European accent.

Aside from the always-hated sales aspect of the job, there isn't too much to not like about the job. It's pretty hard to fuck it up, but as we all know, there are some people who excel in that department. Let me share the story of Scott, a prototype gym guy, complete with a history of steroid use and bad skin to go along with it. He had about a year's worth of training experience before starting at Precision Fitness. He and I were about the same age when we began working together. I was always pretty particular about my clients, taking notes and jotting down which weights they were using and whatnot. Scott, on the other hand, didn't do much. In fact, he would usually start a half hour session with five to ten minutes of bullshit while he figured out what to do with his client. It wasn't a surprise when 99 percent of Scott's clients looked exactly the same after about a year of training with him. In his defense, he was a hell of a bullshitter. In fact, Scott's clients were so fond of him that I'd bet a majority of them didn't give two shits about gaining five pounds of fat while training with him. Likability is a key component for any successful trainer. But like I mentioned, if you fuck things up, things catch up to you. Scott ended up calling in sick and canceling on his clients so much that their loyalty was tested. They got fed up with his antics, dropped him altogether, and ended up training with someone else.

Now let's look at Brad, or "B-Rad," as he was known in the gym. Brad was a mainstay at Body Masters, the next gym I worked at for several years. Brad was reaching that mid- to late thirties realm where things may be going well but you are desperately reaching for more. Brad always had multiple business ideas, many of which did not involve training. Whether it be replacing all the lights in hospitals with a new type of lightbulb that never burns out or charging people fifty bucks a pop to use some piece of machinery he picked up on a trip to South America that was known to cure every possible ailment, Brad always had a scheme. In hopes of getting investors, he shared these ideas with anyone who was willing to listen to him. Brad was also famous for contorting his clients into near pretzel form by any means necessary. It was not uncommon to hear one of Brad's clients wail out in pain while being stretched after hearing what sounded like something tearing. I would laugh to myself as Brad would casually explain that whatever happened was supposed to happen.

One of my personal favorites was catching Brad performing what would later be dubbed as the "tea bag spot." If you're familiar with an Olympic bench press setup, you know that a person will usually spot you from behind the bar, behind your head as it rests on the bench. For some reason or another, Brad decided to take it up a notch and step in front of the supports that are off to the sides that hold the bar in place. This put his crotch directly above the client's face. One thing I should mention is that Brad always wore short shorts, and I mean *short* shorts that were also tight. I can only imagine what was going through his clients' minds as Brad stood over them. But no matter how shady this guy was, he managed to have clients for years on end, so in the ever-challenging world of client retention, I am still clueless as to what approach is the best bet for the long haul.

Perhaps the most entertaining part of working in a gym is the clientele that graces its rubber flooring each day—especially Mondays, otherwise known as National Bench Press Day. That's when all the "Bench Bros" get together for their choreographed lift. Ever wonder why the gyms are so crowded on Mondays? I know better than to set foot in a gym on Monday unless it's between the hours of 11 a.m. and 3 p.m. The freaks surely do show up on this day, if they bother to show up at all. Everybody knows that guy who looks like he stepped off the cover of *Flex* magazine. This guy is freakishly large and always carries a gym bag that could easily be mistaken for a Navy seabag. One can only wonder what equipment is kept in this oversized sack. He will also tend to carry around a gallon jug of water, because lord knows he may become parched lumbering from one side of the gym to the other. I can laugh now, because I was one of those gallon jug–toting choads at one point.

What about the talker? The talker can be a male or female but is most likely a lonely guy who just wants someone to listen. He'll know all the staff by name, even if they don't know his. He'll seem to be at the gym all the time, or at least every time you are there, and never really seem to look any different year after year despite endless hours spent at the gym. This guy will talk any poor soul's ear off if you even make eye contact with him. Hopefully, you are not trapped on a treadmill next to him, or else you will be forced to cut your workout short just to avoid a conversation that is no doubt going nowhere. Sometimes talkers are given the unofficial title of "mayor" or something stupid like that to make them feel good about themselves. I recommend the old "pretend to take a phone call" move when approached by this constant converser. I've discovered nothing deters someone like pretending to talk on your cell phone and acting like your imaginary caller is in great distress. Trust me, behind the scenes, talkers are ridiculed mercilessly, like Daniel LaRusso when he moved to Reseda.

Let's not forget about the loud guy. He can often be mistaken for a talker, but he is anything but. Surprisingly, he isn't usually the biggest guy in the gym, but the sounds coming out of him with a few hundred pounds on his chest will have you thinking he's the Hulk. Everyone grunts and groans a little. I know firsthand in bed there are times I feel like yelling out similar to the way William Wallace did right before getting quartered, but I think better of it and feel better about myself afterward. These guys seem to have no regard for anyone within one hundred yards of them. They will shriek, scream, swear, and spit the whole nine just to get that last rep! It's one thing if you see 500 or 600 pounds on the bar, but when you do a double take and notice only 185 pounds, you really wonder what the fuck they are thinking.

Aside from the occasionally shitty hours (who the hell likes to wake up at the ass crack of dawn, or better yet, who likes working evenings rather than watching the game at happy hour?), there isn't a whole lot to complain about. Your physical labor at its most difficult is lifting a forty-five-pound plate onto a bar or handing a client a pair of thirty-pound dumbbells. It's a great job if you are remotely into health and fitness. You may catch slack if you're over the age of thirty, but just remember that those people who give you shit would rather be doing anything other than what they have to do every day.

So live it up. Enjoy the fruits of your labor. And just remember, despite how some people will view your work, you are actually doing something and you have a good time doing it, which is foreign to most people in the workforce today.

7
LIVIN' THE DREAM

I'm not gonna lie. I was enjoying the fruits of my labor. My job at Precision Fitness was awesome. I was in the midst of what seemed like an endless stream of women who needed my services. I couldn't turn my head without running into a client who was hounding me to "hang out" or "get together." I will be the first to admit that things were quickly getting out of hand, but it was getting so easy that I was beginning to feel like I was on a yearlong tour with Mötley Crüe, complete with all the backstage debauchery one only dreams about. With my managers sending me all the women between the ages of twenty-seven and forty-seven who walked through the doors of the gym, I felt compelled to do what I needed to do to keep this train rolling. I was making great money and having a good time doing it. I wasn't about to possibly jeopardize all that by turning a woman down and, in the process, possibly stopping my steady influx of women from management. As far as I was concerned, I had built up a reputation and needed to uphold it—like when that order of extra anchovies came in, someone had to deliver. Call it some sort of sick pride thing, but I felt obligated to continue my ways. I had also managed to stay drama-free. The way I saw it, I would continue to steer my present course as long as I didn't get caught or experience something that would make me look in the mirror a little harder and seriously reconsider my ways.

So how about Mary Ann? Could I possibly make room for one more? I sure could. She fit the description of my typical female client perfectly: Already in shape, check. Very cute, with a golden-brown tan year-round, double check. In addition, Mary Ann was legally divorced, so any extracurricular affairs would be in the clear, triple check.

Tony, one of the sales managers, introduced us. Within seconds of meeting me, Mary Ann completely shifted her focus to me and seemingly forgot that she had just spent the last ten minutes talking to Tony. It was as if Tony ceased to exist. I hadn't done much more than say hello to her, yet she already had this huge smile on her face. Could she already tell that she would end up in bed with me? When this type of shit happens to an average guy, how could he not think of himself as awesome? Tony just laughed and left us to talk, as he quickly noticed the connection and knew immediately where this was going to eventually lead.

Mary Ann was a petite thirty-nine-year-old Italian woman with a dark complexion that seemed to stay sun-soaked tan no matter what time of year it was. Her hair was a satin-like dark black, and fortunately, she lacked hairy arms, a feature that plagues some Italian women. If there was a trace of a mustache, she must have had that thing well waxed or lasered because I didn't notice a furry upper lip. She had these thin little legs and weighed no more than 110 pounds. She had long, curly black hair and always wore a little extra makeup to the gym. At first glance, Mary Ann didn't appear to be in need of a trainer, but who was I to turn away a paying customer?

With little resistance, Mary Ann signed up for training three days a week. That was quite a lot of time to spend on training, seeing how she was already in good shape. Mary Ann seemed to be on a mission to win me over, but she wasn't verbally open like Raquel and didn't say things like, "Can I please suck your dick after our workout?" Instead, it came in the form of another unexpected perk of the job. Over the course of our first few sessions, Mary Ann would go to great lengths to get on my good side, as if she needed to put in some work to get into my pants. This was my first experience getting gifts from a client for no apparent reason. How many people have worked in a job where people show up on the reg with shit for you? My birthday and the holidays were months away, but Mary Ann would show up with clothes, food, gift cards, you name it. Each week there was something to look forward to. It felt like Hanukkah except it lasted longer than eight days.

Since I was not used to being shown such affection by anyone in my life, this type of gifting created an awkward feeling in my gut. In my opinion, when someone gives you something nice, it's only common courtesy to return the favor. Even after letting Mary Ann know I had a girlfriend and would not be able to return the favor, Mary Ann went on unfazed and continued to bring me things each time she showed up. Try explaining that to your significant other when she knows you never go shopping with her, let alone for yourself.

I wasn't quite sure what all this gifting meant. Did it mean she wanted more than just a fuck? Was she just a genuinely nice person who liked to do stuff for other people? Sure, like it's completely normal for people to buy things for someone they just met and not just once but every week. I had a few regular clients who, in addition to personal training, were getting that "little extra" from me. Why not add another? What did I have to lose? You may ask, how the fuck does someone who has a girlfriend rationalize adding yet another one to his quickly expanding and already ridiculous playlist? Looking back, I would have to ask the same question. How much can one person push the envelope? Turns out, quite a bit if you don't put much thought into it and just do it. Just like some major league baseball players have a bull pen of women waiting for them when they play their away games, I was building a good-sized bull pen of my own except it was getting a little too close for comfort, as it was in my own backyard. It began to feel a little weird when I trained a woman whom I had slept with on Friday followed by a woman whom I hooked up with on Saturday, and then top it off with the one who gave me a hummer just last night. How much longer could I keep this up? Each of these women would walk right by one another as I met them at the front door of the gym. I felt a little like the strip club DJ. He knows he's no prize but continues to tap more ass than he knows what to do with. Outside the strip club, he is your average Joe, but inside that neon-lit, mirrored dome with that horrible Nickelback song blaring from the speakers, he's the king of that castle.

Mary Ann was usually my last appointment of the day, at nine o'clock in the evening. The gym closed at ten o'clock, and the rest of the staff was usually out of the door by 9:55 p.m. whenever possible. I always stayed until the last minute of the hour with Mary Ann. She was so generous with the gifts each time we met that it was the least I could do for her.

One night, a little less than six weeks into her training, we were in the back of the thirty-thousand-square-foot gym finishing up the workout when Tony yelled to me he was leaving and heading to Chotchkies for a few drinks and told me to come by. He also told me the cleaners were coming by that night and asked me to lock the door on my way out. It wasn't uncommon for me to be the last one in the gym, as none of the other trainers had appointments that late in the evening.

Tony tried his best to coax me into going out with him, but I was a little worn out from the previous week. I had a full slate with Raquel, Gina, Sabrina, and my girlfriend each having a night they could call their own. I wasn't really into getting hammered that night, so the last thing I wanted to do was head over to Chotchkies and get a premature headache from too many premixed Long Island iced teas. I figured once Mary Ann left, I would be on my way home for an uneventful evening.

After she finished her last set of stiff-legged dead lifts, I walked Mary Ann to the front door and thought for a minute that I would be home within the next twenty minutes. As Mary Ann grabbed her bag behind the front desk, she reached in and put a lollipop in her mouth. This wasn't the first time Mary Ann put some type of candy in her mouth right after we worked out, but a lollipop? Really? I'll never understand how such an innocent act can give a guy a semi. It didn't help that she was dressed in her usual tight stretch pants and one of those workout bras that I still question whether is appropriate to wear without a T-shirt over it. Oh, well. It showed Mary Ann's perky little boobs nicely and helped the hour go by relatively fast each time we trained.

The Mexican cleaning crew of about eight men and women filed into the gym with equipment in hand. The cleaning crew was no joke. They would have the place looking spotless in the next half hour. I never really saw them in action, but I knew because I would come in on the mornings after they had cleaned and the gym would look great and wouldn't smell like ass. This cleaning crew paid attention to the small stuff that most people would just once over. If only I could have them clean my house today.

Once Mary Ann grabbed her keys, I said good-bye to her and made my way over to the manager's office, which was next to the front door of the gym, to get my stuff. I was slightly freaked out when I heard the door close behind me. I turned around and saw that Mary Ann had followed me into the manager's office. I was planning on just grabbing my stuff and leaving, so I hadn't even turned the light on in the office. The manager's office had only one window, but it was a huge one-way window, about six feet wide by four feet high, that looked out onto the gym floor. My manager and I shared a few laughs in there while making obscene gestures or some other juvenile type of act toward pain-in-the-ass patrons or attractive women as they worked out. Ah, yes. Good times were abound in this temple of fitness. To think I was getting paid for all this. No wonder many of my friends with "real" jobs were jealous of me.

I wasn't sure what to do, so I grabbed my bag and picked up my keys. Then Mary Ann started talking to me.

"You know how good you look in that shirt?" she said. She wasted no time getting to the point now that we were behind closed doors.

My response was that of your average guy who was beginning to gain confidence in himself: "Really?" It was the best I could come up with.

Mary Ann had the "fuck me" look about her as she said, "I'm sure I'm not the first person to tell you that."

If she only knew.

I couldn't help but notice the huge grin on her face. I always wondered why the hell this woman was so happy. I don't know if it was that smile, that scent of electric youth or whatever the fuck cheap perfume Mary Ann would douse herself in, or that fucking lollipop she was sucking on, but I was mesmerized at that moment. Call me crazy, but the smell of a woman's cheap perfume mixed with sweat had me all up in arms.

I don't remember what else was said, but next thing I knew, my back was up against the large one-way window and I was sucking face with Mary Ann. She was a petite little thing, so I couldn't help but let my hands do some exploring and feel that tight little backside that seemed to be on display every time she was in the gym. I quickly realized Mary Ann was obviously a smoker. I tried not to think about my tongue scraping the bottom of an old ashtray and tried to focus on the green apple flavor of the lollipop she had been sucking. Having only made out with one or two girls who smoked cigarettes, this was definitely not something I was into. It didn't turn out to be a deal breaker, as I was ready to bone or at least unleash the dragon.

After a few minutes of making out, Mary Ann mercifully pulled away and slowly went to her knees, caressing my stomach softly with her hands. Knowing exactly where this was going, I was pretty excited, although I would have much rather taken a seat at what my manager called the "captain's chair," but what the hell. Beggars can't be choosers. I had my usual gym pants on that were the tear-away type (a.k.a. "party boy" ones that can be removed effortlessly). Mary Ann's hands then made their way to my waist, where she untied my pants with the giddiness of a kid opening presents on Christmas. Once again, I was fully engorged. I'll never understand how these guys in porn stay soft while a girl puts it in her mouth. To this day, when the word "blow job" even comes out of a girl's mouth, I have full wood.

Without pulling my pants down, Mary Ann reached down into my boxers, slipped my shaft out of my underwear, and began to give me an exquisite blow job. I must say, having a view of this from a standing position was outstanding. With only the dim light of the main gym providing just enough light to see, I watched in joy as Mary Ann did her thing. She would occasionally look up and give me that huge smile, which made me feel somewhat obligated to smile back at her, but I thought better of it for fear of looking like a clown. Leaning back against the window, I tried to look as cool as a guy could look while a girl was kneeling in front of him and giving him head. Mary Ann was performing at the perfect slow speed to keep me from bursting prematurely.

After a few minutes, I suddenly noticed one of the members of the cleaning crew running a squeegee on the opposite side of the window almost directly next to my head. Startled but unfazed, Mary Ann's mouth popped off my cock. She continued to stroke me with one hand and nervously asked if the cleaner could see through the window.

"It's a one-way window. You can only see out from this side," I told her, even though that wasn't entirely true. I had pressed my head up against that window many times and was able to see what my manager was doing inside the office—and that was with the lights on in the office. I never caught my manager with his pants down around his ankles, like the scene that was unfolding in front of this cleaner's eyes. With the lights off, there was no doubt this guy could see everything as he cleaned the window. He definitely could not mistake my back and some girl on her knees in front of me as some fancy piece of furniture. Thank god Mary Ann didn't pull my boxers down far enough so that my frosty white cheeks were pressed up against the window.

Not wanting this to end before I finished, I again reassured Mary Ann to continue. I didn't want to have blue balls, so I gave her some motivation to finish the job. As she looked up at me with my dick in her hand, I said, "I'm almost finished." This horrible yet somehow effective line turned out to be all I needed to rally Mary Ann to finish strong. The cleaner didn't seem to miss a beat during this unplanned time-out. He continued with the task at hand and in fact probably helped me last a little longer than I normally would have. Mary Ann returned to form and took me right back inside her. She took her performance to the next level when, after a few licks, she grabbed hold of my dick and began sucking on each one of my balls. I began to moan, as this was pushing me to the brink.

After a short while, she returned to swallowing my shaft down to the base. Holy shit! I was holding on by a thread. It wasn't until the cleaner was done with the window and had moved on to his next task that I was able to finish. Unfortunately, I didn't think to give Mary Ann notice that I was about to wrap up. She was down there, head furiously moving forward and back, when I got caught up in the sight of it all and suddenly lost it. The moment came so fast that Mary Ann choked a little bit because of the unexpected delivery.

That nasty string of saliva-goo hung from the tip of my cock to her mouth, and Mary Ann quickly backed off. Most of my load had made it unwillingly down her throat, so there wasn't a total mess. She coughed a little to clear her throat, and I immediately felt terrible for letting loose without a warning. Real classy, right? Here is a woman on her knees trying to pleasure me, and I don't even have the decency to ejaculate civilly.

"I'm so sorry!" I said. I pulled up my pants and ran out of the office to grab a bottle of water from the cooler next to the office. I didn't even think to look and see if the cleaners had gathered to talk about what was happening in the office. I rushed back into the office and again expressed my guilt to Mary Ann as I handed her the water. "I can't believe I did that to you," I said.

Mary Ann was standing next to the desk and still having trouble getting a word out. She coughed a little and took a few sips of water. By some miracle, she didn't seem the least bit irritated by it; instead, that huge smile returned to her face and she said, "Next time, give me a heads up before that happens."

Did I hear her correctly? I just blew into this woman's mouth, causing her to choke, and she just reassured me that she'll give me a blow job again? How in the fuck can one guy be so lucky?

This time before walking out of the office, I looked around the gym. The cleaning crew was in the zone; it was as if we weren't even there. Maybe they were so focused on the job that they didn't notice the show that had just happened in the manager's office, but that was wishful thinking. I'm sure the window cleaner came away with a story that still lives on today at family gatherings. Thankfully, this happened before the age of YouTube where we could have had quite a few hits. I walked Mary

Ann to her car and wisely turned what more than likely was intended to be a kiss into a hug before she got into her car and drove off.

On my way home to meet up with my girlfriend, I felt weird having just blown a load into another woman's mouth. The guilt I felt the first time I strayed was much more apparent now, yet it was getting easier and easier for me to say yes to these women. I was turning into a shallow prick. Part of me wanted to end all these extracurricular activities and start to lead a life on the straight and narrow path. But unfortunately, the other half of me was thoroughly enjoying getting treated like Prince Akeem of Zamunda with his personal bathers.

After our first encounter, things with Mary Ann seemed to roll along just like they did with all the others. There were no big expectations, I continued to collect unearned weekly prizes, and she gave me the occasional BJ after training, usually in her car, since my '87 Firebird with its bucket seats and cool bird emblem on the hood wasn't exactly the most comfortable place. It was as if I was Steven Seagal and I was above the law. Mary Ann continued her weekly sessions, and although the blow jobs were nice, I was beginning to wonder more and more about what she looked like naked.

I knew Mary Ann had a kid who was in high school. Being a little freaked out by the fact that I was barely seven years older than her son, I was hesitant to meet up with Mary Ann at her place. What the hell would this kid say if I showed up at the door? What would I say? "Hello, I'm here to bone your mom"? Worst yet, what if her kid walked into the house and found his mom spread-eagle on the couch with me all up in her? It was a scene I wanted to avoid altogether. As with many things in my life up until this point, I wasn't able to use my best judgment when it came to mysterious magic of poontang.

One Thursday, a couple of months after the night Mary Ann and I first bonded in the manager's office, my car happened to be in the shop, so I got a ride to work from my girlfriend, which made this all the more fucked up. As usual, Mary Ann was my last client of the night. My girlfriend was working late, so I would have to find a ride home. I could have asked Tony or Larry for a ride, but I was yet again thinking with the other head.

After our session, I casually asked Mary Ann for a lift home. I did feel guilty knowing that my girlfriend had given me a ride to work that day. But in my own crazy thought process, I compared it to having my girlfriend drop me off somewhere so that I could just bone another girl. Dammit. If only I had my car, I wouldn't have this horrible sense of guilt.

Mary Ann gave me a giddy smile—as if I just asked her if she wanted an orgasm like no other—and said she could drive me home. While in her car, we chatted casually, but in the back of my mind, I was strategically thinking about where we could have sex that night. I wanted to take this relationship to the next level. It's not that I was getting tired of blow jobs, seeing how they are like glazed doughnuts and never go out of style, but I wanted a little more that evening. We could do it in the car, which I had done before, just not with Mary Ann. In fact, the gym's parking lot happened to be a key spot for me, as I would handle my business many nights in my own car or someone else's while parked in a dark corner of the lot shadowed by the gym. I could just ask her to come over to my place and then bone on my couch, which was feeling dirtier with each passing day. Maybe we could go back to her place and do it somewhere that was foreign to me. For all I knew, her kid was maybe at Dad's place on this Thursday night.

"Do you want to stop by your place?" I asked. Yep, I just invited myself over.

Mary Ann didn't hesitate when I asked if we could stop by her place before going back to mine. This made no sense, as it turns out she lived in the opposite direction of me. Oh, what the hell. I wasn't driving. We arrived at her place, and I was happy to see that there weren't any lights on. I followed her into her house. Once inside, I tiptoed and kept my head on a swivel, as if surveying the scene for enemy snipers. Mary Ann walked through the house without any concern, so I figured everything was cool.

We made a beeline right to her bedroom, which was toward the back of the house. Once inside her room, Mary Ann turned on a small lamp on the nightstand next to her bed and then walked toward her dresser. I went right to the bed. We hadn't even said a word since we got out of the car, and there I was arrogantly assuming I was going to get laid. I even kicked off my shoes as I sat down on the edge of her bed.

Mary Ann, with that big shit-eating grin on her face, came over to the bed and wasted no time as she straddled me and began making out with me. All I could taste was the buildup of years of chain smoking. Even though her chewing gum did a fair job of covering up that initial shock of tar, after a minute or so, it hit me with enough force that I opened my eyes. By now, I had full wood, so I dug deep and pressed on despite this obstacle. As she proceeded to take off her top, revealing her small but nicely shaped breasts, I wondered whether her son was home and if we would wake him, as his mother's moans were getting louder.

With her top removed, I leaned back onto her bed and made myself comfortable. I was getting so used to this adulterous behavior that I expected not only to get laid but also to have it my way. Rodeo? The wheelbarrow? Pirate's bounty? The options were endless. As I was running every position I had in my routine through my head, Mary Ann stripped off the rest of her clothes and left nothing but her little laced panties with a small flower sewn right over the center. Using her soft hands, she began to pull my drawers down, removing them completely and leaving nothing but my socks on. I helped the cause and took my shirt off and lay flat with my schlong pointing slightly to the left. Mary Ann went straight for it in this yoga-like child's pose and had me in awe. I propped myself up onto my elbows for a better view as she slowly went down on me, her hands lightly cupping my balls. It never got old watching Mary Ann—or any of my clients, for that matter—put her lips around me and use whatever method she preferred just to make me happy. I quickly forgot all about her teenage son possibly sleeping in the next room.

After several minutes, Mary Ann sat straight up, reached over to the nightstand drawer, and pulled out a Trojan. Wow, this lady was a pro. I began to wonder how many other guys have been right where I was lying now and about to get to know Mary Ann up close and personal. She took the rubber out of the package. This was probably the second time in my life I had a girl put a condom on me. It definitely helped that Mary Ann was obviously well versed in this, as her technique was flawless. Within seconds, it was perfectly rolled onto my wood without as much as a crease in it. She then slipped right on top of me, and I watched as I disappeared into Mary Ann's very wet vagina. What started slow quickly sped up as Mary Ann began bouncing up and down furiously and steadily increasing the volume of her moans. As she got louder and louder, I began to again lose my focus and wonder if her kid was listening with a glass up against the wall in the next room. Actually, forget the glass now. With nothing like a TV or music on in the background to drown out the noise, I'm sure even her next-door neighbors could have heard everything. This momentary distraction was helpful, as it prolonged me quite a bit.

Mary Ann then began squeezing her own breasts and whipping her hair around her head as my hands guided her waist. I thought for a second that she reminded me a little of Boof from *Teen Wolf*. At the speed she was going, I feared the worst: that she would get up just a little too high and come down so fast that my unit would break. That would be a tough one to explain not only at the emergency room but also to my girlfriend. All these extra thoughts going through my mind helped this moment last probably to one of my all-time highs. With Mary Ann's voice approaching ear-piercing volume, I thought I heard the faint sound of a door closing somewhere in the house. Trying not to lose focus, I continued on as she eventually came with her entire body tensing up from head to toe. She finally slowed down her hip thrusting, causing me to explode inside the condom, which I hoped was still intact. Both of us were nearly covered in sweat. Mary Ann hopped off, and I looked at my fatigued yet satisfied copilot as he lay there covered in a transparent yellow jump coat. Mary Ann threw on a robe and walked out of the room. I had no idea where she was going, as I was in recovery mode and trying to cool down.

Then I heard the unmistakable sounds of Mary Ann talking to someone. I sat up in bed, wide-eyed, with the soggy condom still attached. Thankfully, I didn't hear yelling or shouting, just the murmurs of a normal-toned conversation. I could not help but think she was talking to her son. Unless this kid was deaf, he undoubtedly just heard his mother get railed. I'm not much of a mama's boy, but this shit has got to fuck a kid up.

Worried this kid was going to run into the room with a samurai sword, I quickly removed the soiled prophylactic and, without wiping off my guy, got dressed as fast as I could. Moments later, Mary Ann returned to the room with a big smile on her face, seemingly unfazed by whatever exchange just happened outside the bedroom. I was a little more than perplexed and just wanted to get out of this odd scene. Was it her son in the other room? Was her ex-husband still living with her? Whoever it was, it was most definitely a male.

"My son just got home. I just had to say hello to him," she said.

What? You just got boned by your trainer and minutes later felt the need to say hello to your son?

"He didn't…uh…hear anything?" I asked, even though I didn't really want to know the answer to this. But my high school mentality had taken over, and I pictured myself walking out of Mary Ann's room and giving her son a high five on the way out.

"No," Mary Ann said, although her answer sounded questionable.

Despite not having a watch on, I looked at my wrist and said, "Wow, it's getting late and I got an early day tomorrow," which was a lie. Apparently, I did a good enough job satisfying Mary Ann, as she didn't try to keep me hostage. She took off her robe, got dressed, and grabbed her keys to drive me home.

As we made our way through her house, I nervously looked around and checked to see if I had a red dot somewhere on my body. I think I saw the lights under the door to what must have been her son's bedroom and could only imagine what was going through that kid's head at the time. My mom once boned my best friend's dad, but this was ridiculous.

After I made it out of the house unscathed, I couldn't help but feel both terrible and freaked out by what just happened. Sitting in the car on the way home, I didn't really know what to say. I felt like Finch with Stifler's mom. Trying my best to "act as if," I kept the talk to a minimum and just kept Mary Ann entertained by telling her some stories of the other members of the gym. I just wanted to get back to my place with my penis still intact.

When we got to my apartment, I knew I had to hurry and get into my place and in the shower because my girlfriend was coming over after work. Having a sense that Mary Ann didn't brush those teeth when she left the room earlier, I didn't want to go anywhere near that mouth of hers, so I went in for the hug. Mary Ann continued to smile as we said our good-byes. Once I got out of the car and she pulled away, I stood there for a moment to reflect on what just happened. For some reason, the evening's events made me think a little deeper about what I was doing, and I was reluctant to accept anything else from Mary Ann, including another blow job in the manager's office.

When my girlfriend crept into bed with me after work, I pretended to be out cold but my mind was racing. Yes, ladies, men are also capable of this move on occasion. I was feeling more and more guilt about what I had been doing, and things were weighing heavily on me. Several hours later, I fell asleep and ended up sleeping in well past nine o'clock in the morning. Did I wake up a changed man? Maybe for a second or two. But turns out, I was so wrapped up in this fantasyland I was living in that I would not only give Mary Ann another shot but I would also have even more tryouts for my ever-growing team.

8
THE FRONT DESK GIRL

You have to admire the business model that many gyms use. They place at least one attractive, slim, college-aged girl at the front desk to greet you with a big smile and sometimes an even bigger rack on her chest. It's like Hooters or some other second-rate eating establishment that attempts to cover up the shitty food by providing eye candy in short shorts and tight tops while you choke down what is supposed to be a buffalo wing.

I couldn't agree more with the sly business guys who decided to put attractive girls in front as if they were on display, especially since the majority of a gym's clientele will be young males and middle-aged men. Sex sells, so businesses do what they have to do. Occasionally, a gay guy is sprinkled in to mix it up, but otherwise, it's usually a better-than-average-looking girl. How many times have you walked into a gym and been greeted with a polite smile from some heffer? Chances are not often, if at all, unless it's a gym that caters only to very overweight people. I cannot recall for the life of me seeing a porky gym receptionist, but I have never set foot inside a Curves, so I could be way off.

So what's the story with the hot chick behind the front desk? A guy walking through the door may think for a minute that he has a chance with her. After all, she is usually very pleasant toward him every time he walks in. Don't worry, guys—you are not alone when you walk into the gym and give your front desk greeter a good once over as she swipes your gym card.

Many of the front desk girls I've met over the years had great personalities to go along with their good looks, but I'm not gonna lie to you and tell you that I have not come across some evil bitches along the way. As a matter of fact, I'm sure many people have been close to canceling a gym membership based on an interaction with the front desk girl.

Some front desk girls are great at their jobs. They make each person who walks in the door feel welcome, as if they really care about every person. Some will even go as far as friendly flirting with male clientele. One thing for sure is that when an attractive young female is put in front of you day after day, something is bound to happen over time. What starts out as innocent flirting and joking around often leads to something more.

It's common knowledge that sexual relations with coworkers are more often than not a bad idea. But, as you've seen in the previous chapters, I have a tendency to push the limit, if you will. Larry warned me about the dangers of sleeping with clients, but for the life of me, I could not recall a memo on steering clear of coworkers.

Now, this is going to sound fucked up, but as I write this chapter, I have no idea what the hell this girl's name was. She was an attractive twenty-five-year-old blonde who worked the front desk at Precision Fitness and wore these glasses that made her look like the beautiful blonde from Van Halen's "Hot for Teacher" music video. We'll call her Kathy. Before we go any further, I want to let you know that even though I was now twenty-two years old, bad decisions seemed to continue on a daily basis. Even though

Kathy was on the skinny side, I was more than okay with her whole package, since she had a great personality, as well as sarcasm and wit. She also had the added plus of being in great shape because she worked out regularly. I wasn't the only trainer who thought rather highly of Kathy whenever she rode that spinning bike, as she did it better than most. She was in graduate school, and I could only imagine what she thought of a community college guy like me.

It helped to get in good with the front desk staff because they would often refer clients to me and sometimes filter out the potential pains in the ass. I became friendly with Kathy. We would talk regularly at work, but I never anticipated anything to happen outside the gym. I still had a girlfriend, even though I had cheated on her more times than I could remember, much less count. I know—I would have been much better off a single guy, but I was always the relationship type. Kathy was also working out with Scott, and I was pretty sure she was trying to get into his pants, if she hadn't already. Although I was developing quite the reputation, Scott was a fellow player as well.

Kathy started at Precision Fitness at its inception when I did. She was a firsthand witness to my methods and knew very well what was going on with several of my clients. To boot, Kathy met Danielle on several occasions, since she sporadically worked out at the gym from time to time. Fortunately for me, she never set foot in the gym during the evening hours when it was truly my time to shine.

It was more than a year before anything would become of the innocent flirting and daily conversations I had with Kathy. By this time, my little black book included several older women, including housewives and executive types, but no one in her twenties. I was juggling more women than you can imagine. There weren't enough days in the week to handle my current workload, and I was making a conscious effort to refrain from sleeping with more clients. Once again, smaller heads prevailed as I reasoned that sleeping with a coworker would be acceptable, since it would technically fall into the category of a "work relationship." I know. I was a front-runner for being elected prick of the year, as voted by girlfriends and spouses across the country.

One Thursday before my shift ended, Kathy asked what I was doing over the weekend. I didn't think much of it at the time and quickly responded, "Not much."

Kathy asked if I was interested in going out with her sometime over the weekend. I was completely caught off guard to the fact that she was asking me out. Even though I was getting used to this whole being asked out thing, I had yet to have a highly educated coed ask me out. I had witnessed, over the course of our working together, many brave souls ask Kathy on a date only to be shot down, so the prospect of ever approaching her was far removed from my radar. I knew she was single, but she knew very well that I had a girlfriend.

I know a better man would have said no. How could I go out with someone else if I was already in a relationship? I'd like to throw the "I was only twenty-two" card on the table again. So I gave some bullshit lie to my girlfriend and met up with Kathy at a local watering hole on Saturday evening. With work not an issue for either of us the following day, the drinks would flow freely that night.

Kathy had prior college experience and was more selective about where she preferred to hang out. This worked in my favor, since she chose an obscure bar that was out of the ordinary for a guy like me, thus minimizing my risk of running into someone I knew. The bar could have been mistaken for a coffee house, as I could have sworn people were in there studying on a Saturday night. Kathy and I shared some tales about coworkers and life in general over a few drinks. She was going to graduate soon with her master's degree and seemed to have her shit together. And there I was, a community college legend who felt more like Trip McNeely rather than someone who should be with an older girl who seemed to be a little wiser than me.

Once again, things started off innocently enough: just two coworkers having a drink outside the workplace. But, as proven by the many females you see out downtown on any weekend night, alcohol turns even the most innocent girl into a sex-crazed machine. After an hour of talking and three very strong vodka and something or other drinks, Kathy felt the need to let loose a little bit. The scene wasn't exactly happening, and I could tell Kathy was itching to leave.

"I want to go somewhere that will wake me up a little," she said.

I guess she wasn't feeling content like I was with Bruce Springsteen on the jukebox. Since any type of illegal substance was out of reach on such short notice, I suggested we try somewhere else. We decided to go into the city to a club that I had been wanting to go to for some time. I heard that it was always full of drunken people having a grand old time. Why leave a hole in the wall in a part of town you would never be caught in for a huge club that is packed with a thousand people? You would think I would have wanted to stay low-key and out of sight, especially since I had a girlfriend, but I wasn't too concerned at this point. I swear, they should put labels on each glass you order to remind you that alcohol will impair your judgment. So much for staying incognito. I was about to be in a club the size of a warehouse where I was destined to run into someone who knew me. On the flip side, something told me that if we left this bar, I would get laid later that night.

As fate would have it, we weren't even in the club for five minutes before we ran into Gary, a client of mine. Gary was a business owner who happened to enjoy getting shitfaced on the weekends and surrounding himself with younger people. He wasn't the least bit surprised to see me out, but he was a little thrown off seeing me with Kathy, as he knew all about my girlfriend. He was half in the bag and made a comment about what we were up to that evening. He even said we made a cute couple. Kathy and I laughed his comments off. Gary was a pretty cool guy, and he immediately decided to buy us a couple of shots. That's when the shitty Jose Cuervo Gold, which goes down like battery acid, made its entrance to the party. Just the thought of shots these days turns my stomach.

After several hours of drinking heavily to a point that I even cut loose on the dance floor, I was completely intoxicated. I was throwing myself around the dance floor like an epileptic, but with Gary and Kathy cheering me on, I wasn't about to stop. I was working it, doing the bull dance when the lights came up and it was time to leave. As we left, I thanked Gary for the hangover I was about to have the next morning. Despite being seriously impaired, I drove us back to Kathy's house. It was about a thirty-minute drive, but it felt like hours because I was wide-eyed and focused on the rules of the road. A DUI would have brought the party to a quick end. I was drunk, but Kathy was maybe just slightly buzzed, as her years of drinking in college were paying off. She lived with her sister in this house on the river a few miles from the gym, but her sister was staying over at her boyfriend's place that night. One would think the drive to Kathy's place would somehow sober me up and allow me to make a better decision, but I had no such luck. I don't even think I hesitated when Kathy asked me to come in for a few cocktails. How could someone with a significant other think it was a wise move to go into an attractive woman's house after two o'clock in the morning, especially after having more than half a dozen vodka tonics, as well as multiple tequila shots?

This is my advice to all married folks, and you can bet I will one day heed it myself: Do not, under any circumstances, leave your girlfriend, fiancée, wife, or whoever it may be with a guy in his twenties for more than an hour. Better yet, make that fifteen minutes. And over my dead body will she be in the company of one of these sex-crazed animals for an extended period after dusk. I know it may sound shitty, but I'm just stating the facts. When you're young, in shape, and healthy, you're going to try to get in a woman's pants no matter what the cost. If alcohol is involved and it's after midnight, then it's only a matter of what types of things will happen. If you think I'm wrong, you're going to become a victim of this madness. What was I going to be doing over at her place at such an hour? Hanging out just talking? Fuck no! I planned to get something before making the trek back home, and I hoped it would be more than a handy.

I stumbled into her house and plopped down on her couch. I watched Kathy pour me some concoction with more than enough alcohol for the two of us. I had a difficult time deciphering how many drinks I'd had at this point, but it may have been one of my all-time highs. Things progressed innocently, with light conversation about some of the fucked-up members of the gym and some of the even more fucked-up staff members. Talking shit is a favorite pastime of mine, and apparently I wasn't the only one who enjoyed it. I felt really comfortable with Kathy, as I had gotten to know her well over the past several months, so it was easy to let loose around her. She was funny and hot, which is a nice combination, since boring and hot is only fun for a short time.

Kathy and I were sitting on opposite ends of the couch, doing nothing more than talking and laughing. After a little while, something happened. I don't recall where the conversation went, but next thing I knew, Kathy was straddling me and planting her lips on my face. After a few seconds, she took a break to slip my *smedium* shirt off over my head in one graceful swoop and then returned to my lips. Once again, my technique for sealing the deal with these women was doing exactly nothing. In a drunken haze, I marveled at how fortunate I was to have another woman throw herself on top of me. I couldn't help but think of all the effort I used to give just to have even heavyset women turn me away. I was getting really good at this without ever really trying.

This was my out, if there was going to be one. I could have pushed her off, I could have said something, but I was pretty worked up and wanted to see where this thing was going. Besides, I had another problem. Either all that tequila or all the blood in my body seemed to have made its way between my legs because I had a full boner with Kathy on my lap. As uncomfortable as it was, I wasn't about to say a word because I was more than curious as to what would happen next.

Kathy was slowly dry humping me when she put my hands on her breasts. To this day, when a girl places my hands on her breasts, I lose all inhibition. I took that as a free pass to see what lay beneath and ended up ripping her shirt off over her head. Kathy had quite the nice little rack on her, as I never noticed how perky and nicely rounded her boobs were under our required gym attire, which wasn't half as glamorous as the Under Armour getups of today.

Trying not to get too distracted by the suppleness of her breasts, I assisted her in getting her short shorts off. I then shifted my focus to her underwear, which were see-through black mesh with a pink lace trim. As I removed this last piece of clothing, I couldn't help but notice Kathy was not only well kept down below but also smelled of lush lavender with a hint of cinnamon. Kathy was shaved down with just a small patch of hair on top, which kind of looked like a missed spot the more I stared at it.

I laid her down on the couch, and somehow my head ended up between her legs. When your head is between the legs of a woman other than your girlfriend, you really aren't thinking much of what will happen if she finds out. I had a job to do, and dag gummit, I was going to give it my all. The aroma that lured me down there in the first place was not a fancy sort of cover-up. There's nothing worse than sticking your tongue in something that smells of a lush tropical garden but turns out tasting like the top of a nine-volt battery. As my tongue made its way around her sweet spot, Kathy's hands pressed into the back of my head as if to get me in a little deeper. Thankfully, the isometric exercises I had been working on my neck extensors managed to keep my head above water, so to speak. I didn't want to pull up looking like I just went bobbing for an apple and came up with nothing but a wet chin. With a few fingers in the mix, I managed to get Kathy off, or at least I think I did because her legs tensed up tightly around my head.

I came up for air with nothing hanging from my mouth, and seeing how she was neatly trimmed, the possibility of having a shorty sticking out of the corner of my mouth was minimal. Kathy looked as if she was done for the night, similar to my move on more than a few occasions when I got off but didn't exactly return the favor.

Having finished my job with high marks, I was looking for a little reciprocation. I stood up in front of the couch and pulled down my pants to expose myself. Kathy didn't hesitate and proceeded to return the favor. I had my pants pulled halfway down at this point but was topless. I must have looked like that kid in kindergarten who doesn't quite know how to operate the fly on his jeans. As she kept one hand on my cock and steadily sucked away with purpose, Kathy completely removed my pants and underwear with her other hand. With her hand on my already throbbing knob, I couldn't help but think he seemed a bit bigger than usual this evening. Maybe that tequila really did increase the blood flow down there, and maybe I should be choking down more of that shit when I expect to score.

With her hand around my cock and her thumb gently massaging the fellas, Kathy went to work like a graduate student cramming for finals. I felt a little odd standing up while she took me in and out of her mouth. I didn't know where to put my hands, since I felt weird putting them on my hips. I ended up carefully cupping the back of Kathy's head with one hand, while my other hand made its way to the back of my head. When I thought about what I looked like, I felt like a tool. I looked like some guy who decided to try his hand at a mechanical bull.

Kathy had the perfect ratio of suck to lick going on, and it wasn't long before I was ready for launch. Should I advise her that this was coming to an end? If so, what was the best way to get this message across other than the obvious "I'm coming," which makes every guy feel like a jerk-off when he says it? Before I knew it, I let go in Kathy's mouth. She was ready for it like a vacuum and swallowed without a gag or any trace of evidence afterward.

Once I finished, I immediately felt that familiar sense of guilt. This feeling was getting more and more overwhelming each time I dropped a load in front of someone other than my girlfriend. I just needed to be a single guy, I thought. Then I would feel much better about this. There I was with this very long buildup, and once I climaxed, all I could think about was getting out the door. I didn't really know what to say afterward. This wasn't my first time fucking around, but for some reason, I felt guiltier than ever.

After a couple of minutes of awkward silence, we both searched for our clothing, which was scattered about Kathy's living room. I didn't want to make things more uncomfortable, but that's exactly what I did.

"I can't believe we just did this. I'm such an asshole," I said. (Note to self: women don't really want to hear this after you just shared oral sex with them.) My follow-up wasn't much better. "I'm so sorry I did this to you," I said, as if Kathy was the one who had just been cheated on.

Kathy just sat back on her couch with a glazed look in her eyes and calmly said, "Don't worry about it."

I was surprised she was as cool as she was, but then again, she was a graduate student, so maybe that was just how postgrad coeds were. I finished putting on my shoes and looked around her place frazzled as if there was a hidden camera taping our session. Without waiting for some other brilliant thought to pop into my head, I ran out of Kathy's house with my pants unbuttoned.

This was a first for me. I can't remember a time when I acted so strangely after having sexual contact with a woman.

Maybe it was because I'd never had sex with a coworker before. I had no idea what to expect walking into the gym on Monday afternoon after this event-filled evening. Kathy and I never talked on the phone, so I knew I would not speak to her over the rest of the weekend or get a chance to clear the air after my sudden exit. Shit, this was going to be the end for me.

My girlfriend had seen and spoken to Kathy on more than one occasion at the gym, and for all I knew, my girlfriend could walk in at any point during the week and hear all about my big night out. Talk about a precarious position. It was as if I was frying bacon naked, just asking for it. Surely this would come back to bite me. All Kathy had to do to throw me under the bus was strike up a conversation with my girlfriend when she came into the gym. After my odd behavior, why the hell wouldn't she?

As I walked into the gym that Monday, I never felt more uneasy. Sure, I had already slept with several clients, some of whom had back-to-back training sessions and walked right past one another, but this was different. This was a coworker. Who hasn't heard stories of shit really hitting the fan when two coworkers end up doing the nasty? If only I stuck to clients, none of this added stress would be on top of my shoulders. From here on out, I'm swearing off coworkers, I thought to myself.

Could I possibly quit with clients as well? That wasn't something I was quite ready to give up, but based on how I was feeling after this encounter with Kathy, I knew having something with a coworker could quickly turn ugly. I didn't know what the hell to say to Kathy. I thought she was going to be pissed off beyond belief. I pictured the typical cross-armed posture with a look of disgust on her face when I walked in. Fuck it, time to face the music. It was a fun run. Could I really complain if it had to end at this point judging from the unimaginable amount of sex I had over the last year and a half of my life?

I was shocked at Kathy's reception of me. She had her usual smile on her face, and for a second, I wondered if it was the bullshit smile she gave to each member who walked through the front door. Much to my surprise, Kathy was completely cool with the whole situation. It was like a one-night stand that had gone perfectly as planned. She asked how I felt the morning after we went out. Turns out, Kathy was a little more drunk than she had led on. She had some recollection we "hooked up," as she put it, but she seemed to have forgotten all about my abrupt exit. If she did remember it, she didn't mention it. Maybe it was my stellar work when I went down on her. Wishful thinking, I know. Hopefully, she wouldn't have an epiphany one day and realize I ran out of there with my pants unbuttoned, almost sobbing about what an asshole I'd been.

As if I couldn't get any luckier, just a couple of weeks after our big night out, Kathy told me she was transferring to another gym at the end of the month. The rest of the time we worked together, there was no evidence of any bad blood between us. I was shocked, as my prior sexual experiences had never ended on such an odd note, and I was certain my actions that night justified some type of bullshit I would have to deal with. I felt like Rocky with Mickey in his corner. I was unstoppable.

On Kathy's last day at the gym, we had a farewell party for her. You never would have known we had one crazy night together. No one we worked with knew any of the details, and aside from my client Gary, I was certain we weren't spotted out that evening. Ah, yes. To be fortunate enough to have had my run before the golden age of camera phones.

At the end of Kathy's last day, several of us went out after work to the bar down the street from the gym. Kathy was having a grand old time partying like only she knew how, and I was just kicking back, enjoying my sense of relief that this was all coming to a close. This night signaled the end of my worries about something bad happening to me because of my time spent with Kathy. The rest of my clients, well, that was another story, but on this night, I wanted to focus on the good things.

Just then, Larry walked in with a good-looking young blonde girl in tow.

"My man, JD!" Larry said. He always seemed to be excited to see me even if I just saw him at work a couple of hours ago. I waved him over.

"Kathy was one of the greats. I'm gonna miss her," he said as he put his hand on my shoulder.

"You have no idea," I said with a smile. I couldn't help but notice the girl he was with. Larry pulled up a chair for her.

"This is Cindy, the new front desk girl," Larry said.

Cindy held out her hand, and with a big smile and just the slightest wink in her eye, she said, "Nice to finally meet you, JD. Larry told me all about you."

You've got to be fucking kidding me.

9
MOVIN' OUT (JD'S SONG)

Just like those Wall Street titans and lawyers who get burned-out from their careers, I was starting to get tired of the rat race that was personal training. My time at Precision Fitness had been an epic three-year journey with many highs and a few lows. There was once a time when I didn't think I was going to make it, but somehow I succeeded beyond even my own expectations. I was finally making the kind of money I always envisioned, but with all the money and perks that came along with training, there were some aspects of the job I didn't care for. In addition to the endless skirt chasing that, albeit was more fun than I ever dreamed, had my stress levels at all-time highs, the job itself began to wear on me.

Precision Fitness was constantly trying to up their revenue. No matter how much money I made for the gym, it was never good enough. I had started at thirty-five hours a week. A year later, I was working close to fifty hours a week, all filled with training sessions. In fact, I was booked up for nearly three months in advance. I had no time for new clients unless I added more hours to my workweek.

Fifty hours may not sound like a ton of hours, but I was in college while working as a trainer. Even though I was only taking a few classes each semester, it was getting difficult to balance school and work, and I wanted to continue school until I got a degree of some sort. Always trying to squeeze every last bit from me, my manager would tell me how bad all these people wanted to train with me and would give me a guilt trip if I declined.

Next thing I knew, my Saturdays were filled with training sessions from seven o'clock in the morning until five o'clock in the evening. This is hard for a guy in his twenties who likes to go out from time to time on Friday nights. I can't tell you how many times I strolled in on a Saturday morning with my head pounding and my breath reeking of Long Island iced teas. Luckily, my clients were all pretty cool and somehow, someway, I never got sick. I even had KFC for lunch one day and managed to keep it down despite having at least a dozen or so drinks and several shots of Jägermeister the night before. It was pretty easy back then to get something accomplished while hungover from the previous night. Then again, it's nice to be able to eat a buffet of chicken and biscuits and still be able to maintain a six-pack in the process. Being twenty-two fuckin' ruled. Nowadays, just driving by a KFC is enough to give me a bad case of the shits for three to four days. Not only that, but going to sleep past eleven o'clock at night is usually enough to shatter the next day's tasks.

I had come a long way from my first days on the job when I was reminded regularly in those weekly training meetings how much I sucked. Although I was now getting high praises from management, I couldn't help but notice how they always upped the ante week after week. What was originally an attainable monthly goal of a few thousand dollars in training crept up to nearly twice that amount in less than a few months. I was now stressing the fuck out about reaching this goal, which was more and more difficult to reach, since all my clients paid in advance and the ratio of client hours needed to hours I had available was mathematically impossible to reach. It got so bad that management wanted me to ask my clients if they could renew their training package even if they had ten sessions left. This not only annoyed me but also pissed off several of my clients. In fact, I lost a few clients thanks to those assholes. What the fuck kind of business guy drives away a sure thing that probably would have become a lifetime client if only he hadn't pushed shit the client didn't want? I don't hold an MBA, but something tells me this is the type of shit they teach you not to do.

Combine this with the several women who wanted a little more than I could give them. I was one man with one dong and more than a handful of women to please. It was no easy task, even for an American gigolo. Turns out, some of these women were looking for a little more than just a roll in the sheets, and being the nice guy I was, I found that I was extending myself more than I cared to. No, I never agreed to pick up a client's kid from school or anything crazy like that. But I was spending more and more of the limited free time I had going here or there with these clients in addition to spending time rolling around in the sheets. I was stressed out not only from the pressure of making the sale when it was increasingly difficult to make one but also from these constant requests from my clients who wanted more and more personal attention. Although I was making great money with only a handful of college classes under my belt, I was beginning to realize I could not do this for the rest of my life. If I had played my cards a little differently, who knows, maybe I wouldn't have felt that way.

At my apartment one day, I brainstormed and came up with a plan. I had recently visited my friend Craig out in California. It was unlike anywhere I had ever been in my life, and it was awesome. I thought about packing up whatever I had and heading west. I didn't really have anything holding me back. Sure, I had a well-paying job and a girlfriend, but I didn't doubt I could replace those two things out in California. I was still young with minimal responsibilities, so why not give it a shot? Even though none of the possible nightmarish scenarios had come true, I was getting more and more stressed out about the possibility that I was going to get caught. How many more times was I going to dodge bullets when it came to my girlfriend or these sure-to-be-pissed-off husbands around town? All these factors were adding up as I began to think about my future.

Where would I be in five years if I stayed with Precision Fitness? Would I move up the ladder, as they say? Would the bullshit meter run into the red if I made it up to a management position? I also couldn't ignore the possibility that this job would run its course, just like my luck with fucking around might run out at some point. Like the great Philadelphia Phillies Mike Schmidt, I had a chance to go out on top. I could just pack up and go and be done with it all. And that's exactly what I decided to do.

The gym didn't take the news so lightly. They didn't have a replacement for me—that is, a younger guy who appealed to women in their late twenties to mid-forties and who could not only sell them training but also keep them coming back for more. My manager was visibly distraught when I walked into his office and broke the news. It wasn't as if I was leaving tomorrow. I gave him a month's notice so that I could arrange for my move out of state. Like most shady business owners, he asked that I not tell my clients and keep running business as usual. When it came time to renew their training sessions, he advised me to tell them to renew as if I was going to be around for the next several months. Pretty fucked up, considering I was sleeping with some of these clients. It's not that it would change things, but it would be hard not to tell them I was moving, since they had the tendency to get what they wanted out of me.

I reluctantly did not tell the truth to some clients, but I did tell others, and I even told them I wasn't supposed to tell them. Most were appreciative, and others were somewhat pissed—not at me, but at the management for lying to them to get them to drop more money into something they maybe didn't want anymore.

It's hard to say what the relationship between a trainer and a client can morph into. It's different from that of your hairdresser, accountant, or anyone else whom you may pay to be in your life to some degree. Sure, you can fuck any one of those individuals, but it is very seldom that any of those individuals get as up close and personal with you as your trusted personal trainer. Personal trainers spend intimate time with their clients, leading to some pretty strong bonds. You can become close friends and, in my case on more than one occasion, a little more than that. I've been to some clients' family holidays, weddings, bat mitzvahs, you name it. It's difficult to replace that bond with someone else, no matter how good that other trainer may be. Sure, you can throw in a younger version, maybe even someone with a better personality, but the feelings and trust that developed with someone over one or more years will take time to develop. After I moved, I kept in touch with some former clients and discovered that they continued training with someone else but some never lasted long, as they were unable to make that connection with their new trainer.

As I made my announcement to my roster of clients, some were happy for me while others were visibly upset. I tried to reassure them that they would do fine with another trainer and explained that I was missing something and needed a change. For many clients whom I had slept with, it was as if the fantasyland type of existence that I had helped make a reality for them was about to come to an abrupt end. Even though I had a girlfriend and many of these women had husbands, I became more than a guy on the side. I felt like I had several girlfriends at once. They all had feelings for me, and, I have to admit, I had some for them, too. As fucked up as it may sound, I had a soft spot for every one of those women I was sleeping with. What was wrong with me? I knew this was completely wrong, and the big guy upstairs was probably looking down at me and shaking his head. I treated all of them with respect, if you consider banging a woman behind her husband's back in any way respectful. All I knew was that I had to get the hell out of there. I couldn't face another day seeing missed calls on my cell phone while I was out with my girlfriend or having to choose between which women to go out with during the week. I know most guys would be clamoring for this type of attention, but as River Phoenix taught all of us, sometimes no matter how good it seems on the outside, it's pretty fucked up on the inside. And I wasn't about to let that happen to me.

So I packed my bags and said my good-byes, which turned out to be a lot of them. For many of my clients, it would be the last time I would ever see them. Sure, I talked to some of them from time to time, but most of us would never cross paths again. A huge weight was lifted off my shoulders when I left. I no longer felt obligated to run around town trying to satisfy my clients, feeling guilty every step of the way. Most people would scratch their heads and wonder why someone would give up regular sex with half a dozen women or so, but I was over it. I was going to be free of my self-imposed bullshit and could start moving forward with my life.

Did my girlfriend ever find out about the shenanigans I was up to? Did she ever discover that I had gotten a blow job in the office at work or that I went down on someone else the night before she slept over? To this day, I'll never know. Danielle didn't take my moving away too well. I felt like an even bigger asshole seeing how much she cared about me. I should have come clean and told her about what had transpired over the past couple of years, but I was too much of a pussy. Ladies, here's some advice: expect shady behavior from every guy younger than thirty, no matter how "mature" they claim to be. Even worse, Danielle and I didn't even break up when I left. We just kept some sort of long-distance relationship going for a while, which was a terrible idea from the start. Needless to say, it didn't work out and we fell out of touch. I try not to make a habit of keeping in contact with people I have dated. I've always wondered about people who do keep in touch with those they have bedded in the past. Is it just me, or does that invite trouble into your life at any moment? If you managed to have sex with someone in the past, what is going to keep you from going down that road again? Isn't it easier the second or third time or however many times you've done it before? Unless you totally blew it the first go-round and lasted less than thirty seconds, you can probably recreate history with little or no work.

So off I went, like the prospectors of the 1800s heading west to claim their share of fortune and fame. I was hoping this move would give me the change I needed in my life. Personal training allowed me to live a great lifestyle and make good money without a college degree, but I was determined to give up personal training in my new city. How the fuck was I to know that nothing would come close to paying me what I was making as a personal trainer? I did what any young guy would do who didn't have that silver spoon. I did what I needed to do to make ends meet.

I got a job bartending, which turned out to be more inconsistent than personal training and, not to mention, a shady environment like no other. Combine the late-night hours with tips that varied from less than a hundred to several hundred dollars a night, it didn't feel like a step forward. I also tried to be one of those people who sit on their asses for hours on end doing nothing but answering phones, which turned out feeling like I was in a prison. I surprised myself in that I was able to do it for two weeks. I even came close to signing up for easy money by starring in a "tickling" video. I won't even bother explaining what kind of fucked-up shit happens in this type of video. Let's just say I did the right thing and said no.

I had found something in personal training that I loved, but I got fed up with certain aspects of the job. Come on, who the fuck really loves what they do day in and day out, year after year? Maybe there is no such thing as enjoying what you do every day. Maybe that's why they call it work. Maybe if I went back to school and finished my degree like everyone in my family seemed to be advising me to do (even if none of them had ever set foot on a college campus), I could land that dream job. After all, the secret to being successful is getting your degree, right? The bottom line for those kids out there is to go to school for something. Learn some type of skill because life is hard enough, and it's even harder when you have no skills. Sure, learning about dead poets may sound interesting, but good luck trying to make money if that's what you decided to major in.

I justified returning to the game simply because I was able to find a job at a personal training "studio," unlike the large gym facility I worked at previously. It was a smaller, more intimate setting. Body Masters Fitness Studio was more like a lounge. It had a loft and oversized couches in the lobby along with a coffee bar next to the front desk. Local artists would hang their pictures in the lobby and sell them for hundreds of dollars a piece. They even had some dude play an acoustic guitar at the front a couple of nights a week while people worked out. Strange, to say the least.

The pressure of sales was also nonexistent. I looked forward to not having some sales manager on my ass about how much I sold the prior month and how much I was down this month. I worked out a deal where I was only responsible for a small share of the rent each month; my portion was easily covered with just a few clients, and everything else was in my pocket. This was the setting I was looking for. I could work as much or as little as I wanted to. I had keys to the place and had access 24/7, so there was no way I could not find the time to train clients. When I started, I had every intention of playing the game without straying off the path as I'd done before. It was easy at first. I made some good friends along the way who worked at this gym. Similar to myself, the other trainers were about making money and enjoying life.

I knew from my old manager Larry that finding a gym in the nice part of town was key to having success as a personal trainer. Living with Craig helped. He was involved in real estate and had a place near the coast in Southern California. He once said that if a Whole Foods is nearby, then you know you are living in the nice part of town. Not only was there a Whole Foods next to the gym, but also there were exotic car dealerships and no sign of pawnshops or check-cashing centers for miles.

Jason, my new manager, asked very little of us. On occasion, we would be required to give fitness assessments at a local shopping center or college. My friend Pete and I would usually agree to work these events. Sometimes they were on Saturday mornings, which would prove to be difficult with a hangover. Pete and I had quite a few similarities, including the occasional bowl we would fire up in the back of the gym at closing time. And who could forget the remaining cans of beer from the Christmas party that we shotgunned one afternoon before our shift?

One of the more memorable fitness assessments occurred one Saturday morning after a long night at an Irish bar drinking Irish car bombs like they were going out of style. Pete slowly strolled up to the table wearing dark-tinted aviator sunglasses. He didn't say a word as he managed to find the chair and plop down next to me. I had already set up about an hour later than planned in front of the Whole Foods and felt just as terrible, so I could tell it wasn't going to be a productive day. We both agreed that we were too fucked up to attract new clients in our current state of mind. We packed up the table and drove to a nearby client of Pete's who had some of the best weed around. There's nothing better for a hangover than a bowl of Acapulco gold. I could not help but notice how the weed out west seemed to be much more potent.

Things were going well at first, albeit a little slow compared to what I was used to. With no sales manager drumming up business, there weren't a ton of potential clients to be served up on a silver platter. If I was going to make it here, I was going to have to do it on my own. It was as if I was used to the hustle and bustle of city life and had moved to the rural Midwest where things just happen whenever they happen. After a few months of not being very busy, I was starting to get a little nervous, as funds were not as plentiful as they had been at my previous job. Unlike Precision Fitness where this type of shit would not be tolerated, my new employer took a much laid-back approach to the whole situation. Seeing how I was new to the town and didn't know many people, getting referrals was difficult to say the least. I was never the type of jerk-off to annoy the piss out of people whom I'd just met with the "here's what I do" speech and "here's my card" line. I always relied on my work to do the talking for me, but training only a handful of people regularly made it a little difficult.

My breakthrough came unexpectedly. I was lounging in the lobby of the gym on one of our lovely contemporary couches when the phone rang. Robin, the girl at the front desk, answered it. Robin was your stereotypical California girl, with long blonde hair and very attractive features. She looked like a model in my opinion, but I guess out in California, where girls like her were a dime a dozen, she was just a receptionist at a gym. You are correct in assuming I probably wanted to fuck her, but for some reason or another, that never happened. Maybe this move really was the change I needed to grow up.

After a few minutes, Robin hung up and asked me if I was going to be around for the next half hour. I told her I had all the time in the world. She said the caller was a guy who was very interested in training and was going to be by the gym soon to check it out.

"Can you show him around?" she asked.

"Sure. Why not?" I said, not knowing if she could sense my lack of enthusiasm. The last time I showed someone around the gym resulted in me listening to a religious guy tell me a biblical story about some guy with an ax picking away at something or another. I listened to this story for the better part of an hour just to have the guy walk out without buying anything. Hopefully, this would be a better outcome.

A half hour later, the gentleman showed up in a BMW, which is always a good sign. I politely introduced myself. Sean was in his late thirties, worked in a hospital, and didn't look like he really needed personal training, but I wasn't in any spot to turn someone away. After all, I was taught early on that everyone could use some personal training. After just a half hour of talking, Sean threw down his Visa card and signed up for training three times a week. About a week later, Chris, another thirty-something-year-old, who also didn't look like he really needed personal training, walked through the door and signed up for training with me without even meeting me. Turns out, Chris was a friend of Sean's and ended up referring me a few more people, so the snowball began to grow. I had moved out from my comfortable habitat into a whole new world, but I was sure this time I was movin' on up. I was back in action, and before long, my swagger was back as well.

10
TRAINING GAY DUDES

I don't know what it was about me, but at one point in my career, half of my clientele consisted of gay men. Even though frosted tips were all the rage, I kept it simple and styled my hair with a few ounces of mousse and gel. Maybe it was my George Michael scruff look at the time that had these highly successful, sharply dressed gentlemen sent my way. How was I to know that, in addition to meeting more than enough willing and able women as a trainer, I would also become a local gay icon? I did not aggressively seek out this type of client, but I wasn't about to complain when they showed up with credit card in hand and price was never an issue. What started as one snowballed, and in very little time, I was training more gay guys than you would find at an Erasure concert. This was a sweet relief for a guy like me, since this would cut the possibility of sleeping with my clients by about 50 percent, since I never felt the urge to experiment with the same sex.

A few guys I went to high school with played for the other team, but other than that, I didn't have a whole lot of interaction with gay men prior to training them. Even though I grew up in one of the more progressive parts of the country, my only knowledge of gay guys was from watching the original *Police Academy* movie. With the infamous Blue Oyster Bar ingrained in my mind, I expected all gay men to dress like the Village People and have high-pitched voices or lisps. Luckily, I was brought up in a very accepting household and wasn't influenced by people in school who were outward in their intolerance of anyone who had a different sexual orientation.

Some of the other trainers I worked with didn't like training gay clients, but I could care less about what my clients' orientations were as long as I was getting paid. And believe me, these guys had money to burn. As a straight male who was on a recent tear with his female clientele, I was more than comfortable in my sexuality, and training this demographic was no problem for me. In fact, I welcomed them into the lineup, as they were always prompt and usually paid in full, on time. I also knew I wouldn't get mixed up in all the shenanigans I was getting myself into with my female clientele.

Aaron was a good-looking guy in his early forties. I know that line makes me sound gay, but I call them like I see them. He was a cool older guy who seemed to be doing well in his job and had a good sense of humor. He was my first gay client, but I didn't know it off the bat. It wasn't until he came out and told me. Well, he didn't just come out and tell me he was gay. He told me that after football practice in high school, he used to suck his teammates' dicks! This came as a shocker to me, as I was just starting out in my training career and it was the mid-nineties when most gays were still stuffed in the closet. It wasn't until several weeks into our training that Aaron dropped this bomb. He jokingly said that I shouldn't knock it until I tried it. I was dumfounded at his remark and didn't really know how to react. I did know that even though I wasn't about to ask my buddy who I played high school football with to give me a blow job that night, I wasn't going to think any differently of Aaron. As far as I was concerned, he was a paying customer and I was getting paid well, so as long as he wasn't pushing for me to blow him, I didn't give a shit what Aaron talked about during our hour. I quickly developed this mentality that I was open to whatever my clients were talking about, whether or not I agreed or disagreed. This was my first experience training a gay guy and would prepare me for the onslaught of gay clients I would train over the years.

One of the many stigmas of the day was that gay guys would try to turn a straight guy the other way, similar to those Jehovah's Witnesses who show up at your doorstep and try to convert you. I'm not sure of the exact termed used for turning a supposedly straight guy into a gay guy, but something tells me if it's in you, it will come out at some point no matter how hard you try to suppress it. Despite this, I had no problems with my gay crew and never once felt pressured into sucking a dick. In fact, I got more than I bargained for with my time spent training gay men.

For example, I learned which moisturizers were the least oil-based and best for my complexion and which shirt went well with a pair of pants. Did you know that your ring finger should be used when applying moisturizer around the eye? This is because the tissue around the eye is very delicate and the ring finger is the weakest of all your fingers, reducing the risk of damaging the skin around the eye. I am now filled with all kinds of self-care tips that I never would have been aware of had I not trained gay guys. These guys took me to the next level when it came to making me more attractive to the opposite sex. I also learned to appreciate their lives, as these men were, for the most part, stress-free and seemed to have larger paychecks than their straight counterparts. How they did it I have no idea. Many of them did not have kids, so maybe that was the secret. To answer your question, no, I didn't dabble, even if I was told on more than one occasion I would make quite the twink.

I know some people have a stereotype in their head when they think of gay guys, just as I did growing up. They think of a guy with a heavy lisp, complete with makeup and dressed in outrageous clothing. But the gay men I trained sometimes had more manly characteristics than some of the straight guys I knew. Steve was easily six foot four and weighed about 250 pounds. He looked more like an NFL linebacker than he did a guy who spent his evenings watching Bravo TV. This guy could easily kick my ass if he wanted to, but he was as gentle as gentle could be. Steve was also into manly endeavors, such as renovating homes. I'm not talking about decorating ideas and designs on paper. Steve actually did tile work and installed plumbing himself. I would scratch my head thinking about how a guy that big and into as many guy things as he was into could look at woman's vagine in disgust. Well, more for me is the way I would look at it, as this guy could probably get more women than most straight guys if he wanted.

Some gay clients, like Adam, were a little more feminine than others. Adam was your typical skinny guy who didn't have a high voice but had that concerned tone about him. He could always add a little drama to even the most mundane incident. There wasn't a session that went by where Adam didn't throw in a very excited "Oh my god!" when telling me a story or listening to one. Adam was the first of my gay clients to possess better-than-average taste when it came to clothing and decorating. He had a keen sense of style and shared with me how to improve my somewhat dated look. Considering my idea of matching clothes consisted of buying the clothing that was already on the mannequin at any clothing store in the mall, Adam assisted me in learning the basics, such as never wearing a brown belt with black shoes.

I had no goddamned clue about fashion prior to working with gay clients. I was mostly a T-shirt and jeans type of guy whose idea of mixing it up was shorts in the summer. I owned maybe a couple of pairs of jeans and pants. I thought khakis were the best option for any occasion. How these guys knew what they knew was beyond me. A lot of them said they read *Men's Fitness*, as I did. Maybe they paid attention to the clothing ads, which I usually flipped right through. Maybe they actually spent more than five minutes in those horrible stores in the mall called something and Fitch. I learned about clothes—how to wear things that matched and what not to wear—and what to do with my hair. For the longest time, I had a gay client cut my hair, and I can say that I never got more compliments after a haircut than any other time in my life. My gay clients were solely responsible for turning me from a guy with a Joe Dirt haircut and bad clothing into a walking *GQ* advertisement. Even though I was somehow still able to pull in women with my early eighties fashion sense, my gay clients put me over the edge, and it was noticeable every time I stepped out in public. In fact, I felt better about myself when I was styled by a gay guy rather than when a girl would do it. It's no wonder why so many people in Hollywood have at least one gay stylist by their side.

No matter how different their looks, styles, or personalities, my gay clients all had one thing in common: they were very determined to get what they wanted. If that meant losing twenty pounds and getting their body fat to less than 10 percent, they would do whatever it took to get there. I'm not trying to compare gay people to straight people, but laziness is something that I rarely saw in any of the gay men I trained and others I've met over the years. They seem to work feverishly as if they have a chip on their shoulder. I can't tell you how many straight guys or girls I have trained who just didn't put forth half the effort my gay clients would muster up. Some of them had such a driven work ethic, I found myself questioning my own at times. It wasn't common for some of my gay clients to not only work long hours but also volunteer and serve on some type of board that required their time. Mark my words, they would never even think about canceling an appointment.

No matter how bad the hangover or how tired they were from work, you could count on them being on time every time. God, I miss training my gay clients.

It was somewhat foreign to hear some of the stories that came out of my gay clients' mouths at times. Sure, I was used to hearing stories of hookups and crazy times from my straight clients, but I often felt like those stories paled in comparison to their weekly romps of debauchery and good times. A typical Wednesday evening for these guys would often turn into a gay version of *Animal House*. Not to say all gay guys are into some crazy partying, but some of the younger groups of guys I trained were living the lives of rock stars or college kids except after their college years. Maybe it was just the gay men I trained, or maybe it was the area I was living in at the time, which had become a haven for young gay men. To sum it up best, one client once told me, "It's a great day to be gay." I'm not gonna lie—there were times I found myself agreeing with that thought. Considering the times I spent with my female clientele ended up disastrous 99.9 percent of the time, these guys not only knew one another, but they also usually blew one another at some point in time and remained great friends afterward. Wow, how does this end up happening? My ex-girlfriends to this day probably look back on our time spent together and use some not-so-pleasant adjectives to describe me. Getting together for coffee is the last thing on all their minds.

Another thing that always amazed me about my gay clients was their never-ending search for bodily perfection. Some of my gay clients were built better than a lot of straight guys, and women were all over them whenever they went out. Oddly enough, you would think the proclamation of "I'm gay" would be enough to deter these women, but not always. You would be just as shocked as I was when I found out that some women will stop at nothing just to sleep with a great-looking gay man. Some girls truly are fucking nuts. It's even more shocking to hear a gay guy tell you about how he slept with a woman "just because" or "just to shut her up." I can't think of a single point in my life where I threw a woman a shot just to silence her. I know this is not the norm, but I have heard firsthand the story of the fag hag who wouldn't quit until she got what she wanted. So not only were some of them built better and better looking than many straight guys, but they also occasionally slept with a beautiful girl "just because"? What the fuck? This doesn't bode too well for that three-hundred-pounder sitting on his sofa with a mug full of Pabst Blue Ribbon and watching NASCAR. Think about it. How many overweight, out-of-shape gay guys do you know? I know all about those big, burly "bears" who you see out on occasion hunting for that young cub, but something tells me they are a small percentage of the gay community.

Another little detail I've noticed with gay men is that they are similar to rich women in their tendency toward cosmetic surgery and their everlasting quest to maintain their youthful appearance. Like I mentioned before, these guys seemed to have money to burn—on themselves, that is. I admit to having spent thousands of dollars over the years, most likely frivolously, on supplements, lotions, and other questionable items that may or may not have improved my appearance, but I draw the line at cosmetic procedures that cost several thousands of dollars. Microdermabrasion, bleaching, and laser hair removal are just some of the procedures I've witnessed my clients undergo, and no, I was not aware of these procedures until I was enlightened by a gay guy. In addition to the hundreds of dollars they would spend on training, they spent even more on these pricey procedures and who knows what else to preserve themselves as much as possible. But, hey, if they had enough to pay me and would give me some tips from time to time on bringing up my own game, I was all for it.

One of the best perks about training gay men was their surplus of beautiful women. I can't tell you how many unbelievably good-looking girls I met through my relationships with gay guys. If there is one thing I learned, it was the ability to talk to women and do all those things that most straight guys can't stand, such as sit through an episode of *Sex and the City* or the latest romantic comedy. This information proved invaluable, as I became the ultimate professional on how to stay awake during whatever Richard Gere–Julia Roberts movie was out at the time. I found that if I was hanging out with gay guys as opposed to a group of straight guys, I was usually talking to a lot more women by the end of the night. It would never fail. I could go out to a club with several straight friends, drink until I ran out of money, and then find myself going home alone, giving myself a hand job, and waking up with a terrible hangover. It was as if collectively we exuded a female repellant that kept girls more than ten feet from us the entire night. But if I went out with a group of gay guys, I would meet a bevy of girls, manage to charm one of the usual handful that was around, and end up waking up next to her the following morning. How many times have you been out with the fellas and found yourself sitting around mowing down a greasy pizza or, God forbid, sitting down at IHOP at three o'clock in the morning eating omelets that will most definitely give you the shits and talking about girls as opposed to being with them? More importantly, why do guys eat the shittiest food in the wee hours of the morning? I always wondered if women hit up the drive-thru after a long night of boozing. Well, I have found that when I'm out with a girl, we are usually in bed burning calories in those hours instead of consuming them. I'm not saying it's a guarantee you're going to hook up with a girl if you're out with a bunch of gay guys, but I'm here to tell you the odds are definitely in your favor. I can speak from personal experience. The number of times I hooked up with girls by hanging out with gay guys far outnumbers the times it's happened after going out with the fellas.

Like women, some gay guys are extremely sensitive. Anything you say may set them off, and watch out if that happens because that can be the end of you as their trainer. The gay community in many areas is very close-knit. Cross one, and it will cost you in many ways. One bad review from a gay client, and there goes your in to the gay clientele. For example, I once had it out with one of my gay clients. I remember it being about money. Of course, it's always about the money. I could have gone about it in a more tactful manner, but I was young and not too bright when it came to handling money. I not only lost that client, but the next thing I knew, I was also down five more. What would have amounted to a temporary loss of a few hundred dollars ended up being well over several thousands of dollars that I could have made from potential referrals down the road. They can make you or break you. Any prospective trainers out there should shed any fear or uneasiness about training gay clients. I don't care if you're an up-and-coming young trainer with model looks; your business is not going to be the best it can be without the help of gay clients. In retrospect, had I just exclusively trained gay guys, I could have saved myself some close calls or, as I like to say, near misses.

Gay men are often well connected in the area in which they live. They know everyone who happens to be important in town and can help you immensely in succeeding no matter what business you are in. How they are still shunned by people in some parts of the country amazes me. If you get in good with some gay guys, you are most often in with the sophisticated types, and there always seems to be an abundance of good times and soirees that put your average house party to shame. Many referrals of well-to-do people came from my gay clients. If you're not the best networker, as I most certainly was not, you will find it useful to befriend your gay clients, as they tend to be great at rubbing elbows with all the right people. It's those right people who will make your schedule fill up more so than an entire roster of college coeds and hot women, although the thought is nice.

I let my relationships with my gay clients extend outside the gym as well, but it wasn't in the typical fashion I would partake in with my female clients. Gay friendly, yes, but not gay for pay. I'm not saying I haven't spent a weekend or two living it up at the Parliament House listening to Donna Summer and sipping on an umbrella drink. But I was a college student at the time, and I was all about making money. In fact, I would sometimes work as a bartender at private parties on weekends thanks to some connections I made through my gay clients. I know what you may be thinking, but no, I wasn't topless with a bow tie and tight leather pants. It was an easy way to make a ton of money and get more clients. I didn't have to do much work, just talk with some guys and, more often than not, very hot single women. I had no problem mixing some drinks for gay guys for unbelievable money and meeting women in the process. Over the course of a few years, I had more clients than I knew what to do with, not to mention a Rolodex full of girls, all courtesy of my gay crew.

To the best of my knowledge, I have trained a few lesbians too but not half as many as I have gay men. Maybe they are a little less outgoing about their sexuality than gay guys. It's rare to see a flaming gay woman running around like a female Richard Simmons. I did train this young, cute college girl at one point who I think was a little confused about her sexuality. Her name was Christine, and I had been training her for her first two years of college. At the time, I was only a few years older than she was, so I related to her pretty well. We would talk about all kinds of stuff, and at one point the topic of relationships came up. I knew she was in a sorority and had been with guys in the past. But then she started talking about this girl "Billie" she worked with. I know it's not good to judge someone's sexual orientation based on a name, but Billie? Come on, that has "I dabble" written all over it. If her haircut looks anything like the lead character in *The Legend of Billie Jean*, I would forever hold on to that stereotype. To make a long story short, I was lucky enough to hear some stories of their sleepovers. I couldn't believe what I was hearing; I thought two hot college girls going at it only existed in the world of Internet porn. Much to my chagrin, I never had the cojones to somehow find myself in the middle of that situation, which I had fantasized about ever since picking up my first *Hustler*. How could I find myself in between these two young coeds? It's a fantasy that eludes me to this day, and I can't help but think about how awesome it would be. Could I have pushed Christine just a little bit when I had the chance, seeing how other clients seemed to be convinced fairly easily into doing anything I asked for? Could have, would have, and should have, but again, for some reason I found myself having difficulty coming up with the balls to even ask if this was a possibility. That possible scenario will always haunt me when I'm perusing the latest threesome scene on my go-to porn hub site.

So did I enjoy working with my fair share of gay people? You bet. In fact, I think that the fitness industry has a significant number of gay workers, and I noticed the numbers expand exponentially over the course of my career as a trainer. Some of my former coworkers made no qualms about their gayness. They flaunted it, in fact. You think old school bicycle shorts are taboo on men? Not in some gyms where I worked. I was one of the few out there wearing low-cut basketball shorts. Was I ashamed of the outline of my nether regions in a pair of bicycle shorts? Well, let's just say I'm a grower not a shower. I couldn't imagine running around all day with my package bulging out, covered by a thin layer of spandex. I was still at a point in my life where random boners would surprise me in the middle of the afternoon for no apparent reason.

If I could turn back time, I would have traded many female clients for gay clients, as I could have avoided some of the shit that I stepped in along the way. Some of my best clients were gay guys, and I am happy to say I never got into shady situations that would haunt me to this day. To those youngsters out there, go ahead and tap into the gay market. Take a ride on the wild side, and I can promise you won't regret the decision.

11
OLD MAN RIVER

After training for nearly five years, I thought I had experienced everything there was to experience as a personal trainer, as I had trained all types of people: big and small, young and old, gay and straight. But nothing would prepare me for an unusual opportunity to make a few extra bucks outside the gym. I had heard about personal trainers traveling to clients' homes to train them, but I had only trained people within the friendly confines of the gym. Considering my track record, I always declined any opportunity to train clients at their homes for fear of getting into even more shady affairs. How convenient would it be to bypass the whole gym environment and have the bed just steps away when the appropriate time presented itself? If I started training clients in their homes, I knew I wouldn't get much accomplished other than saving a lot of ladies gas money.

Pete, my new partner in crime, primarily trained clients in the gym, but he also had a handful of clients whom he trained at home, and he always talked to me about the extra cash he made doing it. Pete wasn't the most ambitious of trainers. He'd rather be playing video games in the middle of the afternoon than training someone who lived less than twenty minutes from his house for a hundred bucks. Pete truly had the West Coast persona down to a tee. He was laid back and operated at a level that I wished I could. If Pete knew the waves were going off, you could count on him canceling his sessions that day. He was also known to cancel on his clients after a rough night of drinking or especially on opening day of the baseball season.

Pete would share tales of his home-training clients. He told me that, on some days, he would drink a cup of coffee with one of his clients while watching *The Price Is Right* instead of training. Other times, he would end up at a taco stand with his client for the hour sipping on a bucket of Coronas and sharing a chicken quesadilla, all the while getting paid, of course. But one story stood out more than others. Pete said Father John was an elderly gentleman in his early eighties with a ton of cash based on the size of his lakefront Mediterranean-style home. He was a retired priest and happened to have a housemate. Father John did not have just any housemate. Pete said this housemate was a gay guy in his early forties who obviously took care of the décor in the house. I wondered how a retired priest could afford to live in a multi-million-dollar home in the most upscale part of town. I always questioned where those dollars went when that basket was getting passed around at mass. Combine this with the gay housemate, no wonder I question religion as a whole.

One day, Pete called me and asked if I could go to Father John's house for the next week or so and train him because he wasn't able to for some reason. I later found out he just didn't want to miss that day's episode of SportsCenter, which was highlighting the upcoming baseball season. It also happened to be the opening week of the season. This was somewhat understandable to me, as there weren't ten channels of ESPN at the time and TiVo wasn't around yet. Pete liked having multiple TVs on so that he could attempt to watch more than one game at a time—he was that guy. Pete reminded me about the old man's unique living situation. Regardless of how strange Pete made the scene out to be, I was looking forward to getting some extra cash and told Pete I would go to Father John's house to train him. I assured him I didn't have any problems with the whole setup. Besides, this guy was in his eighties. How creepy could it really be? I didn't think I was going to end up putting the lotion in the basket or anything crazy like that.

So I threw on my usual gym attire and made my way into the even nicer part of town, which was hard to imagine, since I was living in a nice part of town. I had a small break in my class schedule that gave me some flexibility to make this whole thing happen. As I drove my trusted steed down the street, I passed intricate gates covered with vines and cars that looked like they just came off the showroom floor. Pete had told me about Father John's house, but my jaw dropped when I pulled up to the huge, two-story home that seemed to stretch far and wide into the large plot of land where it sat. I had only seen houses like this on TV. The landscaping was so perfect and the long driveway of light-brown pavers so clean that I didn't want to park my shitty Jeep on it. The towering Washingtonia filifera that lined the driveway were perfectly spaced out just a few feet from one another and gave the whole place a Mediterranean vibe. How could only two guys live in a place this big? I grew up in a family of five, and our house was probably the size of this guy's three-car garage.

I walked up to the large mahogany front door and rang the doorbell. The door was bordered with mosaic-like glass that resembled a kaleidoscope. It was nearly impossible to see through the differently shaded pieces of glass. I waited for a couple of minutes before ringing the doorbell again. About five minutes later, I finally saw a figure making its way toward the door. It seemed to move ever so slowly, and I wasn't sure if it was a man or animal. I was always a little freaked out by puppets, and this object moving slowly toward the door kind of looked like one. It was difficult to make out a face through the glass. Part of me wanted to say the hell with it and bail out. This shit was taking forever, and I have to admit, I was getting a little nervous.

Then I heard the door click, followed by the rhythmic unlocking of what sounded like five different locks. The door slowly opened, and an old gentleman, bent over and using a walking cane, greeted me. I quickly introduced myself and went through my whole spiel of what he could expect from today's session before I even set foot in the house. "We're going to get you outside and do a little walking and try some stretching," I said.

The old man politely nodded while holding his cane with both hands.

"We might also get you doing some exercises with the Thera-Band, but I'm not sure there will be enough time today," I said.

The old man stood there, seeming to study me as I spoke, and then said, "Uh-oh, sounds like I'm going to need a nap after all that." He then introduced himself in a soft, old-timer voice. "My name is John, but some people call me Father John. You may call me whichever you wish."

Whoa, I hadn't been to church in quite awhile. I really hoped this wasn't going to turn into a Bible-preaching session, seeing how I was guilty of about half of those items on the "thou shall not" list.

Father John slowly turned and motioned with his hand for me to follow him inside. For a moment, I felt like a young Luke Skywalker in the Dagobah system following Yoda into his home. I was surprised to see that Father John had an easy time maneuvering himself around this huge house with high ceilings and a wide-open floor plan. I couldn't help but notice the expensive-looking art on the walls and the very modern kitchen that appeared to have every upgrade imaginable. The kitchen, complete with stainless steel appliances and granite countertops, was so big and immaculate. It looked like one of those kitchens you see in magazines. How the fuck do these rich people keep their kitchens so clean? They probably have no idea how to cook and never use their kitchens.

As I followed Father John down a hallway, I tried to conceal my awe. This was the nicest home I had ever set foot in. I also noticed that the house smelled a little bit like a church. We entered the living room, where an older woman was in the corner dusting something that already looked clean to me. Father John stopped to get her attention.

"Naomi, this is Pete's friend JD. He will be training me today," Father John said.

Naomi looked up from her cleaning duties and smiled. "Ah, you make sure Father John don't give you a hard time now," she said with a thick Jamaican accent. I quickly figured out where Pete got that Jamaican purple we smoked a few days prior.

I didn't know how to respond, so I just nodded in agreement.

"Naomi has been my housekeeper for the past ten years," Father John said. This was all too crazy for my mind to comprehend. I had only seen a housekeeper on my favorite show *Diff'rent Strokes* and never in real life. Did I also mention I once lived near one of Mr. Drummond's residences? It's true, but no, I never did run into Arnold or Willis back in the day.

As we continued through the living room, I assumed we were making our way to some type of gym or recreation room. Considering how expansive this house seemed to be, I thought he surely had a spare room for exercise. After another turn down a smaller hallway, we ended up in what appeared to be a bedroom. I was a little thrown off my game at first because there was no visible workout equipment in the room. A huge king-sized bed was in the middle of the room and a large plasma screen TV was anchored to the wall above an expensive-looking European-style dresser. This was the first plasma TV I had ever seen, since they were just being rolled out in the states at the time. When I found out how much they cost, I almost shit my pants. How the fuck does a retired priest afford a television that costs several thousands of dollars? The room had an old person feel about it with plain drapery and neutral-colored walls, and the only wall decoration other than the TV happened to be a large cross on the wall above the bed. Before you think I showed some geriatric dude my unit for a few bucks, think again. I may have seen and done many things I was not too proud of, but I wasn't desperate. Once in Father John's bedroom, I again reviewed what we were going to be doing as far as training went. I tried to maintain a degree of respectability and professionalism considering the already awkward situation. Aside from my plan of doing a couple of stretches and taking a walk outside in his driveway, which was the size of a small indoor track, there wasn't a whole lot Father John wanted to accomplish.

Nothing I had experienced in my lifetime would prepare me for what came out of his mouth next. As Father John slowly turned to ready himself to sit down on the edge of his bed, he blurted out, "I bet you have a large penis."

At first, I was stunned. I didn't know how to respond. I never once had been accused of this, neither by man nor woman. Had I been one of those right-winged, anti-everything types, I probably would have punched him in the face and walked out of that place, never to return. This guy was not only older than any of my grandparents and on his last leg but also a retired priest, yet he obviously didn't have a care in the world. After all, you can't hit a priest, can you?

I couldn't help but break out into nervous laughter. Pete had mentioned Father John was odd, but it wasn't until now that I began to question if Pete let an old man give him a handy, or worse. Rather than make a big deal about it, I just assured Father John that my penis was of adequate size and I had yet to have any complaints about it. I wasn't about to be a braggart about my junk to some geriatric guy I just met. Thankfully, he wasn't persistent in seeing it to believe it and that was the last question about the size of my manhood—at least that day anyway. It certainly would not be the last of many off-the-wall comments I heard from Father John.

Some of the more colorful commentary I heard from Father John during the first week I trained him included his stance on gay men. While walking him around his driveway one day, I casually asked his opinion on gay men serving in the military, since it was a hot topic of debate at the time.

Without hesitation, Father John responded, "That's wrong and should not be tolerated."

I scratched my head for a minute, seeing how this guy had previously expressed an interest in what I was packing downstairs, and who knows what other not considered straight thoughts went through his mind. I didn't want to probe any further and possibly piss him off, since the money was great, so I avoided further questioning about that topic.

He also seemed to be interested in my sex life and would ask if I had gotten laid the day before seeing him. Really? This wasn't the kind of conversation I was used to having with people Father John's age, but I took a liking to him and began to open up when he asked questions. This seemed to please him in some strange way, and as long as he wasn't asking to see what I looked like in my underwear, I was okay with his offbeat questions.

When I finally ran into Pete at the gym the following week, I asked him why the fuck he didn't prepare me for one of the gayest experiences of my life. His answer was simply that I had trained plenty of gay guys before, so he thought I wouldn't have any problems. Are you serious? You could train the biggest queen in the United States and still have a difficult time figuring out how to deal with a retired religious figure who had a penchant for young men. We then laughed it off, and Pete said he didn't feel like training Father John the following week, so he asked if I wanted to keep training him for a while. Pete also said that Father John called him and said that he liked training with me, so Pete threw me a bone and let me take over. This was indeed a rare occurrence in the world of personal training, since most trainers are not willing to give up a client who pays regularly. Pete hooked me up big with this one. An extra couple hundred dollars in cash a week for just a few hours of work? I would have been insane to turn that down.

My thoughts were all over the place. I was feeling like Michael Douglas in a gay version of *Disclosure*. But in the end, my desire to live a little more comfortably while in school got the best of me. If I could deal with this guy's erratic bantering about shit that you would expect to hear from an old degenerate friend from high school, I could maybe afford a nice dinner out here and there.

Nevertheless, I returned to Father John's sprawling estate the next week. I never knew what to expect at Father John's house. Perhaps a disco ball in the living room or, better yet, one of those pieces of S&M gear lying out on the dining room table, seeing how he was feeling more comfortable with me. Father John would scale back his questioning about my package, but he did dive into my relationships, which I didn't mind talking about. He found some type of joy in hearing about my fucked-up personal life with women. I told him all about my life as a trainer back east. Now that I was a single guy and was finally finding my way around Southern California, I discovered what the late Jim Morrison was talking about when he said, "The West is the best." It seemed difficult to find a woman who wasn't a 9, and I happened to be mingling with a few of them, all of whom I'm proud to say were in no way affiliated with my new gym. Father John would ask me normal questions, such as how I met a particular girl, but then he would quickly change gears and ask how many times she and I had sex the night before or if we had sex before I came to see him. It was as if he wanted to sniff my finger to make sure I wasn't lying about getting my daily dose of sex. I thought about how strange it was to have a guy in his eighties talk to a guy in his twenties about shit that is usually reserved for close friends. After some time, I began to think that my relationship with Father John was probably a good thing, considering I didn't have any remaining relatives near his age whom I kept in contact with. It was somewhat refreshing to hear an old-timer's take on some issues, such as girls, that were of utmost priority to a young guy like me.

The more I visited Father John, the more my curiosity grew about how his odd living arrangement worked. Roger was Father John's "roommate" and half his age. He supposedly had a job but seemed to have most afternoons off, as he was usually there when I got to the house right after Father John's one o'clock teatime. Roger would always be running out the door before I left. He was very polite and concerned about Father John's well-being, but there was no mistaking that lisp of his. It seemed to me that Roger had the ultimate living situation. He could come and go as he pleased, and it appeared that Father John took care of all the living expenses, since he sometimes mentioned to me how bills or taxes were suddenly increasing. There was always a stack of checks on his desk waiting to be mailed out. Roger was out and about most of the time in his late model Mercedes, which I'm sure he didn't pay for. I wouldn't mind a deal like that. Maybe I could ask Father John if he cared for another roommate. Wait, did I just say that? Maintain some pride, JD.

Roger had the entire upstairs to himself. In fact, there was a mysterious gate at the top of the stairs that kept people from going to the second floor. It was similar to those pet gates that keep a dog out of the kitchen, except it was a steel gate with a lock on it. What the hell was up there? I had been in almost every room on the first floor, but I never got a tour of the second floor. I wondered if I would find one of those swings hanging from the rafters or an armoire full of bondage equipment. Each time we walked by the staircase, I glanced up with growing suspicion, similar to how you feel when you walk by a door in some museum that has a "Do Not Enter" sign on it.

One day when Father John excused himself to go to the bathroom, I decided to investigate the upstairs. Father John's bathroom trips were an event in the making. The process took anywhere from nine to thirteen minutes. Each time Father John excused himself to go to the bathroom, I thanked the big guy upstairs because Father John never requested assistance to get into the bathroom—or worse, help getting his pants down. As he slowly proceeded to the bathroom, I excused myself to go to the other bathroom down the hall and instead made a beeline for the staircase. I quickly darted up the stairs, got to the gate, and discovered it was locked. I didn't think this was a problem, however, since I thought I could just climb over the short gate. Unfortunately, I had a pair of party boy breakaway workout pants on and the fabric got caught on the top of the gate, unbuttoning the entire side of my pants right up to my underwear. Fuck! There I was with one leg on the floor and the other up in a semi-split as if I was about to hurdle the gate. I didn't know what to do first—try to button my pant leg up or get my leg off the gate. I hopped around on one leg for a moment trying to keep my balance while pulling my pant leg off the gate. I almost fell to the ground during this whole process but luckily managed to hold myself up and avoid hitting the floor.

"JD, is that you?" I faintly heard Father John call from the bathroom.

Shit! Father John must have heard the ruckus I was making as I tried to free myself from the gate. I don't understand how he could hear anything all the way from the bathroom, since he would always ask me to repeat questions multiple times when I was just a few feet away from him.

"Yes, sir. I'm just finishing up in the bathroom," I lied. Now I am definitely fucked, I thought. I just lied to a priest.

"I thought I heard something upstairs," he said. Why do senior citizens insist on knowing what it is you're doing at all times?

"I dropped my phone in the bathroom," I said. Now I just punched my ticket to hell. Lie number two. I finagled my pant leg off the gate and ever so quietly crept back downstairs and waited in the bedroom for Father John.

Several minutes later, Father John gingerly returned from the bathroom, cane in hand. I stood there feeling somewhat guilty as he made his way back to the chair to continue his exercise.

I regret to say that I never did discover what was on the second floor. Father John seemed to keep close tabs on me after that day. It was as if he had a nanny camera set up in the stairwell and had caught me in the act. For all I knew, the gimp was up there in a box, waiting for his time to shine later on that evening.

Our time together was definitely time well spent. Father John's outlandish remarks provided great fodder for my clients' entertainment. From masturbation to interracial affairs to gays in the military, no topic was untouched. I could always count on his unbiased opinion on all kinds of shit. Unlike many conversations I've shared with people in my family who just asked simple questions like how school was, Father John took more of an interest in my doings outside of the classroom. How often did I get laid? Had I done any drugs? He didn't hold back anything, so I have a great deal of respect for him. As odd as it sounds, he happened to be one of my best clients. Sure, it was very inappropriate at times, but then again, who was I to judge? I was someone who ended up fucking most of my female clients. Did I deserve to have only Fortune 500 CEOs and people with impeccable personalities? If anything, this was something that was a much safer environment for me to be in. There was no possibility for any of the craziness I'd been through before to happen with Father John. I could just do my job for as long as Old Man River hung on. Even though he wasn't in the best of health, he seemed to be a whole lot happier when I stopped by. I don't want to even think about what the hell was going through his head after I left. Thankfully, he never requested I wear a particular piece of clothing when coming to see him. Father John was a lot like my grandfather before he passed. He was witty, very brash, and always told me how it was.

It's been several years since I've been in contact with Father John. I sometimes wonder how he's doing and if he replaced me with a younger trainer. Whatever the case may be, I hope he's enjoying the remainder of his life, sipping on an umbrella drink in the warm sun and waiting for the ten o'clock Chippendale performance.

12
OTHER TRAINERS' CLIENTS

There are several unwritten rules among trainers. Like in any profession, there are things you just don't do to your cohorts. Some of these rules are broken daily but are easily forgiven. Jump on a machine that another trainer is working circuits through, no problem. Chat up another trainer's client before their session, no big deal. I've even seen trainers poach another trainer's client. One might think this would be the worst thing you could do to another trainer, but even that seemed to blow over with time. However, there are some rules that are pretty taboo and could lead to a major shitstorm.

Personal trainers have a special bond with each of their clients. Some are just clients, but some end up feeling like family. Similar to how a psychiatrist spends several hours a week listening to the innermost feelings of his patients, personal trainers get wind of more shit than they care to hear. Sometimes they hear things they wish they never heard. When a client tells you she is lonely or bored with life, you can count on something pretty exciting happening in the near future. But I have to say that there is nothing like a relationship with another trainer or another trainer's client to stir the pot at the workplace. Yes, once again, I found myself at the stove stirring the pot with my own two hands.

I had been at Body Masters for almost six months. With the business model being the exact opposite of the one used at Precision Fitness, it took a little time for me to get rolling with steady clients. I had finally been accepted to a real college. With full-time classes, I was again back in the mix with days that seemed longer than I cared for but knew I just had to suck it up. I made myself available at all times for training. Nights, weekends, you name it. Whenever a client needed training, I was there. Since things were a little slow, I hung around the gym quite a bit and worked out with some of the other trainers and got to know some of them quite well. Even though the money wasn't like it was in the past, I was happy in my new setup. Having access to the gym at all times meant I could go there when I needed a quiet place to study, since life with roommates wasn't very agreeable with learning. I would go to happy hour a few nights here and there with the rest of the crew from Body Masters, and for the first time, I felt complete freedom. I also didn't feel the guilt I was used to feeling from doing things I knew deep down I shouldn't have been doing. However, a few months of abstaining from sex felt like an eternity for me. Little did I know how addictive the power of the panties could be.

In all workplaces, situations arise that can disrupt the daily workflow between employees, for example, a little argument about how someone is or isn't doing his job in your opinion or perhaps an overall disdain for the new company uniform. Keep in mind, this is a gym and it's not as if we are saving the world within these walls. With firsthand knowledge, I can say there is nothing worse than when a client of another trainer somehow ends up in your bed. I was guilty of yet another personal training no-no. For the record, I will maintain my innocence to a degree and claim that I was yet again pursued, not the pursuee.

Nicole was an attractive thirty-three-year-old. She was a petite girl, barely five feet tall and maybe a hair over a hundred pounds, with long curly brown hair. I'm no John Stamos, so I'm probably on a different rating scale, but she was probably a solid 8 in my opinion. What really added to her intrigue was that she was an opera singer. I was slightly intimidated because I assumed an opera singer was automatically a member of the upper class. I'm not sure how many people can say they have been with an opera singer, but I would bet that I stand among an elite fraternity. Some people have a thing for midgets, some for amputees, but I'm pretty straightforward when it comes to women: blonde, brunette, yellow, brown, black, Puerto Rican, Asian, whatever. I don't favor one over the other; I am an equal opportunity kind of guy.

Nicole was not one of my clients. She trained with Tina, another trainer, but I would check Nicole out from time to time. Did I have clients of my own whom I should have been focusing on? Sure, but I thought for a split second that this may help cure my tendency to fish in my own pool. After all, Larry's words were ringing in my ears. With his tried and true philosophies instilled in me, I knew I couldn't count on sleeping with all my attractive clients and expect my retention rate to stay better than average now could I? I was finally on the straight and narrow path. I had avoided trouble for the first few months at my new job, but here I was about to welcome it back into my life with open arms. Sure, Nicole wasn't my client, but sometimes all it takes is a little spark. What kind of guy goes through all the trouble of moving across the country and starting fresh only to pick up where he left off, you may ask? This guy.

My coworker Tina was a veteran to the training game. She was in her late forties but was in great shape and got along with everyone. Tina was one of those happy types; she always had on a smile. Although she was a little older than your average trainer, she kept a youthful demeanor about her that helped her stay busier than most trainers I knew. It is no wonder Tina had been at Body Masters for many years and had developed a great business. When I first started at Body Masters, Tina offered me advice on how to get my business built up and the best ways to network in town, since I was new to this neck of the woods. I appreciated all her help and became very close with her. She became somewhat of a mentor to me at my new job. As a matter of fact, Tina would occasionally try to set me up with people she knew after she discovered I was single. Little did I know that her clients were off-limits. Had I known this was going to piss Tina off a great deal, I would have thought twice about grazing in her pasture.

As fate would have it, testosterone-fueled thoughts prevailed and once again I ended up in the position I was now all too familiar with. It was a Saturday afternoon, and I was done training my clients. I was the only one on the gym floor at the time, working out on my own. Body Masters was a small, private studio that didn't have any members working out unless a trainer was with them. Nicole was in the cardio room finishing a yoga class. As the class let out, I noticed Nicole walk by, and we briefly made eye contact. It wasn't much, but it was enough for her to turn around and say a few words to me. Maybe it was my killer form I displayed on the dead lifts I was doing that drew her in. Up until now, I had only officially met her once and maybe said hello a couple of times when I saw her pass by.

I knew her to be a shy girl, but on this day she didn't hesitate to approach me and strike up a conversation. Her newly discovered courage made me even more interested in her. It was as if I were wearing some type of cologne that just exuded lust in any woman who came within ten feet of me. Did I know at that moment she came up to me and started talking to me that I would be in bed with her within the next twenty-four hours? Yes, I did. After a couple of minutes of small talk, Nicole asked me to attend a work function with her that evening.

I answered without hesitation and then stood there for a moment trying to take it all in. Nicole was a little bit older than me and wasn't exactly out of my league in what I would call the Playboy bunny type of way, but she was out of my league on several other levels. Why did she decide to ask me? Before my career as a personal trainer, I was hit on a total of two times in my life, and both of those occasions occurred in middle school and happened to be by larger-than-life girls.

I was already looking forward to my night out with Nicole. Who doesn't enjoy schmoozing with the elite, especially if you're not one of them? When you are a young guy who didn't come from much, just seeing people with cash makes you wonder what the hell they did to get it. Who knows, maybe I would meet some potential clients. Besides, what the hell else was I going to do?

Nicole met me at my place later that evening. She was wearing a black and white sundress with these little black boots that made her look even more appealing. Her dress was cinched at the waist with a black belt that was tied in a perfect bow, which made me think what lay underneath was my gift for the evening. I was used to only seeing her dressed down at the gym. Her face wasn't plastered with makeup, and her natural beauty impressed me. I had roommates at the time, which was kind of a bummer, considering I used to live on my own and now had to share refrigerator space with other dudes. So without inviting Nicole inside, we hopped into her car and off we went to the nicest hotel in the city.

Having Nicole by my side helped me cope with this scene, which turned out to be a good old boy network that made me want to fucking puke. Seeing how the other half lives was truly an eye-opener, especially since I wasn't one of them. To me, "gourmet" was a double meat foot-long sub with the works, but at this event, I found myself sitting at a huge table with cheeses from god knows where that smelled like shit but were described by someone as "exquisite." I should have known right then and there that this wasn't exactly my crowd.

You can imagine the looks I was getting. Talk about being the odd couple. I was a young twenty-three-year-old with this very cute, sophisticated woman in her thirties. Now I know how Cher's bagel boy felt to some degree. The average age of Nicole's friends, or whoever these people were, was around fifty. These weren't your average older couples either. These people were dressed in clothes that they probably thought would make them look younger but had no idea it just wasn't quite working for them. They were also wearing jewelry that wasn't the kind you find at your average Kay Jewelers. I couldn't help but notice that as dressed up as I tried to be, my attire didn't come close to some of the designer duds the others were wearing. My standard blue jeans and button-down shirt weren't exactly crowd pleasers. It was beginning to dawn on me that people out west spent quite a bit of time on their wardrobe before they left the house.

Nevertheless, I tried to be a good sport and kept a smile on my face as much as possible despite hanging with these pompous assholes. Getting introduced to someone who was known as a "donor" was just weird. These weren't even organ donors but rather people with so much excess cash they were just looking for excuses to part ways with it. I always donated a few bucks to the local no-kill shelter, but something told me these people were donating on a much larger scale. By the looks of their attire, I knew that I was not only severely underdressed but also way out of my comfort zone, especially when the conversation was all about opera music. I knew absolutely nothing about opera other than I hoped to have an opera singer's legs wrapped around me that night. I managed to brush off the looks and comments with several vodka tonics, but I couldn't wait to bail out of that place.

Did I really just want to get to the point and see what this girl looked like naked? Yep. I didn't care much for more unnecessary conversation; I had already done enough of that over the past couple of hours just trying to kill time at this event. Nicole was an artist at heart and probably loved music more than anything, and I was just some guy who loved nothing but sex. Well, I must say that a close second to having sex was making money. I was still somewhat new to town and all and enjoying being officially unattached for the first time in quite awhile. This was my first experience being a single adult, and I was looking forward to enjoying all the benefits that came along with that title.

I can't tell you how many minutes were spent talking to Nicole about things that really weren't interesting to me, but I felt I had put in enough time to get laid. This six-month buildup had me feeling like it was the first time all over again. Nicole and I were polar opposites, but there was this sexual chemistry that needed to be explored. I also knew that this would be unlike my previous relations with clients of my own. If Nicole was one of my clients, I would already know her family history, likes and dislikes, and all the other information needed to make her feel all warm and fuzzy inside before ending up in bed. I didn't know much about Nicole at all other than what she did for a living and approximately how big her rack was. This was just like a one-night stand. Yes, those one-night stands. I know I'm not the only one guilty of going out to a bar, talking to someone for a few minutes or a few hours, and ending the night on top of one another. Does it satisfy your immediate needs? Absolutely. But is it fulfilling on any other level? Nope. Not only that, but the odds of carrying on some type of relationship after that point were slim to none, thanks to my new mind-set. I was single and adamant about staying that way for at least a little while.

After a couple of painful hours in this awkward setting, I was nearing the peak of my buzz and sexual curiosity. When I noticed Nicole had managed to get a little tipsy herself, I knew my opportunity to escape was near.

"If I have to hear one more story that begins with how wonderful someone is, I'm going to hang myself," I said to Nicole.

She somehow found my locker room behavior amusing and laughed. "What are you up for?" she asked with a smile.

That line alone got me hard. I knew Nicole was up for what I was thinking about. "I got a few ideas," I said and took her hand to leave.

Now where could we go to be alone? Certainly not my place, since I had two out-of-control roommates. I could see it now: I would show up with a great-looking girl, and these guys would end up convinced that where there's one, there must be more, and then proceed to bother the shit out of her by trying to get her to invite her friends over. I could just imagine what their reaction would be when they found out she was an opera singer. I'm sure they would not stop badgering her until she belted out a few notes just for kicks. On the other hand, I didn't want to be rude and ask to go back to her place, since I didn't know her very well. At this point, the alcohol had set in and I was in the mood, so something needed to happen fast. I figured what better place to go than where we first met: the gym. I had the keys to the gym, and there were no worries of an intrusion after midnight.

As we drove to the gym, I wondered where to make the magic happen. Would it be the on the bench press? Perhaps my desk? Or maybe on one of those yoga mats Nicole seemed to be very familiar with? My mind was racing to find an adequate surface to make this not only pleasurable but also somewhat classy. Luckily, Nicole was just as much in the heat of the moment as I was, since she drove the whole time with one hand on the wheel and the other ever so close to my semi-hard wiener.

Body Masters was in a strip mall and didn't look like much from the front window but stretched far back where it opened to the gym floor and yoga studios. As we made our way through the lobby and into the pitch-black corridor that led to the gym floor, a light went off in my head. In the back of the gym was a room set aside for massages. Lou, the massage therapist, always had the room set up in a very tranquil manner with incense and candles. Lou was quite the asshole, and there was no love lost between the two of us. Nothing worse than a massage therapist who thinks he's God's gift. He would love to share his knowledge of medical terminology with anyone who didn't have any of their own, especially someone younger like me. He kind of looked like a poor man's Henry Rollins but lacked the coolness. Nicole gave me this cute little smile as I took her hand and led her into massage room.

Trying to make somewhat of an impression, I lit a candle as Nicole lay down on the massage table. I leaned over her and began kissing her neck and working my way down to her chest. She moaned softly as I started to undress her. She wasn't exactly hitting the high notes yet, but it was enough for me to know I was heading in the right direction. Spread out before me on top of the massage table naked with just her boots remaining, her body looked perfect in the candlelit room. The dim light outlined her curves.

One thing I figured out on my own during my training days was the art of foreplay. I let my hands and mouth do the talking for several minutes, which was more than enough time for Nicole. I stood over her and caressed every part of her body until it was go time. I quickly unbuttoned and removed my shirt and could see the excitement in Nicole's eyes. I was pointing due north in my jeans, which required careful removal of my drawers as I awkwardly climbed on top of her. This was my first experience not only with someone who sang for a living but also on top of a massage table, so I didn't know what to expect. I didn't know if the table was going to break or if Nicole was going to emanate soft sounds or break out in song as we went further and further.

This was one of the very few times as a personal trainer that I didn't get a blow job off the bat. I can't say I was disappointed though, as Nicole was quite the kisser and thankfully her breath wasn't foul after a night of drinking. She obviously didn't try any of that goat cheese or whatever the fuck was on that table earlier in the evening. Lying on the massage table, our bodies were locked together and our mouths all over each other. Nicole had these nice perky breasts that fell nicely in the palm of my hand. Her petite size allowed for easy maneuverability on top of the massage table.

I came prepared with a condom. I know this might come as a surprise, considering my history. Well, I was in the process of maturing (and I would find the process to be a long one), and the first logical step in my mind was to carry a condom in my wallet. Perhaps because it had been several months since getting any action from someone other than myself, I had plenty of time to prepare for this event. On another note, why is it that a girl you just met and hung out with for a little while is so wet down there that there is not an ounce of effort required for entry? I must admit, I was a little worried about the integrity of this massage table as I lay on top of Nicole and slowly made my way in and out. I was too nervous to speed up, so I kept it nice and slow. I waited for some type of beautiful music to come out of her as we went at it, but I settled for the soft moans. Surprisingly, I lasted longer than usual because my fear of the table breaking kept my rhythm to a slow and steady pace. We spent quite some time on the table, but when I was about to finish, I stood up at the edge of the table, pulled Nicole closer to me, and held her legs in my hands.

With Nicole still wearing her black boots and her legs in my hands, I watched myself going in and out. I was doing my best Peter North impression. The only thing missing was the spa music in the background. Nicole's soft moans made up for the lack of music and were reaching a higher pitch as she got closer to the verge of climaxing. I was still trying to keep this thing going, even though I still had the tendency to be a guy. I had to slow things down once I moved to the standing position. You have to give me credit for trying. As I had with most of the previous clients I'd slept with, I was determined to make this memorable for both parties. Besides, she asked me out, so this was the least I could do. Thanks to my now single status and the fact that Nicole wasn't my client, I felt more compelled than ever to put on a good show, as I didn't have anyone to go home to. I incorporated some type of rotation into the usual back and forth thrusting in an attempt to prolong the moment. Whatever the hell I did, it worked and then some. Not only did I buy myself another thirty-five to forty-five seconds, but Nicole's voice turned into a high-pitched shriek as I felt her body tense up. As if on cue, I finished into my trusty Trojan the moment she finally eased up and her body completely relaxed.

When I finished, there was that awkward moment that a guy feels after pulling out and standing there with a hard-on covered in a goo-filled rubber. I could only imagine what my facial expression and what was left of my erection with this yellow cap covering it would look like on a hidden camera. As unbelievable as the past nine and a half minutes or so just felt, my interest in Nicole quickly waned as soon as I finished. I rushed out of the room with boxers in hand to wash up in the bathroom. I left Nicole naked on the massage table. When I got back, she had slipped back into her dress and was sitting up on the table.

It was a great night to say the least. Nicole and I both got what we wanted, and I was without the usual guilt I felt after sleeping with my clients. Being single brought a whole new meaning to training. I probably could have continued a relationship with Nicole, since I was available, but I just wasn't feeling it. Yet just a short time ago, I was in a relationship of my own but sleeping with married women whom I occasionally thought about getting even closer to. Now I was beyond the point of no return. Even though I avoided the possible disastrous consequences of fucking around at my old job, I was less than six months into my new job and already stirring the pot once again. Fuck it, I thought. As long as I was a personal trainer, I would be caught up in all the extra perks that go along with it, whether or not they were right or wrong. After this brief moment of reflection, I came to and picked up around the room before we left. To spite the asshole Lou, I left some sediment on the table. I know you're thinking that's disgusting, but the way I look at it, it could have been worse. I could have left the entire remains on the table, used rubber and all. Besides, we all work with a Lou—someone we wish we could just do something fucked up to for being an asshole all the time.

Nicole dropped me off at my place, and I gave her a nice peck on the cheek good-bye to go along with that awkward hug that one does while sitting next to someone in the front seat of the car. After Nicole and I said good-bye, I had a good feeling just knowing that what happened didn't have to be kept as a dark secret from a girlfriend. Nicole was someone else's client, so I didn't have to ask her for money at the end of the month, which was something that truly made me feel like a gigolo. Had I known this would feel this good, I would have slept with other people's clients from the get-go rather than my own.

Reality is a bitch, however. There always seems to be a reality check for everybody at some point. When you do something remotely fucked up in the eyes of the world, the good times don't last long. Seeing how the shit that I pulled over the past couple of years was beyond wrong, I was long overdue for a letdown. Being with Nicole had been way too easy. I would find out rather quickly how wrong it is to fuck another trainer's client. Ever so slowly I was learning the steep cost of trying to be a player, as they say. I often wonder if these pro athletes and entertainers have this much trouble with groupies they encounter on the road.

The following week, Nicole and I crossed paths in the gym. There was no weirdness or tension between the two of us. She gave me a nice hello along with a big smile. Score!

At least, that's what I thought. Every asshole has his day, and who was I to think I was allowed multiple days? Tina got wind of our escapade. I don't know if Nicole told her everything or briefly mentioned that she "hung out" with me recently, but word travels fast in a two-thousand-square-foot gym with barely half a dozen trainers.

Tina was rip shit when she found out. I remember her coming over to me and telling me how fucked up I was.

"Who the hell do you think you are sleeping with my clients?" Tina yelled at me, complete with larger than normal eyes and a finger close to my face. "After everything I've done for you, this is what I get in return?"

I was speechless. It was as if I deflowered her daughter after prom and forgot to call her again. Gone was that very happy person who always had a big smile and was friendly to everyone. Shocked but guilty as charged, I stood there as Tina lit into me. Thankfully, there weren't a bunch of people in the gym at the time. The only thing I could muster in my defense was that Nicole pursued me. I played innocent.

"Tina, she asked me out," I said without even attempting to look her in the eyes. Lucky for me, Tina bought my excuse, which actually was the truth for once. Again, the youthful defense of stupidity prevailed.

Tina didn't remain pissed at me for long. Soon things were back to normal. The camaraderie that I developed with Tina returned, and all was forgiven even while I continued to sleep with Nicole on occasion. Despite our very obvious sexual chemistry, things inevitably turned stale after awhile, probably because we had nothing else in common. Watching the Eagles on Sunday with a basket of hot wings will always trump going to see a performance of *Les Misérables*. After a few memorable sessions, none of which again would occur on Lou's massage table, we mutually decided to stop sleeping together. As it turns out, agreeing to stop sleeping together is much easier than breaking up with a significant other. There wasn't any animosity on either end. This was one of the few instances I officially ended things on a high note.

13
OH, CHERYL

About a year after moving out to California, things seemed to be falling into place. I was training in a great gym, I had built up a steady list of clients, and I had referrals coming in left and right. I thought I had it all, and I was finally free of all the fucked-up things I was guilty of in the past.

I began training Cheryl, a new client whom Jason had passed on to me. She was a semi-cute gymnastic studio owner. By semi-cute, I mean she had a nice body, but I'm not gonna lie to you—she was a bona fide butterface. In my own defense, Cheryl did not fall down the ugly tree and hit every branch. She missed a few branches, or maybe it was just a small tree. Let's call her a solid 6, but her body was easily a 9 and a half. She was thirty-three and ran her own successful business in addition to being a decorated former gymnast. After getting to know her and the disaster that was otherwise known as her life, I wondered how she ever became successful. Other than some plastic surgery and one of the tightest backsides I've seen on a woman over thirty, I really didn't find much else attractive about Cheryl. Despite being from the Midwest, Cheryl had the personality of a spoiled Long Island teenager who was pissed because the BMW her parents gave her for her sweet sixteen was white instead of silver. She was a cunt with a capital C. Her attitude toward most people was like that of the upper class in the movie *Titanic*, but unfortunately, she wasn't on a boat going down. To her, people who washed cars for a living or, God forbid, did landscaping were trash, and she avoided making eye contact with them. I hate to admit it, but the more I think about it, the lone bright spot was her disposable income, which probably made her the way she was in the first place.

Cheryl had no problem throwing down $500 a month for personal training, which was the cost for three training sessions a week. Things on the West Coast were even better than they were back home. It was a nice score for me. She would talk about her shopping ventures, which included purchases at nothing but high-end stores like Gucci and Prada. Thanks to my gay clients, I knew these designer stores were no joke and of course well out of my price range. When I think of my time spent with Cheryl, one thing is certain: if she wasn't paying me so well, I never would have put up with her for as long as I did, but I was a true glutton for punishment. I would soon discover how far a guy would go for the almighty dollar.

On the other hand, I was a bona fide blue-collar guy with a blue-collar upbringing. As a kid, I was given only those items that were considered completely necessary for survival, including the seasonal hand-me-downs from my older brother. My time spent with Cheryl gave me the chance to experience something that was very foreign to me—that is, getting whatever the hell you wanted whenever you wanted it. I had always been intrigued with this type of lifestyle, and this was well before the days of being able to look up celebrity homes on the Internet. This was back when most information was gathered from watching MTV. Who hasn't seen an episode of Cribs and looked at all the unnecessary shit those people have at their disposal? I know

I'm not alone when I say that I wanted to at least have a taste of that at one time or another. Turns out, Cheryl was my ticket to the highlife.

As I trained Cheryl three times a week, I began to realize that, for the first time in a long time, I was adhering to the strict guidelines of professionalism in the workplace. Sure, some time was spent joking around with Cheryl for the sake of entertainment, but no boundaries were broken. When Cheryl left the gym, we put our chatter on hold until the next session. I was occasionally sleeping with Nicole (who, I must reiterate, was *not* my client) when I first started training Cheryl, but other than that, I was keeping it real for the first time in a long time.

Several months went by with nothing but friendly banter back and forth when all of a sudden it happened like a crash of lightning that startles you when you're lying on the couch.

"So when are we going to hang out?" Cheryl asked me.

I felt that uneasy feeling in the base of my stomach when I realized it was more than just a hunch. It had been nearly a year since I had moved, but the memories of those former clients were still fresh in my mind. I could go in one direction or another: I could make the right choice and cancel out all that was wrong in my past, or I could opt for the wrong choice and once again punch my ticket on the highway to hell. I can proudly say for once I made the right choice—at first. I managed to brush off Cheryl's attempt to hang out, but she persisted. As bad as this may sound, if Cheryl was more attractive, I can say the wrong choice would have happened without a second of hesitation. I guess there was still some growing up to do on my part.

I had a full roster of clients, but losing $500 a month would hurt if I upset Cheryl by not hanging out with her. I had come up with excuses for several weeks as to why I couldn't go out, but Cheryl persisted like a drunken sorority chick at a frat party who wasn't used to hearing the word no. She was getting annoying with her requests, which seemed to be coming at least two of the three times I saw her each week. I was all about satisfying the customer, but I wanted to keep it clean when it came to clients. Since moving, I had been able to keep all my relations with my clients at a very businesslike level. After a month of dodging the question, I began to wonder what would happen if I said yes to Cheryl. I felt a somewhat new sense of confidence in keeping a friendly relationship with the opposite sex. Besides, would it really be that bad if we just hung out?

I decided to round up my roommates and a group of friends so that the night wouldn't seem like some intimate event. Yet I once again showed my immaturity and asked Jada, whom I really was interested in, to also come along. Jada was a friend of a friend. She was smart, employed, and hot—the perfect trifecta. Pursuing a relationship with her was something that had been on my mind ever since meeting her shortly after I moved out west. This is where I created a potential hazardous situation well before the night even began. Even though I was going out with friends, I was going headfirst into the danger zone without my wingman, Pete, which was a bad move. Pete was more than capable of helping me out on many a night. Whenever we hung out, if I ever found myself in a precarious situation with a girl whom I wanted nothing to do with, Pete could step in and take control. Somehow, his dissertation on animal rights or student loans would captivate even the toughest listener. With his usually stoned demeanor, he was able to take anyone's attention off me for enough time to allow me to slip out the back door of the bar and make a clean getaway.

This night had doom written all over it from the start. A group of about eight of us went out one Friday night to some god-awful club that, for some unknown reason, I would actually set foot in again on another night after this whole shitstorm occurred. We drove in two cars. I rode with Cheryl and a couple of friends, and my roommate Craig drove with Jada. I thought I would have this whole situation taken care of with little to no effort, but I was wrong in so many ways. Cheryl knew no one in the group other than me, and she wasn't exactly the most socially equipped individual.

When we arrived at the club, Cheryl was hanging all over me, so Jada discovered my shenanigans early on and quickly tuned me out. I was pissed off immediately because I knew I blew it with her. Jada was my age but mature enough to see a true asshole when she saw one. Cheryl, who was petite at maybe five feet tall and barely 102 pounds after hitting the Chinese buffet hard, then decided to put on her drinking shoes. Holy shit. I have never to this day seen anything like it in my life. I've seen some girls drink way more than they should, but not like this. For example, whenever a new song came on—and I mean every time a new song came on—no matter what it was, Cheryl felt the need to welcome it with an obnoxiously loud "Woooooo!" Her sense of entitlement was magnified. She would throw a shit fit if, God forbid, she had to wait for a few minutes to get a drink at a crowded bar.

I'm sure I'm not alone when I say one of the worst nights of my life involved someone drinking way too much, and this night would make the top of that list for me. Not only were my friends, who were occasional weekend binge drinkers themselves, turned off by this demonstration, but it also appeared that the general public was none too pleased either. Cheryl managed to piss off the already annoying people who were at the club, if that was even possible. I was under the assumption that most people at these places were immune to getting pissed off at sloppy drunks, since they themselves were probably inebriated as well and had no idea what they were doing, let alone what anyone else was doing.

For someone like Cheryl who was a quiet and reserved business owner, alcohol seemed to unleash the beast. Again, if she were a little better looking, there might have been a perfectly reasonable excuse for this type of behavior but, unfortunately, she was not. Was I just as pissed off as every poor soul in that horrible club and turned off by this inappropriate behavior? Absolutely. I could go on forever with this one, but to make a long story short, things didn't go as planned that evening. I gave in to the powers of fake breasts and a tight ass. A few shots of tequila and, of course, a purple hooter or two didn't help either.

It was closing time, as the song goes. Jada was long gone. Now that I'm looking back at this night, Jada might have actually became the girlfriend who could have ended this lurid behavior of mine for good if I hadn't screwed things up. The rest of my friends who came to the club were also nowhere to be found, thanks to this annoying girl I brought. She really was a buzz kill. She was slurring her words as we were leaving and gave me the keys to her brand-new Lexus SUV. I had never sat in a brand-new car, let alone driven one. She talked about how I was the first person to drive her new car other than herself and joked about not getting into an accident on the way home. If only I could have gotten into an accident to possibly avoid the bullshit that I was about to fall into.

We ended up driving almost a half hour back to her place, which was no easy feat, not because I was impaired but because she put on a display worthy of someone in the back of one of those short buses you see in the neighborhood. She was cranking up some terrible fucking country music, which I still hate to this day, and writhing around in the front seat like a moron. Ugh, fuck my life. I squinted as I studied this odd behavior and mouthed the words *What the fuck?* while gripping the steering wheel as tightly as I could. A smart guy would have dropped her off and called a cab for a ride back to his own place. Not this guy; instead, I ended up accepting her invitation to go into her apartment.

Inside her apartment, Cheryl popped open a bottle of Bud Light. Classy, I thought. If this scene happened today, there is no doubt in my mind Cheryl would have cracked open a Bud Light Lime. I passed on more alcohol and opted for water. After sitting on her couch for just a couple of minutes listening to her slur her words with her eyes half closed, I was beginning to get tired. It's funny how too much alcohol can make an already unattractive person even more unattractive. I then realized there was nothing to talk about. I was about to get up after a thankful moment of silence, but Cheryl suddenly straddled me and began making out with me. Did some sick part of me want to see those funbags in real time? Yes, a part of me did, so I dealt with her breath, which was an odd combination of fish and beer, as she continued to suck my face. Lucky for me, Cheryl had enough after several minutes and decided she wanted a little more than just kissy face. She got up and led me to her huge bedroom, which had one of those gigantic California King–sized beds. I wished I had access to some mouthwash to kill whatever it was that seemed to linger in my mouth.

Cheryl was giddy like a little kid as she jumped onto the bed and aggressively undressed me like a dog in heat. I returned the favor and took off her top to set those mounds free. To those who have not had the pleasure of experiencing artificial boobs, I can say they are something else when installed properly. That being said, I have seen my fair share of good fake ones and bad fake ones. As I grabbed Cheryl's left breast, my face probably spoke volumes. These things were definitely not built for speed. They were solid as rocks. In fact, they were so solid it was quite the turnoff as I continued to play with them. Whatever. They looked a lot better than they felt.

Cheryl soon had enough of my very nonsensual and probably very probe-like hands. She removed what was left of my undergarments and went right down on me as I stood at the edge of the bed. As I disappeared in her mouth, my head turned upward as if to thank someone up there for yet again sending me this gift. I truly am a sucker for blow jobs, as I've rarely turned away a willing participant.

Standing at the foot of Cheryl's bed, I couldn't help but wonder what was going on down there. If there were such a thing as a bad blow job, Cheryl would be the culprit. I think at one point she was actually blowing instead of sucking. Aside from getting my first blow job in high school by an obviously untrained teenager, this had to rate as one of the worst. I couldn't finish with this type of tomfoolery going on down there. I took a step back to prevent further emotional and possibly physical damage to my wiener.

Cheryl then took off her lace panties and tried to be as sexy as a hammered woman can be as she rolled over onto her back. This also was a sign of things to come. Cheryl was very vanilla when it came to fucking. If I wasn't doing the work, there would be no work at all, since Cheryl didn't like to move much while having sex. So much for the theory that gymnasts are great in the sack. I went all in, literally. Aside from her groans, which amplified her breath, there really wasn't much going on. I actually had to go back into the Rolodex to assist with finishing off. Maybe it was her demeanor throughout the night that lessened the experience. Maybe I was truly just a complete asshole at this point in my life. Whatever the case may be, the highlight was finishing on those attractive yet rubbery boobs.

A few days later at work, I spoke with my manager, Jason. He wasn't your typical gym manager. Everyone wondered what he was all about, since he was about thirty and seemed to show the same affection for both men and women alike. He wore those string bracelets, and I believe he wore a thumb ring on a few occasions. Who the fuck wears a thumb ring? Whatever his deal was, he was at least a little more tolerable than the sales-driven guys who are usually in charge. He sat down with me on one of the couches in the front lounge of the gym to talk about Cheryl. Unlike my last place of employment where there were some skeletons that never found their way out into the limelight, news traveled fast in this small studio. Luckily, Jason wasn't too pissed about the ordeal. I told him I had unfortunately been down this road a time or two before. He then proceeded to tell me some words of advice that I should have heeded.

"So, I hear you're dating Cheryl," Jason said.

What? I had literally fucked her a few days ago and somehow this guy heard we were "dating"?

"More or less," I responded reluctantly. For the first time since I started working at Body Masters, I got the hint that Jason was more concerned about keeping Cheryl around as a client.

"I hope it goes well for you," he said, as if he somehow knew I was going to be in for a rough ride. I was relieved that he wasn't pissed at me for sleeping with a client. I was used to getting high fives from my old management team. I was then given the "honeymoon period" lecture.

"You know, after the first six months or so of being with someone, things usually get a little dicey," Jason said.

I tried to play cool. "Yes, sir. I'm not really thinking about that right now," I said. Even though this was not my first rodeo, I had been with enough women to realize the honeymoon period exists in every relationship. Aside from Danielle, I never made it through this supposed six-month period, and at this point, I really didn't think Cheryl and I would ever amount to anything more than a few dates. Once again, I thought I was above all this. No way was I going to let this little slipup cost me my finally budding business. But did I think that getting involved with this woman was going to have me worrying about honeymoon periods or any of that shit that goes along with relationships? Hell no. I really had no interest in her as a person other than the silicon 34 Cs on a petite frame and, from what I had seen so far, a lot of coin in the bank.

Our next scheduled appointment was odd to say the least. It was about four days after our night out, and I hadn't talked to Cheryl since then. I didn't know how she would react after that first night even though I had been in this same position more times than I could count.

"You haven't called me," Cheryl said.

"I've been very busy the past few days," I said.

She quickly followed up with the line that many guys love to hear when they're horny and would rather share the experience with someone rather than take care of things themselves: "What are you doing tonight?" she asked.

So what did I do? You guessed it. I gave her the go-ahead to come on by. This time around, it was a weeknight, so I didn't think things could get too out of hand, but I realized I was wrong when she showed up in what looked like a Catwoman outfit, along with what would be her trusty six-pack of Bud Light. She knew very well I wasn't a Bud guy, and if she really gave a shit about anyone but herself, she could have shown up with a bottle of Grey Goose. I was still living with roommates at the time, and thankfully, they were not home when she showed up. I really couldn't imagine having to explain this one to them.

We sat on my couch, and I watched SportsCenter while Cheryl helped herself to her Bud Light. It was as if I was the hideous chud and she needed to get annihilated before sleeping with me. Meanwhile, I just wanted to fuck her and get her out of the house before my roommates got back. About twenty minutes later, I had Cheryl naked on the couch and I was on top of her. It was disappointing knowing that her body was mostly just for show, but it was more than enough to get me worked up. I slipped my dick out of my underwear, grabbed her legs, and tried to work my way into her. Cheryl was very tight, almost virgin-like tight—not that I've ever experienced that, but this was what I imagined it to feel like. After I worked it around and partially in and out for a couple of minutes, Cheryl loosened up just enough to let me in. Once again, I was doing all the work, but I couldn't help but think how good this felt, even if there were several things I didn't care for much. Hey, I was getting laid and not having to pay for it, so I would call it a win-win.

Something different happened as I worked my hips into and out of Cheryl. For the first time, I felt a sense of guilt well before I shot off. Usually, my head was completely clear no matter whom I was fucking—married, separated, MILF, you name it. But now I was feeling bad *while* I was doing it. After about fifteen minutes of noneventful screwing, which was on the longer side for me, I let loose inside her. Nope, the condom didn't make it on this time. Just when I thought I was growing up, I managed to regress in more than one way. Not only was I being irresponsible sexually, but I was also tapping into the well that I was drinking from. I thought I left all this type of bullshit behind me. I lasted over a year doing it the right way, but now I was getting myself involved in dirty deeds again.

This time it was Cheryl who left shortly afterward. I sat back on my couch after she left and watched the end of SportsCenter. I had no idea what was in store for me after this encounter. The more I thought about it, the more I realized I should have just taken care of myself, but somehow things weren't that simple for me back then. Knowing what I know now, I could have avoided this mess and what turned out to be almost eight miserable months of my life. A small part of me thought that everything was just fine and that I may be in the clear, just as I had been every other time since I started working in this field.

A few days after our second "date," I had the chance to do the right thing but managed to blow it. Cheryl and I began our training as usual with a warm-up followed by some circuit training. Between sets of walking lunges, Cheryl said, "So what is going on with us? Other guys have been asking me out, and I don't know what to tell them."

Could I have gotten out at this point with a "get out of jail free" card? Absolutely, as there is always an out. It's just a question of whether you have the balls to use it. Even though my twenty-three-year-old balls had gotten plenty of work, I didn't quite understand how to use them in a situation like this. Shit, I was certain a lower body circuit with walking lunges, step-ups, and squats was more than enough to keep her somewhat out of breath. And come on, she was not much of a looker, so who the hell else was trying to get in her pants? Of course, I totally discounted that she was a petite female with a nice body and a large fake chest. What normal guy wasn't going to take a shot at her? Shit, I was buttonhooked.

I'm somewhat of a sensitive guy, and around this time, I was growing more sensitive for some unknown reason. I could have saved myself future anguish and possibly gotten away with another month or two of training sessions from Cheryl without any commitment on my part. Instead, I made perhaps the biggest blunder of my training and dating career. Somehow, someway, the words that then came out of my mouth that day were misconstrued into "I want to be your boyfriend." As a good friend of mine once said, "You got yourself a girlfriend."

Did I want to have a relationship with Cheryl? Absolutely not. Did she have a nice body? Yep. Did the prospect of sleeping with her on occasion sound good? Yes, because what guy doesn't like getting laid? I don't have to explain how things get weird after sleeping with someone, especially if it's not a planned deal and it's spontaneous. Let's just say that you can safely multiply the weirdness factor by ten when you're training a person who is also your girlfriend. The old me would have thrown her a shot every now and then and continued to pursue other attractive young California girls, but I guess I was feeling the need to "grow up" a little bit. Should I have thought twice about getting involved with her before things got out of hand? Yep, but I obviously had a lot to learn.

Then things quickly went south. Cheryl proceeded to drop the hammer exactly the way some girls do. Not even a month after we officially started dating, she decided not to renew her training sessions. Bummer, there goes $500 a month. Who could blame her? Why pay the piper when you're already getting the pipe for free? Not only was I not getting paid each month for spending time with this girl, but her uncontrollable drinking was also getting out of hand.

Most people stop by 7-Eleven for a lotto ticket and a Slurpee after a long day at the office, but Cheryl was good for a six-pack and whatever wine whose label appealed to her. This wasn't a habit just a couple of days a week but rather a daily occurrence, and weekends were usually much worse, thanks to bars staying open until the wee hours.

So why did I decide to stick around someone I really despised as a person? I will tell you exactly why, and I'm sure just about every guy or girl is guilty of this at least once. Did I like wearing new duds from Armani? It was an easy question to answer when the nicest piece of attire I owned at the time was a shirt from Abercrombie and Fitch that was gifted to me about five years ago. How about going to restaurants that don't have coupons and the average dinner plate goes for fifty dollars? Seeing how I thought Olive Garden was classy, this was something I was more than happy to be a part of. And did the occasional all-expenses-paid trip to Vegas or South Beach make up for the constant shit I had to eat along the way? In my mind, during the early part of our courtship, it did.

Since I never had extra cash to throw around to the degree that Cheryl did, being with someone who did not have to care about money was a sight to see, but being with her made me feel less of a person. She just sucked at life. I didn't see the signs or more than likely just turned a blind eye when we were first training. Our initial conversations were not too in-depth, and I didn't train her for more than a couple of months before the cat was out of the bag. And yes, she had cats, and I fucking hate the entire species to this day thanks to her. I had made a rookie mistake even though at this point in my career I was far from being a rookie. Shame on me. I did, however, find some solace in that I was with a wealthy woman who lived a lifestyle beyond anything that I had ever seen. I also want to pull the "guy" card on this one, which calls for you to be removed from any responsibility in situations when an older woman seduces you and that older woman also happens to have a lot of cash in the bank.

Of course, everyone around me saw the signs of Cheryl's troubled personality well before I did. If she wasn't rolling her eyes at the front desk girl for no apparent reason, she was a loud cell phone talker. No matter where she was—in the gym, at a restaurant, or even at a funeral—Cheryl was *that* important that she not only would answer the phone but also have a lengthy conversation with whoever called. My coworkers and friends were polite enough to tell me that they didn't want her around when we went out. Like a true jackass, I ignored all the warning signs. I stayed with Cheryl for what felt like forever even though it was less than a year. Turns out, Cheryl became the equivalent of Danielle. I continued to date her but cheated on her without remorse. In Danielle's defense, she wasn't half the bitch that Cheryl was, even on her worse day. Cheryl was about to feel the wrath of what happens when you go through life as a stuck-up bitch. I was going to treat her exactly like she treated everyone else in her life—like shit.

Cheryl sealed her fate one night while we were at a concert. I had somehow gotten tickets to see Pearl Jam. These were the guys I grew up listening to. Their *Ten* album was on repeat throughout my high school days. Whenever we traveled for a football game, that was the tape of choice (and yes, it was a tape). It was also the soundtrack for many drunken Saturday nights—you could hear it blaring out of someone's Camaro while parked at the back of a dead-end road.

The band was just passing through town, so the show was at a small club that held barely a thousand people. Having seen them at a huge arena a few years prior, I couldn't wait to see them in a small venue. So who does one take to a concert when you have two tickets? Of course you take your fucking girlfriend. Normally, this wouldn't be an issue, but Cheryl had no fucking idea who Pearl Jam was and preferred country music. Yeah, I know—of all the girls I could have dated, I chose to date the absolutely worst one.

When we got to the small club where the concert was to be held, the line was out the door because they weren't letting anyone in until eight o'clock. Some brilliant manager decided to sell drinks to us poor folks standing in line. I didn't buy a drink for myself because the only options were Bud and Bud Light. It just so happens that those two choices sent Cheryl into a frenzy, being the beer chick she was. I was always amazed at her steady diet of Budweiser and shitty takeout food; she had anything but a gunt downstairs. After close to forty-five minutes of waiting in line and about five Buds for Cheryl, we finally made it in. I should have known that when she opted for the Bud over her usual choice of Bud Light she was on a mission to get hammered. We found a place on the second floor near the railing overlooking the stage and main floor.

I wanted to enjoy every moment of the concert, so I was determined to stay sober and refrained from alcohol altogether. However, I kept feeding Cheryl bottles of Bud just to shut her the fuck up. It was like that scene in *Back to School* when the great Thornton Mellon gives the waitress instructions to bring a pitcher of beer every fifteen minutes until someone passes out and then to bring one every thirty minutes.

Once the band was doing their thing and sounding unbelievable at the one-hour mark, Cheryl was shit-faced. I was sick of having to get up to get her a fucking beer every fifteen minutes, so I finally stopped her flow of alcohol. This did not go over well with Cheryl, and she began to pout like a toddler. Cheryl then took a big swig of some stranger's drink. This very large and obviously angry individual noticed this petite woman slurping down his Jack and Coke, or whatever the fuck it was, like water.

"What the fuck!" he yelled.

Cheryl took this as a challenge and started slurring some type of babbling bullshit at this guy, who was at least six foot five and built like a truck. I put my head into my hands and then tried to diffuse the situation by taking the guy to the bar and buying him a drink. He happened to be cool enough about it all and could see the writing all over my face when I had to explain my "girlfriend" to him.

When we got back to the spot by the railing where we had been standing, something was missing. Cheryl had wandered away like a kid who loses her parents while shopping at Kmart. I don't even know why I bothered to look for her. The band was still playing as I tried to put an end to this monkey business. I decided to go downstairs to visit the bathroom and then search for Cheryl.

Of course, the bathroom attendant was trying to guilt me into dropping a buck into the jar for a squirt of soap and paper towels. I gave him a dollar and surveyed the table filled with breath mints and cologne. Fuck it, I thought. Even though my dollar entitled me to grab a mint and spray of whatever cologne I wanted, I didn't give a shit what I smelled like or how bad my breath reeked. As I walked out of the bathroom, a large bouncer walked toward me. I looked around to see if he had mistaken me for someone else and hoped he was making his way into the shitter to take of business. No such luck. He approached me and asked me to come with him.

I followed him to the entrance of the club and immediately recognized Cheryl's small frame. She was sitting against the wall like a kid who missed the school bus. Her hands held her legs close to her body, and her head was buried in her knees. She looked pathetic. What the fuck? I had no idea I would end up babysitting a woman in her thirties who had a shitload of money.

"We had a complaint that she tried to take some lady's drink, so she's gotta go because it looks like she's had enough," the bouncer said to me.

I stood there observing this mess of a woman whom I had fucked several times but really didn't care much about. As this was going on, I heard the crowd go crazy as Pearl

Jam started playing "Alive." You have got to be kidding me. I guess this was payback in some way.

The bouncer then said, "I didn't say you gotta go, but she does." He seemed to have a smile on his face as he said this, as if he could sense my pain and wanted to help. Once again, I was presented with an out. Call her a cab and go back in to the concert and hang out with Eddie and the guys. But since she was my girlfriend of several months, I ended up carrying her limp body out of there and heading home.

That night, I vowed to not give a shit whatsoever about her from then on and to collect all the cash and prizes I could. As sorry as she was when she sobered up the next day, I didn't give a shit. I had made up my mind: she would remain my girlfriend as long as I was getting something out of it other than sex because the sex wasn't that great with her anyway. A couple of weeks later, Cheryl referred a massage therapist to me. If I thought my time with Cheryl was turbulent, I was in for a big surprise.

14
TRUTH IN ADVERTISING

Every trainer goes through occasional downtime where clients seem to be few and far between. Whether or not it is the holidays or the dog days of summer, no trainer is immune to this unless of course you happen to be one of those celebrity trainers. As much as every trainer counts on regular clients who come in each week, month after month, trainers sometimes are forced to think outside the box to bring in new clients.

Although things were going pretty well at Body Masters, I hit a little dry spell. Not in the usual sense—I had more than a few regulars—but in the influx of new clients. The gym had recently hired a few new trainers, so any customer walking in the door would be going to those trainers to build up their business. I had to rely on my own clients to send me referrals or find new clients on my own. Body Masters was a small gym. It wasn't like the huge factory one I worked at previously where potential clients were everywhere.

Not being much of a marketer, I didn't know the first thing about approaching people outside the gym and talking to them about coming in for training. In fact, I hated those jerk-offs who seemed to promote themselves endlessly whenever they were out in public. Who doesn't know someone who always seems to work business into every conversation? I never really thought much about advertising because I always seemed to do well without it.

I was in college at the time—real college, by the way. I had moved on from what seemed like an eternity spent in community college. It's no wonder why most people don't make it past the ranks of community college. It sucks in oh so many ways. By the time I started college six months after moving west, I was a couple of years older than most of the people in my classes. I was far from being in Blue's category, but I wasn't your typical fraternity guy, and the young eighteen- to twenty-year-olds didn't pay much attention to me. That didn't matter too much to me because I wasn't looking for a relationship while I was in college—yet I managed to maintain a steady relationship with Cheryl, whom I probably should not have been with, in addition to sleeping with a few clients along with other women I met outside of the gym. Yes, something about Cheryl made me slip back into my old ways. I was on a dead-end street with Cheryl but kept her hanging on for who knows why. It was like déjà vu, except in a different area code.

One random afternoon while sitting in class, I brainstormed ways to attract more clients. This was a few years before Facebook. Mr. Zuckerberg was still probably a year or two away from his first wet dream. It was getting close to spring break, so I decided to design a flyer that said, "Get in Shape for Spring Break." How original. I had no idea if that phrase had been used before and could care less about copyright infringement at that time. I recruited a classmate to put a graphic on it depicting some cartoon character lifting weights. Genius, I thought. I went to the computer lab and printed a ton of copies on different colored paper. Once printed, I picked up a few rolls of tape and went on a mad tear putting my flyers on every parking structure, newspaper vending machine, empty wall, and bulletin board I could find. It must have taken close to three hours to plaster these flyers all over campus. I was beyond proud of myself. I thought I was going to net a huge stable full of college-aged girls with this latest effort. After all, the college had close to 40,000 students. Even if less than 5 percent saw my advertisement, there was bound to be at least more than a handful of phone calls.

Just one day after I posted these signs all over campus, the phone rang. I was ecstatic because the call was from a number I had never seen before. I answered in a tone I thought would match the coolness of my flyer but instead sounded like a kid who lost his ball on the roof.

Some overeager, miserable bitch whose job more than likely involved sitting behind a desk at the university all day attacked me without giving me a chance to chime in: "We have taken down as many of these flyers as we could find today, and I would advise you to take down the rest, as this is a violation of school code." Blah, blah, blah. I couldn't help but flashback to my high school guidance counselor.

When I finally had a chance to get a word in and ask how to go about advertising for something like personal training, she said that was not her department. She was also quite cunty when I asked who would be the best person to talk to about advertising on campus. No wonder universities are more backward than the government when it comes to running smoothly and efficiently. To that woman whose name I'll never remember, may you discover your husband balls deep in the neighbor and may your cushy state-funded job go by the wayside during the latest round of budget cuts, if it hasn't already happened.

Talk about feeling deflated. I thought those flyers were a guaranteed home run. I didn't know what to do next. I wasn't hurting that bad, but with summer right around the corner, I knew things were going to slow down even more. Without the gym's help in giving me new referrals, I was clueless as to how to get new people through the door. I was able to stay afloat with what I was currently pulling down, but things would be a little easier with just a few more clients. I always seemed to want more, no matter how much I already had right in front of me.

Just when I resigned myself to doing the best I could with what I had, the phone rang about a week after I posted my flyers all over campus. This time the call was not from a middle-aged college administrator who was bitter about her own life and toward everyone else who dared to cross her path. Her name was Alana. She saw my flyer in a parking garage on campus and was interested in starting to train right away. To top it off, she was training to compete in a bikini contest! You have got to be kidding me. The one person who responded to my ad was a college-aged girl whose aspirations were to enter a bikini contest? The man upstairs sure does work in mysterious ways.

Having only talked to Alana on the phone, I had no idea what to expect when she walked through the door to meet me and discuss her training. Would she be a pleasantly plump coed who was getting ahead of herself by entering this contest or perhaps a smoking hot sorority girl whose mom and dad picked up the tab for everything their little girl ever wanted? Thanks to another little secret talent I discovered over my years in the business, I could tell by her voice that she was at least a solid 7. Call it a sixth sense, but after making countless cold calls from my gym to new members about personal training, I could gauge not only how big they were but also how attractive they were. I never said I was perfect though; there have been a few times I was more than surprised when I was certain at least a 9 would walk through the door only to be disappointed by a larger than life 3. Regardless, I was looking forward to getting paid. I would be lying to say I didn't think I was going to get laid as well—that is, if Alana was up to par.

Alana came into the gym one late Thursday afternoon. I hoped the image I had in my mind after our first conversation would turn out to be a reality. Once again, I'm sure someone was looking out for me for some reason. Not only was Alana already better than average looking, with long, shiny blonde hair, but she also looked like she had already spent years working out. Combine this with the fact that she was in graduate school and planning to go to medical school, I was at a loss for words. How can one very average guy be so lucky? I had no idea, but working as a personal trainer seemed like the job that kept on giving.

Alana and I sat down at my desk to discuss what we would be doing for training. I was certain to collect my money up front. Who knew how long this thing was going to last? I wanted to make sure I got paid before any shenanigans were to happen. I then gave Alana a short tour of the place. I couldn't help but notice her long, tanned legs as we walked through the gym. As we passed Lou's massage room, I couldn't help but chuckle. What an asshole. We returned to my desk to set up our schedule. We planned to meet in two days, and then said our good-byes. At this point in my training career, I knew exactly what was going to happen.

We started off training three days a week. Not exactly chump change for a college girl, but Alana worked as a bartender while she was in school, so money wasn't that much of an issue. We had entirely different majors and our classes were at different parts of the campus, so I never did run into her at school. She would come to the gym late in the afternoons to train, right before my regular group of clients. Cheryl wasn't training with me anymore, so I didn't have to worry about her setting foot in the gym. I was more than a little hesitant about hooking up with another client because Cheryl turned out to be a huge mistake, but there was something about Alana that appealed to me. During our sessions, Alana talked a little about herself but didn't open up the way most of my older female clients would. She was smart, to say the least. I was a little thrown off at first. Seeing how she was much younger than the usual ladies I was accustomed to training, I didn't know how to go about getting together. Imagine that. After several years of nonstop debauchery thanks to my job, I still felt like a nervous freshman asking a girl to the big dance. I was so used to being pursued that I had no idea how to do the pursuing.

I was unable to come up with anything remotely catchy to say or do to attempt to get to know Alana outside the gym, so I resorted to my signature move, which seemed to work well for me in the past: I did absolutely nothing. I gave her my complete attention while training her, talking to her about her classes and keeping her as entertained as I possibly could. Funny how just making someone laugh can open up the door to a whole lot more. Two months into our training, not only did I manage to get her in even better shape than she was when she first walked in the door, but I also managed to get a rise or two out of her during each session with whatever comedic genius came out of my mouth. Because I have seen this approach yield a tremendous bounty over the years, I don't recommend this type of approach for the layperson, as I found that it doesn't work well outside the friendly confines of the gym.

Eventually, Alana finally broke the silence and asked when we were going to hang out. Yes! Persistence in doing nothing paid off yet again. We ended up meeting at a tapas restaurant for dinner one night. This was no day date, my friends. I was in. I was so nonchalant about sex at this point that I mistakenly assumed I would be getting laid before midnight. After all, whenever I heard the phrase "hang out," I was used to my pants coming off sooner rather than later.

Alana showed up in a simple red dress and didn't seem to be done up to the degree that many of my previous clients were when I met them outside the gym. I'm not saying Alana skipped the shower, but her long blonde hair was down and she didn't reek of cheap perfume. There was something different about Alana than most of the clients I had been with, or maybe there was something different with me, but something was different indeed.

We kicked off the night with a pitcher of sangria and ordered some appetizers. For some time, we talked about her upcoming bikini contest and what to expect, as if I had any clue what to expect at those types of things. Once we exhausted that topic, we switched gears and went right to the personal details, like what we wanted to do with our lives and what we were attracted to—all the things we never covered during our time in the gym. After several hours of conversation and drinks, we parted ways with nothing more than a hug. My penis looked up at me when I got home to urinate, turned its odd-shaped head to the side, and said, "Really?"

It wasn't that I didn't want to find out if the carpet matched the drapes on Alana, but it just didn't feel right. I didn't know what the fuck was going on. Was I suddenly growing a conscience? Was I looking at Alana as more than just another someone to keep me occupied from time to time when I wasn't busy with someone else or doing my own thing? I didn't really know what to think. For less than a second, I actually thought that I was going to have some type of meaningful relationship with Cheryl, but I saw how awful that played out. Now here I was about to get involved with another client, but I was confused in more ways than one.

Spring break rolled around, and I was working more because I was staying in town. If I could turn back time and just once be able to go to South Padre Island or Cancun in the spring to see what all the hype was about, I think I could officially say I have done it all. That would be my ticket to a threesome for sure because who doesn't have a threesome on spring break?

On an early Tuesday afternoon, I got a call from Alana. Thinking it was about rescheduling or things of that nature, the last thing I expected her to ask was if I wanted to come over and hang out at the pool. Of course I could hang out at her pool. Alana lived in one of those monstrous off-campus apartment complexes that seemed to be full of college kids doing god knows what. I was about to find out firsthand the awesomeness of living right across the street from campus. I got to her apartment complex just a few hours later with the sun still beating down. Yes, I got lost more than once, as driving through the labyrinth of buildings took more than enough talent when cell phones weren't that smart yet.

I finally arrived at her building and walked to the pool area. As I strolled through the winding pathway, I couldn't help but think of how many hundreds if not thousands of barely legal college kids went crazy at this place on a daily basis. Alana was already lying poolside, looking beyond hot with just the right amount of sweat creeping down her back between her two-piece bikini. I showed up in my awesome cargo shorts that doubled as my poolside attire. Not a whole lot of people were at the pool, since most of the lucky ones were at some faraway beachside resort doing body shots at this exact moment. I threw down a towel next to Alana and tried to slyly stare at her very shapely ass out of the corner of my sunglasses. As I lay poolside with Alana, I was thinking how this unbelievable run had come to this point. I was hitting home runs each time I stepped up to the plate and couldn't remember the last time I struck out.

Without trying to overanalyze the situation, which I seemed to be doing more and more since moving, I returned my focus to the task at hand. I had to see Alana naked. Seeing how I was gazing at her 95 percent clotheless body, I was hoping to get the green light to proceed to the next step. Besides, she was training for a bikini contest, so it would only be fair to see what she had to offer under that top to give her my honest opinion. This was one of the first times I would potentially get laid in the middle of the afternoon. Most of my rendezvous occurred in the wee hours, and who says nothing good happens after two o'clock in the morning? I had more than a handful of memorable experiences after the witching hour. Seeing how the sun was bright, I didn't know how this was going to affect my performance. Not trying to psych myself out, I thought about how this scene would unfold and how I could go about prolonging this session. This, by the way, seemed to always be on my mind because I have had more than my fair share of early takeoffs. I could eat all the kiwi, asparagus, carrots, and almonds in the world, but I have found that if it was going to come to an end early, there was no superfood or supplement that could stop it. But if there was a sufficient amount of alcohol, drugs, or both involved, I could sometimes go for longer than Ron Jeremy himself. But it was only late in the afternoon, and other than water, I didn't have anything in me that could possibly help the cause. Even if I somehow got my hands on some wine coolers, I was on my own. The last thing I wanted to do was disappoint this young coed. She would be scarred for life if I only managed to get a handful of pumps in before calling it a day.

Yet again, I was not the instigator in getting the party started. Funny, I thought. Before becoming a trainer, I invested countless hours of conversation in usually ill-fated attempts to score with girls. Now, here I was just a couple of years removed from those dark days and all I had really done was show up. Whether it be to the backseat of a car, a local watering hole, or someone else's house, I found myself putting in much less effort and getting a whole lot more.

I was surprised to see Alana, who seemed to possess above-average intelligence in addition to a better-than-average body (thanks to her recent workouts), take the reins and ask me to come up to her apartment. Trailing behind Alana as we made our way up the three flights of stairs to her top-floor apartment, I kept my eye on the prize.

Her one-bedroom apartment was a small but decent-looking bachelorette pad. It was decorated nicely, unlike my place, which still had a blacklight Led Zeppelin poster on the wall. I was looking around, admiring her simple way of life. Alana wasn't about the designer wear that Cheryl seemed to collect weekly. She was a breath of fresh air compared to the hell I experienced with Cheryl. She had a medium-sized German shepherd mix that excitedly wagged its tail as it came over to greet me.

After less than five minutes of entering her place, Alana led me to her bedroom. She closed the door behind me and immediately threw her arms around my neck and planted her lips on mine. I was wide-eyed and more than surprised at her prowess in the bedroom, as I expected anything but this. Maybe some making out on the couch, but even with that, I expected her to regulate me to a few-second grab of the boobie before she would back off and say, "I really want to, but I just can't right now." That was the reaction I envisioned with your typical college student, especially one who was on her way to medical school. Rather, I was happily surprised as Alana threw her body onto me and we stood there entwined, just a few steps from her bed. Fortunately, she didn't take notice or at least seem to mind the large erection I had, which my cargo shorts did a terrible job of masking, by the way. Not wanting to take away from Alana's plan, I decided to intervene as little as possible and let her run the show.

After several minutes of making out, we tried unsuccessfully to keep our lips locked as we moved to her bed and made the transition from upright to horizontal. Once on the bed, she wasted no time as she unbuttoned the zipper of my shorts to expose my fully grown wood. She had that look in her eyes that told me right away this was going to be more than a good afternoon. Still in her two-piece bikini, Alana slid down toward the foot of the bed. With one hand on my shaft, she went right down on it. When I closed my eyes, it was as if I was transported to my own personal happy place, complete with little fairies dancing among waterfalls. After a few moments, I came to and looked over at the sliding glass door, which was open to the balcony. The sun was still shining brightly, and I thought, who the fuck cares about spring break when I can have this without having to spend a dime on travel? I returned my attention to Alana, who was now on all fours working her magic on me with both hand and mouth. I was astonished as to how well versed she seemed to be in this sacred art form. I tried to keep myself together as her long blonde hair slowly weaved around my midsection.

Alana got up onto her knees and removed her top to expose her perky white boobs. I think I just maybe fell in love. Without a word, she lay down next to me and pulled me on top of her. I kept my serious face on and tried as gracefully as possible to make this the best Alana had ever had. I really felt a need to get her off, which is something I didn't think about most of the time. There was no mention of any form of protection, so once again my other head prevailed. Just when you thought I was growing up, think again. Alana was so moist at this point that as soon as my tip came into contact with her, I felt her whole body seize up. Keeping my fingers crossed that this was not going to end up being the trip of a hot dog down a hallway, I slowly entered Alana. For not only her pleasure but also my hope to prolong this rare afternoon delight, I crept into her like a snail making its way across the sidewalk. As each inch went in, I breathed a sigh of relief and felt her tighten up around my wood. Not seeming to care much about the open sliding glass door to the patio, Alana let out her moans of pleasure with increasing volume as I mixed up my delivery and put my hand under her ass, pulling her up as I thrust back and forth, getting deeper and deeper each time.

With no end in sight for me, I got a little courageous and flipped Alana onto her side for something new. She had these nicely toned legs with very skinny ankles that were easy to support with one hand, so I held one leg up and kept the other on my shoulder as I pulled her closer to me each time I worked myself in and out. Her moans were steady, and I felt my confidence grow. Oddly enough, without the long day and night and the help of any stimulants or drinks, I was putting on a show for the ages. I think I was getting close to my all-time high, and although I would discover later in life that males' sexual peak is from their early to mid-twenties, I wanted to be stuck in this moment. Sweat was beginning to reappear on both of our bodies from the intensity of this workout and the heat from outside. I then was on my way for the cycle when I turned Alana over on her stomach. She propped herself onto her elbows and seemed to push her backside toward me. No, I didn't take a ride down that old dirt road. I'm sure I could have, but it was never one of my favorite roads to travel.

By now, Alana was nearly dripping wet as I placed my hands on the sides of her ass and without guidance pushed myself back into her soaked pussy. With her body at a slight downward angle and my wiener still pointed toward the stars, I seemed to hit the right spot. Alana was moaning heavier and heavier as she grabbed my hand, a move that seemed to silently ask me to fuck her harder. More than happy to oblige, I forcefully thrust myself in and out, putting a little more hip of my own into it. I felt like Ron Burgundy on his way to Pleasure Town but had to shut down mid-thrust when I felt something breathing heavily behind me. Both shaken and disturbed, I quickly pulled out, still at high noon, and said, "What the fuck?"

Alana turned to see what the commotion was all about. Her dog had managed to open the door and climb halfway onto the bed to partake in the festivities. His hind legs were on the floor, his paws on the foot of the bed. Who could blame him? Who wouldn't want to be a part of this? After several minutes of laughter, Alana wrangled the dog out of the room and closed the door, but unfortunately, the moment had passed. It had been close to twenty minutes of what could have been a performance eligible for an AVN Award, but this scene would be missing a climax. Partly expecting a hummer to finish the job, I sat on the bed for a moment, but Alana began to get dressed, not in her bikini, but in shorts and a shirt. Fuck, I thought. This really was too good to be true. Later that evening I found out the true meaning of blue balls.

That wasn't my last encounter with Alana outside the gym. She continued to train with me throughout the rest of the spring semester, and we would meet up either at her place or mine from time to time to share some intimate moments. This was turning out to become something more than just the occasional fuck. I felt like Alana would make a perfect girlfriend. After all, she was single, which was something I could not say for many of the clients I had slept with before. She was very close to me in age, unlike many of my clients. And the more time I spent with her, the more I wanted to be with her. Strangely enough, I didn't care if I slept with her each time I saw her, although I wasn't quite ready to say no once we started sleeping together. I was still technically with Cheryl, but I was fed up with her and could care less about her feelings. I didn't want to find myself in another relationship. With school and work, it was a little difficult to focus on everything as it was. Things would just get more complex if I factored in another girlfriend, even though Alana was more than worthy of that title.

History has a tendency of repeating itself. I found myself exactly where I was just a few short years ago. I had a stable that was less full than the one I had at my old job, but it was beginning to fill up. In addition to Cheryl, there was Nicole, a few others, and now Alana. The balancing act was truly beginning to wear on me again. Sure, there were the favorites, the trusty standbys I could count on with short notice, and who could forget the seemingly endless additions of gifts and food. It was as if I were some Roman emperor whose only task in life was to be the admiration and desire of those who were fortunate enough to come across my path.

I decided to let things end with Alana before they got out of control. I don't think she had any idea what was going on behind the closed doors of the gym. She was someone whom I could have pictured myself being with, but on my current path, it was probably best that things ended before someone got hurt. I never really took into account anyone's feelings before. Maybe I was growing up, or maybe it was just another sign that I wasn't cut out for the job anymore. Maybe it was just that she was closer to me in age than those whom I'd had previous encounters with.

Once the semester ended, Alana told me she got into medical school and would be leaving in the middle of the summer to go upstate. She also told me she didn't win that bikini contest. It's probably for the best, though. If she won, who knows if she would have bothered to take school seriously after having been named Miss Hooters International? Even though she wasn't moving too far away, it was far enough, in my opinion. I know there are people who have done the long distance thing for years at much further distances than a four-hour drive, but I knew better. With me in school, working the job I was working at the time, it wouldn't be long before I found myself getting into more trouble, as some might call it. Alana made a subtle yet obvious hint that she wanted me to come with her, but that wasn't an option for me. I was a year away from graduating, and I had no desire to move to some other college town and start again in a place that I really didn't want to be. Sure, who wouldn't want to spend time with a soon-to-be doctor—and a hot one at that? Unless she went on a beer and Twinkies diet while in school, I could see Alana looking just as good after graduating from med school as she did when she started. I'm pretty sure Alana could have been my out once and for all if I had been willing to put in just a little bit of effort, but it just never happened.

We kept in touch for a short while once she started school, but between the demands she had with her classes and my nonstop school/work/hangout schedule, we drifted apart. I seemed to have ended it just the right way by going out on good terms rather turning it into some bitter breakup.

After training Alana, I ceased all forms of advertisement. I was already taking on more than I could handle without the added pressure of new clients, which was almost similar to starting a new relationship. You go through that initial awkwardness of figuring out what to talk about and what the other person likes and dislikes, and you carry on with the sole intention of getting into that person's pants. It was feeling all too overwhelming for me, so I decided to just stick with the regulars I had, and if they happened to refer someone to me, I would be more than happy to accommodate, but no more going in blind. Truth was, I was getting tired of it all. I know—how can someone get tired of counting reps and getting laid? I would find out in what would officially be my last hoorah. I had moved thousands of miles to turn things around, and in a year's time, I had managed to find myself in exactly the same place I was before I moved. I was proving to be more than a slow learner. Unlike the farewell tour of the Stones that seemed to keep coming back every few years, this one really was coming to an end. This next episode, as I like to call it, gave me more than enough reason to walk away from the game.

15
BITTERSWEET SYMPHONY

Just like some of the NFL greats do, some of us hold on for too long. Very few of us ever get the opportunity to go out on top. It's extremely difficult to give up something that you love to do, especially if it's the only thing you have done in your adult life. Everybody knows that all good things must come to an end. Whether it is a job, a relationship, or perhaps a great run that yielded you a ton of money in the stock market, things are inevitably going to come to an end. We all come to a crossroads where the next decision we make will have a significant impact on the rest of our lives. You may find yourself very happy or always questioning what could have happened.

I never once thought things would happen for me the way they did, but sometimes an unexpected event can bring life as you know it to a screeching halt. Looking back, I'm happy this event happened when it did. Could I have kept my current freewheelin' lifestyle going for the next five, maybe ten years? Absolutely. I could have packed up shop and moved to the next city or state I found appealing. Personal training was second nature to me. I was confident

I could do this line of work anywhere and be successful. But after all that had happened to me over the years, I still had a conscience, although you can argue that it was absent for most of the time I was working as a trainer.

Having gone through it myself, I can't help but notice people holding on when the writing is on the wall. It would have been an easy choice to give up personal training if my only client was a relative who had some sympathy for me and had the money to spare. Maybe if I kept the shenanigans out of the workplace, I would still be training today. As hard as it may be to believe, I was better than most trainers and was learning more and more about the finer details of the job through the years, despite getting laid by my clients a large percentage of that time. Maybe my abrupt end was just payback from the guy in the sky for all the bullshit I had caused in other people's lives over the past several years.

I would be lying if I said there isn't a piece of me that feels at times like I'm missing out on the party, but as I recount this next event, I feel a sense of relief. Every time I walk into the gym and see that young buck with his smedium Under Armour shirt on, I reminisce for a moment or two. As I watch him train that perfectly put-together soccer mom with a huge rock on her ring finger and see them laugh together and have a great time, I'm brought back to my formative years in the business. I wonder if this guy is about to or already has taken the same path as I have in the past. Chances are he is as naïve as I was about the potential damage your penis can cause to your mental well-being. Sometimes I want to say something to this guy, however inappropriate it may sound coming out of my mouth, but then I figure, fuck it, let him live and learn like Joe Public told me to do. When I see this all too familiar scene, I breathe a sigh of relief and can honestly say I'm happy to be out of the game, and this time for good.

Lisa was a referral from my ex-girlfriend Cheryl. If you remember Cheryl's story, you can imagine her sentiments toward me when I continued to train Lisa long after we broke up. As small as Cheryl was, I do believe she had the collective bitch strength you would find in an entire feminist movement group. Cheryl didn't like not getting whatever she wanted. She assumed I was boning Lisa from the get-go, even though I didn't really have any interest in Lisa other than being paid on time by her each month.

Lisa was kind of attractive, but she was no Miss America, so from our first meeting, there wasn't much interest on my part. What did you think? I was sleeping with nothing but perfect 10s? I probably averaged a 7 throughout my personal training career, with the lowest going to Cheryl, who was a solid 6, and that was only because of the tight body. Anyone who says they are only fucking models is lying, by the way—unless of course they are in a band or somehow hang out with Leonardo Dicaprio. Unlike Cheryl, Lisa was not a butterface. She was petite with an athletic build and the added plus of fake hooters. Even though she was about fifteen to twenty years older than me, she was somewhat decent looking, which made me wonder what she would be like in bed.

Little did I know that Lisa was attracted to me from the beginning. Once again, my testosterone seemed to be at an all-time high and ruled over my better judgment. But this time, there were other variables involved other than just getting my wiener wet. There was also the opportunity to stick it to my ex one more time.

I caught Lisa lying about her age on more than one occasion. It was just a minor slipup on her part, but it was a sign of the shit to come my way. I truly started out with the utmost professionalism and went above and beyond to accommodate Lisa's hectic schedule. I had just finished things officially with Alana and had no intention of finding a replacement. Lisa had aspirations of competing in a fitness pageant, and since I had some experience training a few clients who had entered similar contests, I was happy to take on the challenge. She claimed she was in her late thirties. I never really knew her true age, but she had several kids, including one who was finishing high school. If she was in her late thirties, then I would be in my late teens. It just wasn't possible. This lady had to be in her early to mid-forties, based on the eye lines alone, which read almost as accurately as tree rings. The tiny white lies aside, I wasn't complaining, as she was one of my better clients. Not only did she pay cash, but she also ended up giving me more referrals than any other client. In fact, thanks to Lisa, I was busier than ever since I had moved. After my whole semi-unsuccessful self-advertising campaign on campus, this was a welcomed change.

I was still trying to juggle work and school, but I was happy knowing that my decision to move was getting me somewhere in life and wasn't for naught. I was able to move into a place of my own, since the money was rolling in. Lisa was making great progress and referring new clients to me left and right. I honestly thought I turned the corner and found one great client who was going to be successful in meeting her goals, which would lead to more clients, and so on. Not to mention, I would be accomplishing all this without crossing that boundary I had crossed so many times before.

If only I thought for a few more seconds before making a choice, I might have avoided a lot of shit in my life that I don't ever care to relive. If a situation arrived that was a matter of sex, I could have excused myself to the restroom to take care of myself and simultaneously released the poison that was fogging my thoughts. I wonder if one of our former presidents ever rolled out of bed some days and scratched his head thinking, "I probably shouldn't have done that." I know, Bill. I'm right there with you. It's refreshing to know the former president and I had something in common: we both had a pretty good thing going but managed to fuck it up for a little tail.

Several months into her training, Lisa decided to dance with the devil. Her first mode of attack was simple enough:

an open invite to a concert with a bunch of other people. I said yes, but before you start thinking what I was thinking, let me tell you, prior to this point, I received not only thousands of dollars worth of clients but also extra cash each week in addition to my regular payments. It's funny what the power of additional c-notes will do. I received gifts for my house, gift cards, tickets to games, you name it. If anything, I felt as if I owed it to Lisa to go to this concert with her. Besides, it was just one night and there would be other people around, so what could go wrong? Unlike things with Cheryl, I was getting a ton of perks by just training Lisa and not having to deal with the cunty behavior that came along with sleeping with Cheryl.

Before the concert, we had a few drinks and a few passes of the bowl in the car. My member remained in my pants that whole night. I don't even remember the slightest brushup against my pants while dancing. And I'm proud to say I did not receive a handy while we were saying our good-byes in the car. The best reassurance I got was that there wasn't even any weirdness at our next training session. I felt great. This is what I envisioned my personal training business would be like after all my hard work. I had a cool client who thought the world of me and didn't expect anything. Little did I know that I was still naïve to the ways of the world. After all this time in the business, how could I not see this coming? When a woman wants something, there is little that she won't do until she gets it. Blinded by Lisa's polite gestures, I became roped into this woman's fucked-up web.

Lisa worked as a massage therapist at an upscale spa. It wasn't one of those Asian spas you see scattered about in most towns. Lisa offered to come over to my house and give me a massage. Who doesn't love a massage? I was in no position to say no to a free massage. Who the fuck in their right mind turns something like that down? Once again, I was guilty of inviting trouble into my world. There was no voice of reason reminding me how good things were going and that I should think twice about what I was about to do.

One Thursday evening as the sun was just setting, Lisa came over to my place. She wasn't dressed to the nines but was still looking good nevertheless and wearing a semi-revealing outfit that showed off her new and improved physique. Her training over the past several months had paid off for her big time. Her decreased body fat was noticeable, and her arms and legs displayed the outlines of muscles to go along with a tan that accentuated it all. She brought a massage table into my spare bedroom and wasted little time setting up shop. I was roommate-free at the time, so the coast was clear from unwanted guests. I was also single now, so I figured what the hell?

Lisa threw on one of those relaxing CDs, maybe Enya or one of those other new-age bands that uses a lot of chanting, and lit a scented candle. Before I knew it, the smell of lavender and sage engulfed the room and I was passed out on my stomach as Lisa kneaded my back into a dream. I don't know if it was the aromatherapeutic effects of the candle or the hypnotic melody in the background music, but I was out cold. It must have been well over an hour because when I came to, I felt like I had a full night's sleep.

Lisa gently brushed her hand up against my face to wake me up. I probably had lines all over my face from the head support. With my eyes barely open and my hair in a slight fro, Lisa's voice suddenly took on a sexy tone and asked me how everything was. It's not like she usually sounded like a dude when she spoke, but the tone she had now quickly signaled what was in store for me.

I reluctantly opened my eyes and smiled as I sat up on the edge of the massage table. Without a single word, I stood up and made my way to my bedroom. I would be lying if I said I didn't know exactly what I was doing. With not even a bit of resistance, Lisa followed me. I laid down on my bed and utilized the move I picked up many, many years ago in one of the first porn movies I ever saw: the ol' hands behind the head move. I believe it was one of those seventies pornos where everyone seemed to have big, bushy hair and the music was unforgettable. With my shirt already off and nothing but my shorts on, I waited with great anticipation for my happy ending. Come on, I had a massage therapist in my own place. I felt I would be cheating the male population as a whole if I did not complete this fantasy that most of us have dreamed about since we started having wet dreams.

I felt extremely relaxed now, and a blow job was not something I was going to turn down. In fact, a blow job was the only thing I felt like at that moment, since I was in a haze and could have fallen asleep right there. I hoped Lisa did not have any expectations of boning that evening, as my back was just right and any heavy thrusting would have compromised what she just spent so long working at.

Lisa seemed to know this was her cue to finish the job. She removed her loose blouse, revealing her new physique in addition to those hooters. Yes, another pair of fake ones indeed. I was and always will be in a trance when I see these things live in person. I also couldn't help but admire my work as a trainer and those perfectly sculpted mounds when she climbed on top of me.

She didn't waste any time. She stayed below my waist, slipped my shorts off, and then began to stroke my already engorged cock and started to hum, literally, as she began to give me one hell of a hummer. In between her subtle moans of excitement and her teasing tongue all over my cock, she was driving me crazy, as I feared premature release. Lisa had something I had never experienced before: adult braces. These were common my freshman year of high school, but that was a time when blow jobs were still years away for me. Sure, I once made out with a girl who had braces. In fact, I think I had a set of my own at the time, but this was taking orthodontics to a whole new level. I was somewhat nervous about those sharp metal objects getting close to my pal.

Nevertheless, I was ready for the show to go on and placed one hand on the back of Lisa's head.

Lisa then started to slowly lick me up, down, and all around. She was moaning the entire time as if I was the one doing something for her. Amazing, I thought. This must be how those rock stars feel when they are getting head from a groupie backstage; with no effort on their part whatsoever, they manage to get a girl off, or at least it seems like she is getting off. Then I began to wonder, knowing that Lisa was a masseuse, what were the chances she had been in this exact same scenario a time or two with clients of her own? Oh, well. No time to think of that kind of shit. I attempted to prolong this feeling like I have so many times before. Not only did Lisa do a terrific job, but she also paid attention to all parties down there.

A few minutes in, I could not help but watch her in the act. If only I had a camcorder. Unfortunately, this was well before the iPhone; I could have kept this memory for future dates with my left hand, as this was one hell of a blow job. Soon, Lisa had me going crazy. At one point, she had one nut in her mouth while stroking me ever so gently. I was lying there trying my hardest not to writhe around, which may have affected Lisa's performance. It was so good I didn't want it to end. A quick closing of the eyes to envision Ms. Heffernan, my fifth-grade teacher, butt naked except for her old lady glasses was not enough to avoid the inevitable. At the moment of impact, Lisa put her lips over my dick and took every last bit of what I had to give.

Wow, I just got a great massage and a legitimate happy ending, not just some bullshit spank from someone who does a job no better than my opposite hand. And she finished completely with no remnants leftover on my bed. Not only that, but at no point did I feel a hint of metal on my sensitive areas. Lisa just smiled when she finished and didn't attempt to come anywhere near my lips. As gross as I'm sure people may think I am based on my history, having my own load or even just a trace of it anywhere near my mouth makes me gag just thinking about it.

"That was amazing," I said. That was all I could come up with when I finally regained my senses and sat up in my bed.

"I thought you would like that," Lisa said.

"I'm ready for bed," I said, getting up to put my shorts back on.

Lisa seemed to understand that was her cue to leave. She put her shirt on and packed up her table.

"Can I see you again?" she asked as she was about to leave.

After some of the best fellatio I've ever had? "Of course you can," I said, and we said good-bye.

I shut the door behind her and stood against the door for a moment. Did I just get a massage *and* a blowie of epic proportions for free? Yep. How could I be so lucky? It was as if I kept winning the lotto each time I played. Sure, maybe I experienced a little hiccup every now and then with a client, but for the most part, I was getting a whole lot more than just money from this job. I loved being a personal trainer. If this whole school thing didn't work out for me, I figured I could do this forever. I was beginning to feel like getting some type of sexual favor in addition to work was perfectly normal behavior.

This type of thinking on my part was probably when the whole party began to come crashing down. As fate would have it, this little rendezvous was the beginning of something very bad. I made it very clear to Lisa that I had other interests and did not want a relationship. Lisa, in turn, made it clear that she did not want a relationship either and just wanted to make me "happy." I assumed this response meant some sexual favor whenever I felt the need. Like the great Bill Clinton, however, I can honestly say that I did not have sexual relations with that woman. If our former president can say blow jobs don't really "count," then so can I. Lisa gave me a handful of oral pleasures. In fact, I only kissed her on the mouth a couple of times (and no, never after a blow job) and did not see her completely naked on any occasion. I saw her in some fancy lingerie once or twice, but I never saw her downstairs, and I can only hope to this day that she didn't have any surprises down there.

Up until this point, everything that transpired between Lisa and me sounds like a problem most guys would love to have. You mean to tell me I could watch *Caddyshack* and get head if I chose? That's probably every man's wet dream. Only I, like Bodhi, should have known that nobody rides for free. We all end up paying the piper at some point.

Unfortunately, there was an X factor—Lisa's *ex*-husband, or maybe he was still her husband. Lisa certainly wasn't the first attached woman I had slept with in my career, but she was the first to forget to mention it before getting to know my cock and me. In all my years training, nothing had ever caught up to me, but it looked like my luck was finally going to run out. To this day, I have no idea who exactly this guy was—a rogue Federale, drug kingpin, or perhaps a career criminal? I would discover soon enough that I didn't want anything to do with him, his wife (or ex-wife), or this job anymore.

It started one Sunday morning as I was calling my clients to remind them about their appointments that week. I called Lisa's cell phone to see what time she was going to come in on Tuesday. I had no intention of asking her for some head perhaps later that day. Much to my surprise, a guy with a thick Hispanic accent answered the phone. For a minute, I thought I had been had—she really was a dude! And not just any dude, but one with an accent. Fuck!

The guy on the phone was immediately pissed at me and accused me of fucking his wife! Holy shit, that was a shocker. I had no clue Lisa was married to a psychopathic Hispanic with a vengeance. I was both pissed off and upset. I was upset because I swore that I would not do another married woman, and I was pissed because she never mentioned a word about this guy prior to wrapping her lips around my cock. I wondered if letting him know she only blew me would lighten the tension and put his mind at ease.

No matter how much I wanted to stand my ground, I decided to take whatever he was going to dish out. Even though I had a hard time understanding most of what he said, I couldn't help but notice that "fuck you" sounds pretty similar no matter what ethnicity of the person who's yelling it. The rapid-fire Spanish gibberish that he was spewing was beginning to wear on me. After a few minutes of this verbal abuse, I hung up the phone. Shaking my head, I knew right then and there that I had gone too far and that this bullshit had to end. Not just with Lisa, but with everything. How was I going to let some of my clients know we could only be strictly platonic? It would be like a recovering alcoholic working at a bar. My head was beginning to spin. Before moving out west, I was fucking more times than a porn star with nothing but my own guilty conscience to worry about. Now I was doing the same, but all those horror stories I dreamed about were coming true. Between the bullshit with Cheryl and now this with Lisa, I had gotten much more than I bargained for since I began taking my clothes off with clients. I knew I wouldn't be able to play it straight after all the shit I had pulled over the years, so the answer was crystal clear to me.

A few hours later, I got a call from Lisa. "I'm so sorry he called you. He was at my house picking up my son and decided to answer my phone," she said.

"Who is he?" I asked.

"My ex-husband," Lisa said.

"Well, he seems to think he is still your husband," I said.

"Don't worry about him."

Don't fucking worry? I didn't know what to believe at this point. I buried my head into my hands, not knowing how to respond. I decided to just remind her about her appointment on Tuesday and quickly got off the phone. In case you are wondering, she had paid in full and I didn't give refunds, so I had to finish the job.

The date of Lisa's first fitness show was coming up, and she was looking more than ready. But her Tuesday appointment was different, to say the least. My phone had been ringing off the hook with obscene and threatening messages in broken English. I was not in the mood to deal with high school–type hijinks. To think I used to be the one making prank calls at all hours of the night back in high school, and now I was the victim. This was when Lisa got crazy. I guess if you marry a freak, you must have some freakiness in you, too. The soft-spoken, sexy-toned politeness that would accompany a blow job was just a facade.

"So this very pissed off guy who said he is your husband continues to call me daily," I said to Lisa, without saying hello, when she met me at my desk in the gym.

"I told you don't worry about him," she said.

Dumbfounded, I tried to keep my cool. "Lisa, he's calling me nonstop, and I don't think I mentioned this the other day, but he said he wanted to fucking kill me!"

"It's all just a big misunderstanding," she said.

Are you fucking kidding me? A misunderstanding? If I discovered my wife was giving oral favors to another guy, you can bet it would be a pretty big fucking deal. I realized I was going in circles with Lisa and this conversation was going nowhere. I should have known better. Any referral from Cheryl was destined to be as fucked up as she was.

I wasted no time and told Lisa I was going to call the police. "I'll just let them deal with this because I don't have time for this," I said.

Expecting a voice of reason, I instead got a scene like something you'd see in *Cops* when the police come to take away a degenerate man who just beat the shit out of some girl, and the girl is looking all frazzled outside her trailer.

"Please, do not do that," Lisa said.

I was shocked, but then again, crazy people are difficult to figure out.

"He doesn't mean any trouble," she added.

I tried not to laugh as I attempted to analyze what was going on before my own eyes. This fucking guy, who sounded like he genuinely meant it when he said he was going to kill me, had his ex—or whatever the fuck she was to him—taking his side. Is this the same woman who swallowed yet another load of mine just a few nights ago?

"Just leave him alone," Lisa said, as if I were the one causing problems. What the fuck! I was furious because Lisa had never once mentioned anything about this guy when we first started training, and now she was sitting there making me feel like the asshole. I wanted to assure her that I would not have given her the green light to suck my dick had I known she was still "attached" in some way, shape, or form, but it was useless at this point.

I told her that I would see her at her fitness contest that coming weekend, but after that, I thought it would be best if we parted ways. She didn't take that too lightly and got upset. I was at a loss. At this point, I was already checking under the hood of my car each time I got in it for anything that looked out of the ordinary. I couldn't take this unbelievable drama that came with what I assumed was just an innocent blow job on a few occasions. It was then that I knew that the party was over, and any other massages and blow jobs I received would cost me a pretty penny from here on out.

The next day at the gym, I got a surprise visitor beyond my wildest dreams. I was in the main gym with another client, which made the whole situation look a million times worse. A large Hispanic guy who looked like Steven Seagal, complete with the attitude and a ponytail, came up to me, ready to throw down. With a furious look in his eyes, the towering figure looked down at me and said in what was obviously not his native tongue, "Are you JD?"

What does one do in this situation? I didn't know if I was about to get Aikido'd into the wall, but without a moment of hesitation, I boldly responded, "That's me."

The guy had a seedy look about him, and punching me in the face probably wasn't even close to the worst decision he made in his life. I wasn't sure what to expect next. Should I risk everything, get the first punch in, and possibly end up behind bars with some fellow who happens to be quite fond of the backside of a young guy who works out?

The guy's eyes were now popping out of his head, and he was livid, yelling at me in Spanglish. I thought for a moment that I was watching a John Leguizamo comedy special when he would describe his conversations with his family. There were quite a few "fucks" and "my wife" being thrown at me. I had a difficult time following him, but I got the general gist of things. He was clearly upset that a woman he was once, or was still possibly, married to gave me oral. Hey, I would more than likely be just as angry.

As this shouting was going on, my client, who happened to be a large guy himself, looked mortified. I somehow managed to talk the Hispanic guy down and get him the fuck out of there. Don't ask how this was accomplished, but I do recall saying the words "No, I did not" and "policia" at some point. It was even more embarrassing when Jason, who very much had his Chi harnessed, came over to me after the Hispanic guy left and asked me what the hell was going on. I felt like the biggest jerk-off. The price of a few blow jobs was more than any dollar amount I could imagine.

This scene, in addition to the one with Lisa, was the reinforcement I needed to shut it down. Luckily for me, shortly after I stopped training Lisa, she started fucking a coworker of mine named Andre, so the Hispanic's attention was deferred from me and I was finally left alone. Andre unknowingly took a grenade for me; within days of banging Lisa, he told me about some angry fellow calling him and giving him a hard time. I felt a little bad for him, but I was more relieved than anything.

I was at my breaking point in the business. I had come across many fucked-up situations and unfortunately didn't always do the right thing. I had some great times and more than my fair share of sex from more-than-willing women, which was something I still had a hard time wrapping my head around. I am still the same guy I was before getting a job as a personal trainer. I still continue to watch *Coming to America* whenever it's on, no matter how many times I have seen it, because it's hilarious even when edited for regular television. I give myself a dutch oven every now and then just for a laugh. I also hate showering more than once a day, even if I'm covered in sweat from working out after a long day at work. I did absolutely nothing differently but get this job and suddenly I went from being the one who was always looking to being the one who was always getting looked at.

But as strange as it may seem, even after all the women I pulled from personal training, I didn't feel the least bit more confident once I was done with it for good. It was as if the past several years were just a kind of alternate reality that I was fortunate enough to be a part of, even for just a little while. Perhaps a man of integrity would not have made some of the decisions I made. Maybe I am a rogue wave among a sea of purity, and the fitness world as we know it is filled with wholesome, morally correct younger trainers who truly look after their clients' best interests. I don't want to sound like Jose Canseco, but without calling out names, there's unfortunately a lot of monkey business in personal training.

Now that I tarnished my reputation in two cities, thousands of miles apart, I personally felt terrible for all the shit and problems I caused. Even if I wasn't the instigator in some of these shady situations, I was still a willing participant who eventually caused a lot more pain than the pleasure I got out of it. I'm not gonna lie to you, the memories will last forever, and I'm happy to leave it at that.

16
THINKIN' ABOUT THOSE GLORY DAYS

I should apologize in advance because there are no surprises here. It has been nearly a decade since I left my last personal training job, and I haven't experienced any of the run-ins I envisioned. I used to wake up in cold sweats with many scenes from *The Godfather* running through my head. I was always on guard. I worried that one of those fictional scenes where someone is about to get knocked off could one day become a reality for me. How many guys out there wouldn't go to extremes if they found out their supposed soul mate was sucking off the guy at the gym? I was nothing more than a personal trainer and, in some people's eyes, just a glorified rep counter, yet somehow I managed to bed a millionaire's wife and a millionaire's daughter, among others. As morally bankrupt as I had become, I knew my time was up. I couldn't keep this unbelievable ride going. Even though part of me really wanted it to continue, I knew it would never be a job that ensured my cock stayed in my pants.

Just a few short months after the incident with the large Hispanic guy, I put in my two weeks' notice. I had to move on to something a little more respectable. I had no idea what that would be, but I was getting close to finishing my degree, so I figured some type of "real" job would be on the horizon. Would I possibly walk away from all this without as much as a scratch? After all the shitty things I'd done—the lying, the cheating, the using—it just seemed like I was long overdue for a huge letdown. It was as if I lived on the Bunny Ranch for the past several years with no regard for anyone or anything other than getting myself off. The wrath of the Hispanic dude with the ponytail was still fresh in my mind, but I also continued to replay encounters I had with some of my clients over and over in my head. I couldn't help but think that at least one of their significant others had to know. There was no way someone's better half didn't question why his wife was coming home so late or going out in the middle of the week. Even though I wasn't screwing attached women exclusively, I had no doubt that things would end badly for me, but somehow I was spared.

I sometimes wonder if the women who were married when they fucked around with me are still married. How they could justify their actions and remain married is a mystery I'll never be able to figure out. Did they ever admit to their significant others what happened, or are they holding that secret with them to the grave? I never confessed to my former girlfriends. Like a true guy, I denied every allegation that was thrown my way. I became so well versed in the art of lying that it came naturally. Since leaving the profession, I've had to change quite a bit, and lying is just another habit I'm still in the process of breaking. I feel some guilt from time to time about the lies I've told and the things I have done, but there's nothing I can do about it now. I can only imagine how some of my ex-girlfriends would feel if they knew what I had really been up to. It didn't matter if my relationship with my girlfriend was good or bad; I would still find myself screwing around with sometimes three or more women at any given time. I feel bad for those past girlfriends, even Cheryl, who maybe was the definition of a cunt but deserved better.

As for the women who weren't attached, I don't feel that much guilt; instead, I just feel bad for them. Many of them were looking for a little more than just a fuck, despite what they would say to entice me into the bedroom. Who knows what these women were thinking. Were they really thinking I was the kind of guy they wanted to be with? I was in such a haze throughout my training days that I really didn't give much thought about what I was doing until I was done altogether. I was *that* guy in so many ways—the guy people just look at and shake their heads. To my peers and upper management, I was awesome, and I really thought I was for some time. But the laundry list of those whom I fucked over in more than a few ways was something I could not shake. I'm sure each woman felt like shit for a while after I stopped calling or simply said things were finished. For all I know, maybe they were using me and I was the asshole for thinking it was anything more.

Putting the past behind me was just what I did. I stuck around Southern California and worked there for a couple of years in health care after I quit my job as a trainer. It was quite an adjustment for me to work a real job, seeing how personal training was so great that it barely felt like work. It sucks getting up early each day just so that I can spend more time than I ever imagined just trying to get to work. I was essentially my own boss after several years of working as a personal trainer. Now, I'm pretty much someone else's bitch. I guess that's why they say that's what life is.

Having to drive by Body Masters several times a week might have contributed to my strong desire to leave town altogether even though I was finally settling in at my new job. Driving by the old gym conjured up memories, which weren't all bad, but I knew I needed to make a clean break in order to move on with my life. Still being near that place and having some clients who were still looking for some training, even if it was only every now and then, was just a little too tempting for me. Part of me still thinks that if I had continued to work as a trainer, the whole incident with the ponytail guy would have seemed like a welcomed event compared to what could have happened to me.

After I finally finished school and got a real job, I knew it was time for me to grow up, settle down, have a family, and do all that stuff that is driven into your head as a kid whether or not it's anything you want to do. After all, that's just what you're supposed to do in order to be accepted as a "normal" adult. After having worked for several years at a grown-up job, I really do wonder if that's the right thing for everyone to buy into. Nevertheless, I was ready to move on with my life, even if there was a part of me that didn't want to give up the lifestyle of having more females at my disposal than I knew what to do with. How many others out there can say they worked in a setting that not only afforded that type of behavior but also encouraged it at times?

I ended up moving one more time. This time I headed back to the East Coast, far enough from the original scene of the crime but close enough to visit every now and then. I continued to work in health care and even went on to get my graduate degree. Now, after nearly ten long years of working in my new career, I can say that I miss my old job of personal training more than ever. It's difficult to go from being looked up to at the workplace and having fun on a daily basis to looking at the clock just hoping it is close to five. It's true what most people say: work sucks. My real job afforded me none of the luxuries I had when I was a personal trainer. If I was running late to train someone, all I had to do was call up the client and tell him or her to warm up to kill some time until I got there. Try running late more than once to your real job, and you will find yourself getting "written up." I don't even know what the fuck that really means exactly. Is it like when a police officer pulls you over and gives you a written warning instead of a ticket?

How about being able to joke around with everyone at work? This was just part of your average day at the gym.

Whether it was talking shit about a peculiar member or busting a coworker's stones, it was all in good fun. At a real job, jokes are very PG-rated, and you will find yourself in the manager's office for a sit-down about "professionalism" if you participate in any R-rated humor. With everybody so fucking sensitive these days, I find it best to keep my mouth shut at work. In fact, I have toned it down so much that I'm looked at as the "quiet" guy. I would rather be known as the quiet guy than a choad, and everyone knows a few of those around the workplace.

And last but not least, how about the pay? There is some personal satisfaction from being somewhat in control of how much you earn. At the gym, the option to train someone else was always there. If you wanted to add an additional hour or two to a day whenever it was convenient for you, then you'd have a few extra bucks in your pocket without ruining an entire day. With a real job, just be happy cashing that check for the same exact amount each week with very little control over it. Want to work overtime? Sure, just kill your entire Saturday or Sunday or stay for another few hours on top of your already long day. I know there are some exceptions, like with sales jobs and such, but you get the point. There is a lot more bullshit that comes with being a responsible adult with a real job.

I always thought I would move up to a white-collar job, but it's extremely difficult to make the jump from blue-collar to white-collar, and it looks like I'm always going to be wearing the blue one. But at least I can say I'm happy to have spent some time in a job I considered fun. While working as a trainer, I always thought that someday I would be much better off working in a professional setting like a hospital or doctor's office. Now that I find myself working in the health care industry, I have quickly realized that it's not all that it's cracked up to be. Sure, there's steady money and jobs are easy to find unless you have some type of criminal history, but I think dealers in Vegas have it better than the poor souls who work in health care. It didn't take long to see that I was working among not only the unhealthiest but also the unhappiest people. How could this be possible? I went from a job that was thought of as a joke to one that is respected but so full of burnout that very few people last long before their health and happiness is ripped to shreds. Shit, maybe this was just another bad decision on my part.

Thankfully, it took only a few job changes to find myself in an improved workplace that I actually enjoy going to each and every day. The good times still pale in comparison to the occasions I had while personal training. Okay, I may be lying about going to work and enjoying what I do each and every day. I was pretty much my own boss when I was a personal trainer. Now I feel as if I have eight bosses. I find myself hustling more now than I did when I was in my twenties, but I do have what is considered a real job and the money is stable. With that, however, there are some things that seem to have disappeared forever. Gone are the profanities being thrown around daily and the days of showing up late after having a rough night. Also gone are the unbelievable cash bonuses and gifts that were bestowed upon me seemingly every couple of months. But there is satisfaction not only in what I am now doing but also because I don't have to deal with all the drama that went along with my previous career. Some days when I am at work, I wonder if anyone has any idea what it was that I did before I got to my current job. Sure, they all knew I was a personal trainer, but do they have any clue about what really happened?

If Facebook and all those other social media networks had been around back then, my illustrious run would have ended prematurely, no doubt. I can see it now: a bunch of messages requesting a late-night visit or, God forbid, a "Thanks for a great time!" written on that fuckin' wall. There is no doubt in my mind that things would have blown up in my face and ended faster than I could have imagined. I have come across a few former clients on Facebook.

Fortunately, they didn't try to "friend" me, but some did send messages to say hello. I can't tell you how many times I've been on that fucking website and an instant message shows up, causing my heart to drop. How people can stay out of trouble these days is beyond me. I don't think I can name three hundred people I know personally, but somehow I have three hundred friends on Facebook.

I look at how people get to know each other these days and wonder what happened over the last ten years or so. I remember meeting women at the gym, getting to know them by actually *talking* to them in person for a few weeks, and then ending up in bed with them. Now, people are lazy in so many ways. They don't even want to make the effort to talk to someone in person. I don't care how good Ashley Madison advertises. The second you use some type of outside source to hook up, you're only screwing yourself. Maybe I'm showing my age, but whatever happened to the days when you actually had to put in some real face time before getting laid? Nowadays, it seems that all the conversation is unnecessary, and with a few keystrokes, you can have yourself some sex. With all these high-tech methods of communication, people don't have to spend time in front of another person and actually converse. What about those people who swear by Craigslist as a means of hooking up? Sure, I did it, but it was just once and that is a story in itself. I have to say that it is the equivalent of putting your dick in a glory hole. Maybe I was just fortunate enough to be in a field where interaction with people was unavoidable. I have yet to hear any stories from my friends about a workplace that offered anything close to the kind of exposure I got to the ladies as a personal trainer.

My cell phone, back in my personal training days, was the size of a box of Girl Scout cookies. It pretty much stayed in the car, and texting was so difficult, you were bound to end up sending some cryptic message from hitting the 7 button four fucking times just to type a single "S." I still own a flip phone because I have a computer to do all the other shit I need to do. My phone rarely rings past ten o'clock at night these days, and there are no more random texts asking for an extra session. I laugh when I turn the phone on after a long weekend away and see zero missed calls, since back in the day I was performing my own sick version of triage in terms of who would get my attention first and who would have to wait. I still wonder how I pulled it off. I'm a guy who had no moves, and I definitely didn't have what some call "game," yet I was able to bask in a sea of wanting and willing women.

Do I ever look back and regret what I did? Some days I feel a little worse than others, especially when things in life seem to be going badly. I wonder if karma is just running its course when anything goes awry. Whenever anything bad happens to me, I feel in some way that I deserve it due to my past actions. I'm not going to sit here and tell you I became born again, but I have made a conscious effort to live a better life, especially when it comes to where my wiener goes. Should I be in a church right now? Perhaps, but I'll take my chances doing this on my own. There is some relief when you don't have countless secrets you have to keep from a significant other. Although there's still stress in my life, I don't feel the need to fuck around to feel better about things.

On a lighter note, some good has come from my time spent as a personal trainer. A friend of mine from high school continues to thank me profusely for convincing him that his wife should train with a female instead of a male. After I dropped some of these stories to him, he said I increased the likelihood of his marriage staying intact by at least 75 percent. I have also been able to tell others how to avoid getting ripped off by trainers who tell prospective clients that, in addition to training with them, they absolutely *must* take a supplement that of course only they sell. These people have no idea that they are about to get involved in a pyramid scheme that forces them to sign up for an auto-ship program that takes a shitload of money out of their account each month for this so-called wonder pill. So I'm happy to say that at least some good has come out of my wrongdoings.

Long gone are the days of late-night booty calls and having a long list of women to choose from. Today, there are a lot more movie nights, and I can't tell you when was the last time I stayed up past three o'clock in the morning. Maybe things are different after your twenties, or maybe things just come to a screeching halt when you decide to stop playing the field. On that note, whoever still manages to hang out until the wee hours of the morning after their twenties has to be on some type of illegal substance. I can sleep eight or nine hours with every intent on staying out all night the next night, but when the clock strikes eleven, that's it for me. It blows my mind to think some of the women I hooked up with were older than I am now and probably had a hell of a lot more responsibilities than I ever will, yet they were partying like twenty-one-year-olds. I can't imagine going through all that bullshit just to get laid. I know there are many people my age who make it out to the local watering hole several nights a week, but something tells me very few of them are getting action on those nights as well.

I would encourage anyone in the personal training business to play it safe, especially if you're looking to make a career out of it. Keep your pants on. You can have a pretty lengthy career as a personal trainer, even though many people still don't consider it a real job. If you're looking for some action, you may find exactly what you're looking for, but take my fucked-up escapades as warnings—it can all come crashing down.

You may think that it appears I got away relatively clean, so why can't you? Keep in mind that I believe I'm very lucky to be where I am today considering my past. I'm happy to say I'm done with it all and living life on the straight and narrow path. Little things in life like walking the dogs and hanging out at the beach bring more excitement than I could ever imagine. I even have a serious girlfriend whom I've been dating for the past couple of years and haven't cheated on her once. No matter how pretty I try to paint the picture, is it really better than getting a hummer from a hot chick in the office after closing? We all have to grow up at some point, so the grown-up answer would be yes, it is.

I loved my old job, but I wasn't happy with my old life. Sure, sex with multiple women most days of the week sounds good, but in the end, there is no satisfaction. It took me many years to realize this, but you can hit Dave Navarro numbers and still be unsatisfied. I was just a regular guy who never imagined I would have the opportunity to be with so many women. Friends who took that job at Enterprise Rent-A-Car certainly did not have half the stories I showed up with whenever we hung out. Shit, I didn't even play the guitar, yet there I was with pseudo-groupies who, for some reason, liked a guy who held a clipboard and instructed people on how to exercise. It was a surreal feeling that I knew deep down wasn't real life. Of course, there's that evil little head over one shoulder scolding me and calling me a big pussy when I sit down to watch *Road House* on a Saturday night for the 528th time. It's these occasional, uneventful, and sometimes boring nights that remind me what I had and what I gave up. Not to mention, the times when I'm regulated to YouPorn and my left hand to take care of business. On the other shoulder, I have the sweet little angel who is not as cool as the little devil but gives me a smile when I'm in bed before eleven o'clock each night and I choose to turn off the computer instead of searching for porn.

There are many trainers who will pick up where I left off, and there will be many more to come. Despite the warnings, a select few will take the risk. When you are inside that beautiful housewife with a perfect body and a seemingly endless sex drive, it's difficult to think about what may happen after that moment of pure ecstasy. I can't tell you how many times that happened to me over the years. And yes, it does feel awesome. But when I think about how bad things could have ended for me, I'm thankful I'm still intact with nothing but emotional baggage. Things ended much worse for that guy in *Goodfellas* who looked at Joe Pesci and talked to his pal Ace that way. It doesn't matter how clear the warning is, there will always be those who choose to dip their feet in the deep end. So, guys, keep an eye out when your girl says she's going out with her trainer for a few drinks. And, girls, don't think you're exempt. If your guy is training with a nice-looking female trainer, you might want to sniff his fingers when he gets home a little later than usual.

My time is done here. Now that I'm a grown-up with a real job and real responsibilities, I have to wake up like the rest of America, and it sucks. As I write this, I wonder how many personal trainers are chatting with their clients or maybe several drinks in to what will inevitably become a bad decision. As for me, I'm off to bed with my beautiful girlfriend, who just so happens to be a former client.